Birds of California

Birds of California

A NOVEL

Katie Cotugno

HARPER ⬤ PERENNIAL

NEW YORK • LONDON • TORONTO • SYDNEY • NEW DELHI • AUCKLAND

HARPER ● PERENNIAL

HarperCollins books may be purchased for educational, business, or sales promotional use. For information, please email the Special Markets Department at SPsales@harpercollins.com.

FIRST EDITION

Designed by Jen Overstreet

Library of Congress Cataloging-in-Publication Data has been applied for.

ISBN 978-0-06-315914-3

22 23 24 25 26   LSC   10 9 8 7 6 5 4 3 2 1

You know what? I wrote this one for me.

Birds of California

CHAPTER ONE

Fiona

The Heidelberg jams again on Thursday, so Fiona is standing on her tiptoes with her fingers twisted deep inside its mechanical bowels when the bell above the door of the print shop chimes its echoey hello.

"Hey there," she calls, straightening up and coming out of the workshop, wiping a smudge of toner on the seat of her overalls as she takes her spot behind the counter. "Can I help you?"

The guy nods. "I'm picking up a banner." He's probably five years younger than her, twenty-two or twenty-three maybe, dressed in a short-sleeved button-down festooned with a hundred tiny Hula girls and a USC cap turned backward. There's a braided rope bracelet looped around one tan, beefy wrist. "Sigma Tau cookout?"

Ah. "Sixteenth Annual Spring Weekend Sausage Fest?" she asks.

Hula Shirt grins. "*Bratwursts Never Say Die*," he confirms, muscly chest puffing a bit. "That's us."

Fiona nods grimly, pulling the poster tube from a cubby on the wall behind the counter and unrolling the massive banner for his inspection. It turned out fine—better than fine, even, considering Fiona herself caught three different spelling errors in the digital version they sent over—but when she glances up for Backward Cap's approval she finds him peering back at her, eyes narrowed above the plastic frames of his sporty sunglasses. She braces herself like a boxer about to take a punch.

Sure enough: "Hey," he says, pointing with one thick finger. "Aren't you—"

"Boss!" Richie pokes his head out of the workshop, dark hair swinging. He's still screwing around with the printer, waving the manual frantically in her direction. "Sorry. Can you give me a hand back here?"

"Sure thing." Fiona shoots him a grateful look. It's their tacit agreement: he rescues her from conversations like the one that is about to occur with Fratty Matty here, and she doesn't give him a hard time about coming into work baked out of his gourd four out of five days a week. "Sorry," she tells Sausage Fest, rolling up the colorful banner and tucking it safely back inside its cardboard tube. "My colleague will take over."

The guy ignores her. "You are," he says. He's still pointing, smiling the self-satisfied smile of a contestant on *Jeopardy!* who won with the wrong answer by only betting a dollar. "Riley Bird, right?"

And there it is. Fiona sighs. She's come up with a lot of creative answers to this question over the last five years, but lately she finds she's too tired to muster anything but the truth. "Yup," she admits. "I used to be."

"I knew it." The guy grins, pulling his cell phone out of his pocket.

Fiona cringes. "Oh, can you not—" she starts, but he's already snapping the picture, thumbs flying as he sends it off, presumably, to all of his fellow Sigma Tau Bratwursts with a caption she would be willing to bet is not *Look at this private citizen minding her own business at her place of employment.*

"I can't believe you work here now," he says. "My roommate had a poster of you up on our wall last year. The one with the lizard," he adds helpfully, as if it would be any other poster besides the one with the lizard. It's amazing how many people still tell her that, honestly; it's probably the second most common thing they say, after *I saw on Twitter that you died.*

By now Richie has stepped in to ring him up, swiping his credit card and handing him the banner, sending him on his merry way. Fiona is about to go another round with the Heidelberg—her dad is the only one who really knows how to fix it properly, but since he's basically stopped coming into work, she and Richie have been holding it together with spit and tape—but instead of leaving, the guy reaches out and grabs her wrist across the counter.

"Listen," he says—completely oblivious to the way she flinches at the contact, her whole body coiling like a cat knocked off a sill. "Sausage Fest is usually a pretty good time, if you're around this weekend. I know my roommate would love to meet you." He winks. "Although, who knows, maybe I won't even tell him. Might want to keep you all to myself."

Fiona manages not to laugh in his face, but barely. "That

is . . . quite the offer," she says, extricating her arm from his damp, sweaty grip, "but I've got plans."

Sigma Tau fixes her with a deeply skeptical look, gesturing around at the empty shop. "What," he asks with a smirk, "too busy working here?"

Fiona's spine straightens. She hangs on to her temper with claws and teeth these days, but she can feel it starting to rise in her chest and her shoulders, Bruce Banner popping a button or two. Her parents started this business before she was born. "Electroconvulsive therapy," she whispers sadly. "Shock treatments."

One benefit of having been exhaustively captured on film doing all kinds of extremely questionable shit is that for a moment she can tell he has no idea if she's serious or not. Then he shakes his head. "You know what?" he says. "Forget it."

"Don't worry," Fiona assures him, "I definitely will."

Sausage Fest's mouth twists meanly. "Crazy bitch," he mutters, then shoves the poster tube under his arm and stomps out of the store, the chimes above the door ringing cheerfully one more time.

"Sorry," Richie says once he's gone.

Fiona shrugs. "It's fine," she assures him. It's not, really, but that isn't Richie's fault. They go through some iteration of this one-act play at least once every few days, with bicycle couriers and equipment repair technicians and brides-to-be selecting fonts for their letterpress wedding invitations. Once there was a stretch of nearly a month where no one recognized her; another time, when Darcy Sinclair's gossip blog posted a blind item—*Which notoriously wild Bird has returned to the family nest with her feathers tucked between her legs?*—they had to close for a full week until people got bored and stopped hanging around outside hoping for a lookie-loo. It occurs to Fiona that they should print up a sign like they keep in warehouses to track how long it's been since anyone lost an arm in a baler: *No one has asked Fiona about the lizard poster in _____ days.*

It's not like she doesn't get why people are curious. She was a child actress, the squeaky-clean teen darling of the UBC Family Network—starring in their flagship critically acclaimed dramedy *Birds of California* as the plucky daughter of a widower ornithologist who lived in a wildlife sanctuary—for four wildly lucrative blockbuster seasons.

And then, to hear everyone tell it, she lost her fucking mind.

Eventually she and Richie get the Heidelberg working again and print off a batch of alumni newsletters for a fancy prep school, plus an order of pamphlets about gingivitis for a local periodontist's office. Fiona spends an hour sitting at the worktable with the folding tool to get the creases straight, securing the tidy stacks of brochures with rubber bands and packing them neatly into a box for shipping. When she was a kid she always thought she'd die of boredom if she had to work here, but now she finds she actually kind of likes the anesthetic repetition of it, the numbing tactility of the paper in her hands. Sometimes it's nice, being able to forget.

For lunch she runs around the corner for a burrito bowl and eats it standing up in the workshop, scrolling idly through the anonymous social media accounts she maintains for the sole purpose of looking at rambling old houses in New England and rescue dogs living safe and happy lives. She hardly ever bothers checking her email anymore—there is literally never anything that requires her immediate attention—but today mixed in with the junk and the occasional unsolicited dick pic is one message that catches her eye.

Sender: LaSalle, Caroline
Subject: Checking In

Fiona gasps before she can quell the impulse. Caroline hasn't been her agent in seven years. She hasn't had an agent at *all* in seven years, but still the sight of Caroline's name has her swallowing down an instinctive flicker of dread, the humiliation of having disappointed someone deeply, even though she hasn't, as far as she knows, done anything wrong today. Ghost shame.

Hi Fiona,

Gosh, it's been a while! I hope this email finds you healthy and well. You might have seen that I left LGP and started my own agency last year—or maybe not! Not sure how much you keep up with that kind of inside baseball anymore. In any event, I've got an opportunity I'd love to chat with you about. Can you do a call sometime this week?

Fiona winces as if someone has slapped her. *Can you do a call?* is what Caroline used to say when Fiona had screwed up in some public and embarrassing way: *Can you do a call because you flipped off a photographer; can you do a call because you were visibly inebriated on a beloved morning talk show at the age of nineteen. Can you do a call so that I can tell you that your show is canceled, your career is over, you've ruined your entire life and cost who knows how many hardworking people their jobs all because you couldn't bother to keep it together for a little while longer?*

No, Fiona thinks, shoving her phone back into her pocket without bothering to read Caroline's two follow-up messages and tossing the rest of her burrito bowl in the trash. She can't do a call, actually.

"You good?" Richie asks. He's eyeing her warily from the counter, where he's folding scrap from the recycling bin into an intricate origami fox. He's got an entire menagerie of three-dimensional paper animals tacked to the bulletin board in the workshop, next to the mandatory OSHA posters and a flyer he put up for a gig his ska band is doing at a dive bar downtown.

"Totally fine," Fiona manages, watching as he flips the paper between his nimble fingers. She's thought about asking him to show her how he does it, but Richie is, like, the one guy in the universe who's never assumed he could sleep with her and she doesn't want to give him any ideas. "Never better."

"Okay," Richie says, heading up to the counter at the sound of the phone ringing. He hands her the tiny paper sculpture before he goes.

Her dad is sitting in the yard in a lawn chair when she gets home, which is an improvement—yesterday he was sitting in front of the TV in the darkened living room, the blinds drawn against the

Sherman Oaks sunshine and a slightly unwashed funk permeating the air. "Hey," Fiona says brightly. "I picked up some stuff for dinner." Then, when he doesn't answer: "Dad?"

"What?" Her dad blinks and comes back to himself, smiling vaguely. "That's perfect. Thanks, honey."

She waits for him to get up, but he doesn't, so after a moment she goes inside and sets the bag of groceries on the kitchen counter, then opens the slider to the backyard, crossing the dry, prickly grass and letting herself into Estelle's house next door. "Hey," she calls. "Anybody home?"

"In here!" her sister Claudia calls back.

She finds them sitting in Estelle's den watching TV and wearing identical Korean sheet masks, highball glasses of ginger ale sweating on malachite coasters on the coffee table. Brando, Estelle's dozy pit bull, snores happily on the sofa between them. "Hi, sweetheart," Estelle greets her—at least, Fiona thinks that's what she says. With the mask on her face it's hard to tell. Estelle has lived next door for as long as Fiona can remember; she isn't the casserole-making kind of neighbor, but she left Lean Cuisines on their doorstep for a full month after their mom took off.

"How was school?" Fiona asks Claudia now, perching on the boxy arm of the midcentury sofa. Fiona dropped out when she was fourteen, and she loves to hear the details of what it's like for her sister, the more mundane the better: the menu options in the cafeteria and who got in trouble for talking in study hall, which of her teachers is the best dresser. Part of it is just that Fiona loves Claudia desperately, but more than that is the mysterious allure of actual high school, which feels like either a disaster she narrowly avoided or a glamorous vacation she missed due to illness. Maybe both.

Claudia peels off her sheet mask, revealing the same high cheekbones as Fiona and a spray of freckles scattered across the bridge of her seventeen-year-old nose. "Stultifying as usual." She's still looking at the TV, where a busty nurse in oddly low-cut scrubs is yanking a shaggy-haired doctor into an empty exam room while a soulful acoustic cover of an eighties pop hit plays in the background. "Although a kid in my AP Chem class got suspended for lighting a Pop-Tart on fire inside his desk."

Fiona blinks, both at the anecdote and at the television. "Wait," she says after a moment, registering for the first time the broad slope of Sexy Doc's shoulders, the familiar quirk of his mouth. Right away, and very stupidly, she feels her cheeks get warm. "Is this—?"

"'A genius in the operating room,'" Estelle intones, echoing the tagline on the dramatically lit billboards plastered all over LA. "'A fool in love.'"

"Oh my god." Fiona laughs, but only to avoid some other reaction. She steals another quick glance at the TV. "This show is an abomination," she says, though she hasn't actually let herself watch it. The entire conceit of *The Heart Surgeon*, as far as she can tell, is that the title character—a handsome and charismatic savant with an international reputation for greatness—cannot keep his dick in his pants.

"Don't be mean!" Claudia chides, bumping Fiona's knee with her shoulder. "It's good. I mean, it's bad-good, but it's still good."

"Uh-huh," Fiona says, leaning forward to take a sip of Claudia's ginger ale. "See, now *that's* what they should put on the billboards."

"I'll grant you it's not exactly *Masterpiece Theatre*," Estelle concedes. "Still"—she points at the doctor, who's pulled his own shirt off to expose a six-pack you could use to scrub grass stains out of your dirty laundry—"one might argue the aesthetics are equally pleasing, in their way."

"Fiona dated him," Claudia reports, reaching over to rub Brando on his smooth pink belly.

That gets Estelle's attention. "Did she, now?"

"False," Fiona corrects. Sam Fox—the eponymous Heart Surgeon—played Fiona's cool older brother on *Birds of California*; he starred in a couple of teary YA adaptations for Netflix after that, then turned up as a three-episode love interest on virtually every network drama before finally landing what is, according to *People* magazine, his big leading-man break. Not that Fiona reads *People* magazine. Or Sam's IMDb page. Because she doesn't. "I definitely did not date him."

Claudia looks unconvinced. "But you kissed."

"One time," Fiona reminds her. "And I don't actually think it counts if it happens in between getting kicked out of a Wendy's for flashing the assistant manager and falling off the stage at the MTV Movie Awards."

Estelle tuts. "You should have worn different shoes that night," she muses.

"Oh, for sure," Fiona agrees, nodding seriously. "It was the shoes that were the problem."

"Well, my darling, I think it's fair to say they didn't improve the situation." Estelle peels off her own mask, chunky bangle bracelets jangling on her delicate wrists. Estelle was a costume designer for MGM in the seventies and eighties and still dresses like it, all scarves and patterns and designer separates in bright, jazzy jewel tones. Two of the three bedrooms in her house are full of rolling racks crammed with immaculately preserved vintage gowns, which she's promised to Claudia after she dies and not one second sooner. "And if you didn't date him, you should have. He's delicious."

"He's symmetrical," Fiona counters. "And freshly waxed."

Estelle fixes her with a look that suggests she isn't entirely buying it. "There are worse things to be."

Fiona glances down at her own scruffy Converse and the baggy denim jacket she stole from her dad and supposes she doesn't have much to say in rebuttal. On TV, Sam and the bosomy nurse are still going at it, his bare back tan and muscular, his big hands cupping her face. Fiona ignores the weird, involuntary thing her stomach does at the split-second flash of his tongue, then stands up and nudges her sister gently in the side. "Homework in half an hour," is all she says.

After dinner Fiona does the dishes and wipes the counters, then flips through a pile of mail. She's got a postcard from Thandie, who's filming on location in Paris: just four quick lines about a violinist she heard on the street in Montmartre and the pigeons that roost on the wrought iron balcony of her flat. Leave it to Thandie to make even city vermin sound glamorous. Thandie is probably the closest thing Fiona has to a best friend, though they've communicated almost exclusively by mail for the last few years. If you asked Thandie, she'd probably say it's because she likes the old-fashioned quality of a handwritten letter, but Fiona knows the real reason, which is that she herself is easier for Thandie to deal with if they don't have to talk or text.

Now she tucks the postcard into her back pocket and heads down the hall to her bedroom, clicking on the true crime channel for company. *Wives with Knives* isn't on for another hour, so she listens with half an ear to *Hometown Homicides* while she changes into a pair of boxers and a tank top, scooping her mass of curly hair into a knot on top of her head. She feels itchy and out of sorts tonight, her skin and clothes and life all half a size too small.

She uses the antiaging cream Estelle got her for her twenty-eighth birthday. She stares out the window for a while. Finally she plucks her phone off the nightstand, the screen spiderwebbed with cracks from where she dropped it on the patio a couple of months ago filming Claudia doing an impression of Benedict Cumberbatch reciting the lyrics to Rihanna's "Desperado," and opens up a new browser window.

S-a-m, she types into the search bar. *F-*

That's when the thing starts to vibrate in her hand.

Fiona drops it on the mattress, blushing furiously. She feels like she just got caught doing something weird and a little perverted, like masturbating in church or peeing into an empty bottle of Arizona iced tea at a red light.

She's so startled, in fact, that it takes her a moment to register the name on the screen.

Shit.

She fully intends to send the call to voice mail, but her finger jerks or her brain shorts out or maybe she just really is as crazy and self-destructive as everyone thinks she is, because all at once she's hitting the button to answer, lifting the phone to her ear. "Caroline," she says, then immediately, deeply regrets it. Back when she was in the hospital her therapist used to tell her to count backward from ten before she made any rash decisions. Her impulse control is . . . not great. "Hi."

"Fiona!" Caroline says warmly. "It's so good to hear your voice."

Fiona smiles at that; she can't help it. Muscle memory. "Yours too," she says, and for a moment she truly means it. Back when she was a teenager she used to worship Caroline—tall and blond and coolly beautiful, the kind of person who never seemed to have a blemish or a bad day. Fiona remembers thinking that she was the one who should have been on television.

"I'm sorry to be calling you out of the blue like this, and so late," Caroline says now, though of course it isn't out of the blue, not really, and both of them know it. "I did reach out by email, but then it occurred to me that maybe your address had changed, or . . ." She waits a moment, presumably for Fiona to explain herself, then presses on. "Anyway. I got a call from Bob Arkin last week. I guess he wasn't sure how to get in touch with you other than going through me."

"He could have ordered a Sausage Fest banner," Fiona offers reflexively.

Caroline's frown is audible. "What?"

"Nothing." She's stalling, that's all. "What did he want?"

"Well, Bob and Jamie Hartley," Caroline clarifies. "They're interested in rebooting *Birds of California*."

An earthquake shakes the house just then, knocking the books from her bookshelves and the pictures from her walls. At least, that's what it feels like, so when Fiona looks around dizzily she's surprised to find everything just where it was a moment ago. "Seriously?" is the best she can manage.

Caroline laughs, though it doesn't sound like she's finding any of this particularly hilarious. "Fiona," she says, "do you think I would be calling you if they weren't serious?"

Well. Fiona can't argue there. Bob is the head of the Family Network; Jamie played her dad, but he was also the creator and EP, the whole show a love letter to his childhood as a zookeeper's kid on some island off the coast of British Columbia. Last she heard, he had a massive fantasy project in development at HBO. *"Why?"*

"I—" Caroline sounds as baffled as Fiona feels. "Nostalgia?" she guesses. "Money? They seem to think it's a good idea, I don't know. I get the impression Jamie's in the position to be doing pretty much anything he wants right now."

"Not this," Fiona says.

Caroline sighs. "Okay," she says, "before we go any further. Can I make a suggestion? As an old friend?"

The house shakes again; Fiona can feel it. Back when everything was really bad—the year or two after the show got canceled, her blotchy face on Darcy Sinclair's website every day—the only time she ever cried was when Caroline dropped her as a client. "Please," Fiona begged, "I can do better." That was before Caroline stopped taking her calls.

"We're not friends," Fiona manages now, wanting to crawl out of her body at the memory of it. For a moment she's not entirely sure which one of them she's trying to remind.

Caroline pauses before she answers. Fiona can imagine her on the other end of the phone, her painted red mouth just slightly pinched. "Okay," she says finally. "That's fine. As your former agent, then. I don't know what your situation is these days. Maybe you're happy being out of the game forever. I can respect that, after everything you've been through. But if you have any interest in ever acting again—in ever having any kind of career on the screen—then I would think long and hard before I turned my nose up at this offer. This kind of second chance doesn't come along that often, especially—" She breaks off.

"Especially for people like me," Fiona finishes. "Noted. Thanks for the tip."

Caroline sighs again. "Fiona—"

"You can tell Bob Arkin I'm not interested," she says. "And you can tell Jamie Hartley to go fuck himself."

Fiona hangs up before Caroline can answer. She drops her phone on the bed, then gets up and bolts through the still-quaking house, past the living room where her dad is staring blankly at Guy Fieri and the kitchen where Claudia is hand-washing her bras in the sink.

"Whoa," Claudia says, poking her head out into the hallway. "Where are you going?"

"Out," Fiona snaps, then immediately feels like a piece of shit, but it's too late for her to do anything about it, because her legs are already carrying her down the front walk, her fingers already fishing around for her car keys, her lower lip already trembling in a very dangerous way. She sets her jaw and peels out of the driveway, opening all the windows to the hot, dry air.

She drives for close to an hour—palm trees silhouetted darkly against the last blue dregs of daylight, neon blurring by on either side. She doesn't stop until she runs out of road. She leaves the car running in the parking lot at the beach and heads for the shoreline, the driver's side door gaping open behind her; it's not until she feels the heavy grit of the sand between her toes that she realizes she forgot to put on her shoes.

Fiona wades in up to her knees, gasping at the shock of it: the water cold and endless all around her, the wide black canvas of the sky. She stands as still as she can, for as long as she can manage. Then she gets back in her car and goes home.

CHAPTER TWO

Sam

Sam wakes up on Erin's couch with a hangover the following morning, head pounding and mouth like the inside of a gym bag.

Also, his dick is out.

"Why am I naked?" he asks in alarm, peering down at himself and then over at Erin, who's perched at the breakfast bar in jeans and a smart-looking blazer, cup of coffee clutched in one tawny hand. He sits up so fast he gets the spins. "Wait, we didn't . . . right?"

"Oh, we did," Erin reports grimly. She's scrolling through emails on her laptop, not bothering to look up at him. "Honestly, Sam, the pure masculine allure of you in those tight leather pants was finally too much for me after all these years."

"You're hilarious," Sam grumbles, swinging his legs gingerly onto the floor. He pulls the throw blanket off the back of the sofa, wrapping it around him like a toga; the room tilts underneath him, then rights itself again. "Also, those pants aren't *leather*. They're coated denim. It's a different thing."

Erin shrugs. "Whatever they are, you were wearing them

when I went to bed," she tells him. "I don't know what happened to you after that." She shuts her laptop with a tidy click. "You owe me a new throw blanket, PS. That thing is going straight into the trash."

"Well that's just silly," Sam points out reasonably. "By that logic, you'd also need to replace the couch."

"You want to buy me one of those, too?" Erin fires back. "Frankly you're lucky I didn't toss your bare ass directly onto the street first thing this morning. I've spent my entire life purposely trying to avoid a faceful of male genitalia. I'm not about to start tolerating it in the sanctity of my own home."

"You know I sleep hot," Sam mumbles, scrubbing both hands through his hair. He vaguely remembers waking up around three or four, sweaty and anxious, yanking irritably at his clothes before falling back into a restless, half-drunk sleep. "Can I have some coffee?"

"Get it yourself," Erin says cheerfully, standing up and setting her own mug in the dishwasher. "And lock the door on your way out. I've got an interview in Pasadena." Erin's a freelance writer for various culture and entertainment outlets around LA, and the fact that she can afford to live alone in an apartment with a dishwasher is a testament to how very, very good she is at it.

Sam frowns. "Can you push it back?" he asks, a weird current of panic zinging through him at the thought of her leaving him alone. "Let's get breakfast."

Erin stops at the door, her dark eyes narrowed. They were roommates for three years back when she was still blogging and

Sam was hustling for walk-ons; she's the closest thing to family that he has in LA. "Are you okay?" she asks.

"I'm fine," he promises, though it comes out too quickly to sound terribly convincing. "I mean, I'm hungover as all hell, but other than that? Never better."

"If you say so." She turns back to the door. "In that case, I'll see you later."

"Wait!" Sam blurts, almost losing his blanket-toga as he scrambles to his feet. "What happened with the hipster glasses girl you were talking to last night?"

"Okay, seriously." Erin huffs out a breath. "What's going on with you?"

"Why does something have to be going on with me to ask about your romantic life?" Sam asks, wounded. "I'm sensitive."

Erin snorts. "I don't know if *that's* how I'd describe you, exactly."

Sam hitches up his blanket and shuffles over to the coffee maker. He has a bad, anxious feeling, and he probes the origins of it carefully, like he's feeling around with his tongue for a rotten tooth. The nights have sort of started to smear together lately, if he's being honest, but from what he can remember it was a good one: a bunch of people out on the patio at a Mexican place in West Hollywood, oysters and tequila and guacamole with lobster ceviche on top. A cute blond girl from a CW show who kept telling him how funny he was, even though he was pretty sure he wasn't saying anything that hilarious. More drinks afterward, and the bartender coming back with his credit card: "It didn't go through."

Aha. It's weirdly satisfying to figure it out, even though it makes him feel specifically, rather than generally, bad. All at once the memory is as clear as if Sam didn't drink anything at all: "Whoops," he said, smiling at the bartender even as dread and embarrassment wound a double helix up his spine. "Would you mind trying it again?"

"I tried it three times," she reported.

"Once more?" he asked, tilting his head to the side in a way that gets him what he wants, usually. It got him what he wanted this time, too, but a moment later she was back again, sliding the card across the shiny bartop with a shake of her head.

"Sorry," she said—quietly, which Sam appreciated. "No dice."

In the end he had her run his debit card instead, which worked, thankfully, but when he pulled up his banking app he saw that not only had he maxed out his Amex, but that last round of cocktails—and he'd paid for everyone, he was feeling magnanimous—had left him with exactly $314.83 to his name.

It's fine, Sam tells himself now, staring ineffectually at the coffee maker. He'll get paid again in a week or so, though once he makes rent and his car payment and sends some cash home to Adam and his mom—

"Go for a run or something," Erin advises, snapping him out of it. Sam swallows the anxiety back down into his chest where it belongs. "Or at least take a shower." She raises her eyebrows, opens the door. "At your own house, even."

"Your water pressure is better," Sam protests weakly. Erin flips him the bird.

Once she's gone he sits back down on the couch with his coffee and digs his phone out of his discarded jeans, blinking at the screen when he sees he's got 412 text messages. Dread surges up like groundwater until he can almost feel the squish of it underneath his feet: he didn't even have 412 text messages after the pilot of *The Heart Surgeon* aired last year. Right away he's worried he accidentally tweeted something offensive about little people or made a sex tape when he wasn't paying attention. He scrolls through the first few texts, the dread creeping coldly up past his ankles and his knees.

Dude, his trainer said at four forty-five this morning, tough break.

His agent, Russ, texted at five, which is when Sam knows he makes calls from his Peloton. Don't panic. Call me. Let's have lunch today.

Even his mom back at home in Milwaukee, a couple of hours ago: I tried calling, but you didn't pick up! Remember we love you no matter what.

The dread is up to his neck now, and rising fast. Sam takes a deep breath like he's getting ready to dive, then opens up his browser and types his own name into the search bar. The first news article to come up is from the *Hollywood Reporter*. The headline reads: "Midseason cancellations: *Riptide*, *Lightning Jones* done at ABN."

Well, that's okay, Sam thinks, his eyes flicking over the article. He's not on *Riptide* or *Lightning Jones*. He keeps reading.

"Also axed: *The Unlikelies*, *Half-Moon Bay*, *The Heart Surgeon*."

The Heart Surgeon.

Oh, fuck.

Sam jumps up off the couch, looking around wildly at Erin's tidy living room. Belatedly, it occurs to him that he's still completely naked. He doesn't know what's worse, the show being canceled or the fact that it was the third one down on the list of "also axed." He thinks of his empty bank account. He thinks of the mortgage on his mom's house in Wisconsin. He thinks of his Tesla sitting outside Erin's apartment right now—she drove it back to Silver Lake, he remembers suddenly; he was too drunk—and feels a little bit like he's going to be ill.

He knew this could happen, obviously. He just didn't think it would happen to *him*.

Sam sets his coffee down on the end table and checks the clock on his phone: 9:48. Almost noon back at home, he reasons. Already after lunch on the East Coast. "Fuck it," he mutters out loud, then opens Erin's freezer and pulls out a bottle of vodka.

He calls Russ and gets his assistant, a bleached blond named Sherri who tells Sam to meet Russ for lunch on the patio at Soho House. "How you doing, kiddo?" she asks him. Sam doesn't know why it's Sherri of all people being nice to him that kind of makes him want to lie down in the middle of Sunset Boulevard and wait to get run over by a Star Tour.

Still, he goes home and jerks off in the shower and fools around with his hair for a while, smooths his eyebrows down with a little bit of Vaseline. He puts on his favorite shirt, a white linen button-down he knows for a fact makes his tan look very natural, and between all that and the a.m. cocktail he's feeling a little bit steadier by the time he hands his keys to the valet. He loves Soho House: the glamour and the romance, the lounge chairs and the lanterns and the faint whiff of bleach from the pool. Even more than when he's out at a club or on set somewhere, this is where LA always feels the most like LA to him, when it hits him that he's actually doing what he always said he was going to do.

Well. He *was* doing it, anyway.

Now he guesses he's unemployed.

Russ is sitting at his usual table on the far side of the patio, a seltzer with lemon on the table in front of him. Even after living here all these years Sam still pictures every agent as Ari Gold from *Entourage* but in fact Russ looks more like King Triton from *The Little Mermaid*, with a salt-and-pepper beard and longish hair and extremely muscular pectorals. When he gets up from the table at a restaurant, there's always a second when Sam expects him to have fins instead of feet.

"Hey, buddy," Russ says now, like he's Sam's dad, or how Sam imagines his dad would talk if he had one, which he does not. Russ is wearing an extremely fitted button-down shirt and a pair of buttery-looking leather loafers, a Jaeger winking discreetly on his wrist. "How you holding up?"

"I'm fine," Sam says automatically, trying to affect the experienced nonchalance of a seasoned professional. It's important to him, for some reason, that Russ think he's a cool, collected man-about-town. "I guess I'm just . . . a little confused? I thought the numbers were good." That's not strictly true. Sam knew the numbers were not good, actually, but everyone kept telling him it was fine and he mostly didn't question it, because it made his life easier and less stressful to believe them. A weird by-product of having gotten famous when he was a teenager is that people still treat him like a teenager a lot of the time, and it's not actually as bad as it sounds.

The waitress appears at their table before Russ can answer. "Are you gents ready to order?" she asks.

"Absolutely," Russ says, though Sam hasn't looked at the menu yet. Russ orders a Cobb salad, so then Sam panics and orders one too even though he doesn't like blue cheese or hard-boiled eggs and he hasn't let himself eat bacon since Obama was president. The waitress is smiling in a way that could mean either that she recognizes him or that she doesn't but thinks he's nice to look at; Sam gets so distracted smiling back at her that for a moment he forgets both that he's out of a job and that he just accidentally ordered a disgusting lunch he has no intention of eating.

"You shouldn't take it personally," Russ tells him once she's gone, glancing at his phone before setting it facedown on the table. "These things happen, that's all. On to the next. I've got an audition lined up for you tomorrow, maybe another one at the end of the week."

"A movie?" Sam asks hopefully.

Russ shakes his head. "Not this time."

Sam tries not to look too disappointed about that. He's been trying to get a movie for ages; he was in that teen weeper a few years ago about the girl with scoliosis, but after that it was all guest spots on paramedic shows and "nice-but-bland guy who makes the heroine realize who she really loves" until he finally booked *The Heart Surgeon*. He's thought about trying his luck with a different agent, but that feels like a lot of work for who knows what outcome. He's been with Russ for a long time.

"Anyway," Russ says now, like possibly he knows Sam's eye is wandering, "that's not all the good news I've got for you." He checks his phone one more time. "There's interest in a *Birds of California* reboot."

Sam blinks. "Wait, really?" He hardly ever thinks about *Birds* anymore; the contract he signed back then was basically one step up from indentured servitude, so it's not like he's seeing a ton of residuals checks. "On the Family Network?"

"Well, yes and no," Russ says. "They're launching a streaming thing, looking for an anchor. I've had a couple of calls. Arkin sounds very eager. Hartley's written a few episodes already."

"And Fiona said yes?"

"Well." Russ raises his bushy eyebrows. "That's the question, isn't it. They don't want to do it unless she's attached."

"Could they even insure her?"

"Let's not get ahead of ourselves," Russ says. "My understanding is that she's reluctant to commit, which is probably wise of her. The girl is a car wreck."

Sam winces a little at that. He always liked Fiona fine when they were working together. She had a wicked sense of humor; she always knew her lines. And yeah, it kind of seemed like she was going through some shit toward the end there—he thinks suddenly of the last time they saw each other, the taste of wildness at the back of her mouth—but by the time she really started to lose it he was already off the show, so it wasn't like it was his problem.

He remembers she was always reading books in her trailer. He remembers she had a really excellent laugh.

Now, though? Sam has no idea. He guesses at some point she must have gotten tired of shuffling barefoot through Malibu and breathing fire at reporters, because he hasn't seen her on the blogs in a while. He read a rumor she was dead, though he figured someone would have called him if that was true.

"Anyway, it's been suggested to me that you might want to give her a call and talk to her about it," Russ says now, nodding a hello at someone over Sam's shoulder. "She finds out you're signing on, the whole thing looks a little more legit—"

"Wait." Sam is confused. He's been working in LA for long enough that he knows he should have a better understanding of how these things come together, but he feels like the window has closed and now it's too late to ask—that if he admits he doesn't always totally understand what the fuck is happening in his career he'll be exposed as the fraud he worries he is. "Is it *not* legit?"

"No, of course it's legit," Russ says quickly. "You think I'd be bringing it to you if it wasn't legit? I think she just needs a little coaxing, that's all. Hartley seemed to think you were guy for the job."

"Jamie did?" Sam grins at that. He loves Jamie. And if Fiona never particularly struck him as the kind of person who could be *coaxed* into doing much of anything, that doesn't mean it's not worth at least talking to her about it. The whole project kind of sounds like fun.

More to the point: Sam really needs a fucking job.

"Okay," he says now, smiling his thanks as the waitress drops off their revolting salads. "Sure. I'm game."

"Of course you are," Russ says, glancing at his phone one more time before picking up his napkin. "Eat your lunch."

CHAPTER THREE

Fiona

Fiona has rehearsal that night, so once she's done at the print shop she cranks the air in her roasting car and heads downtown, crawling through rush hour traffic while Kate Bush wails away on the stereo. She feeds a handful of quarters into the meter before she heads inside, traipsing down the stairs and through the long, pee-smelling hallway until she gets to the theater, where Georgie and Larry are already sitting in the house arguing about a meme Larry saw on Facebook.

"Frances!" Georgie calls, waving one plump, manicured hand in Fiona's direction. "Settle something for us, would you?"

"What are you going to ask her for?" Larry asks crabbily. He's wearing a baggy plaid button-down and dad jeans, his salt-and-pepper hair springing up in every direction like baby arugula. "People her age don't vote."

"I vote," Fiona says, which is mostly true. "Warm-ups in five."

She drops her backpack in the second row and digs out her battered script, propping her feet on the back of the seat in front of her and rereading the scene they're working tonight while Larry and Georgie gripe at each other and the rest of the cast trickles in. The Angel City Playhouse was a porn theater back in the eighties before it was taken over by a development corporation as part of an urban renewal project that never materialized. Now it's a black box with a dressing room the size of a walk-in closet and a bathroom they share with the nonprofit that rents the office space upstairs. The theater seats eighty-three people. As far as Fiona understands it, they have never sold out a run.

She fishes a pencil out of her bag, scribbling a couple of last-minute notes to herself in the margins. She never intended to act again, obviously—not that this even really counts, because it doesn't. But last winter she was dropping off a bunch of her mom's old stuff at the Goodwill across the street when she saw the hand-written sign on the door of the building:

ANGEL CITY PLAYERS. AUDITIONS TODAY!

Fiona still has no idea why she went inside. It was the same part of her that thought it would be a good idea to let some guy from Justin Bieber's entourage give her a DIY tattoo in a bathroom at the bar at Sunset Tower, she guesses—the reckless part of her that acts first and considers the implications later. She scrawled a made-up name on the sign-in sheet and rattled off the same monologue she always used to do when she auditioned, Helena's *Love looks not with the eyes* speech from *A Midsummer Night's Dream*. It used to get a ton of laughs when she was a kid—the randomness of it, probably, like she was a dog who could bark the alphabet.

Diane didn't even chuckle. "Thanks," she said when Fiona was finished, yanking one of six pens out of her bright red bun and writing something on a legal pad, barely looking up. "We'll let you know." Fiona went home and immediately forgot about it until three days later, when Diane called her cell phone and offered Frances Fairbanks the role of Elaine in *Arsenic and Old Lace*.

That was eighteen months ago. Since then she's played Catherine in *Proof* and Mollie Ralston in *The Mousetrap* and Juror 3 in an all-gender production of *Twelve Angry Men*. Every time the lights go down Fiona fully expects this to be the last time, for someone in the very back row to jump up and point at her like she's a witch from *The Crucible*, but so far she hasn't been caught.

Probably because there are only ever a dozen and a half people in the audience.

"You guys ready to start?" she asks now, getting to her feet and tying her hair up. Two months ago Diane and her wife started fostering a set of twin girls who'd just gotten out of the NICU, which is how Fiona wound up moonlighting as director of this season's show, a modern-day imagining of *A Doll's House*—not because she knows anything about directing, but because she was sitting in the front row of the theater eating a smoked salmon bagel when Diane got the call from the social worker. "Can you take over?" Diane asked, shoving her marked-up script into Fiona's hands before speeding off to Target for car seats and diapers. There's still a smudge of scallion cream cheese on the front of the folder. Fiona had never directed anything in her life—she literally went home and ordered a book called *How to Direct Theater* from

Book Soup—but to her surprise she's found she actually likes it a lot: imagining each scene in her head before rehearsal, talking to everyone about their characters and what they want. It makes her feel like she's in control of something, even if that something is a low-end production of an overdone Ibsen play. It makes her feel very calm.

"Okay," she says once she's hopped up onto the stage, looking around at the rest of the cast—Larry and Georgie and Hector and DeShaun, Pamela who keeps ferrets and always dresses all in black. Fiona knows it's only a matter of time until one of them figures out who she is and she has to quit forever. She's trying to enjoy it while it lasts. "Let's get to work."

When she gets home from rehearsal she makes some toast and heads out onto the patio with a pen and a book of vintage LA postcards, settling herself at the wobbly metal table. The ancient party lights strung through the pergola cast a speckled glow across the yard. Fiona is quiet for a long time, listening to the hum of Estelle's A/C unit and the far-off howl of a coyote. Finally she grits her teeth and ducks her head to write.

Dear Thandie, she starts, then immediately rips the postcard in half and reaches for another one. She's supposed to be writing a breezy three-line note here, not asking for a letter of recommendation to graduate school.

Hey lady! she tries, feeling herself blush as soon as she sees the words on paper. Ugh, there is no fucking way. It's always like this when she tries to write to Thandie: a million false starts and a ream of wasted paper, the fog of her own cheery bullshit too thick to see through with any kind of clarity. She remembers when they talked so constantly that everything they said to each other felt like one long, continuous conversation. She remembers when they talked so constantly they didn't actually need to talk very much at all.

Bonjour, mon petit fromage,

Paris sounds completely dreamy. I like to imagine you, as I imagine literally all French people, wearing a beret with a baguette tucked neatly under your arm for safekeeping, even (especially?) while sleeping or taking a shower.

    Things are good here! Quiet, which is always the goal. I'm thinking of asking Estelle if I can join her book club, which reads only BDSM erotica, though my understanding is that there's a rigorous hazing and I'm not sure I want to voluntarily put myself at the mercy of a dozen randy septuagenarians with a thing for whips and ball gags.

I really, really miss you, she writes before she can stop herself, then crosses the whole thing out and starts again.

The next day dawns smoggy and overcast. Her dad's having a tough morning, so Fiona leaves him sitting at the kitchen table in his bathrobe and makes the twenty-minute drive to open the shop by herself. Sausage Fest was right that business isn't exactly booming—the truth is they barely do enough to stay afloat, year to year—but her parents bought the dilapidated building in Eagle Rock back in the nineties, then watched the neighborhood gentrify around them like a garden bursting into vaguely alarming bloom. Now there are three different cycling studios on this block alone.

Fiona turns on the lights and powers up the printers, breathing in the familiar smell of toner and forced air while she waits for the computer to boot. They've got a couple of digital orders that need to get out the door today, plus a suite of wedding invitations with half a dozen finicky parts. She's going to have to wait for Richie to come in to start those—even after twenty years of watching her dad do it, she still always fucks up the letterpress machine—so she flicks on the radio and unpacks a shipment from the paper mill instead, tucking reams of card stock onto the shelves in the workshop according to color and weight. She's just finishing when the bell above the door rings. "Just a second!" Fiona calls, breaking down the last of the boxes with a neat zip of the utility knife.

When she straightens up and comes out to the counter, Sam Fox is standing on the other side of it, Dodgers cap pulled low over his eyes.

For a moment Fiona just freezes. Then she turns around and marches back into the workshop, where she stares blankly at the Heidelberg for a full ten seconds, seriously considering sneaking out the back and driving all the way to Mexico. But: Claudia, so instead she grits her teeth and goes out again to where Sam is still standing at the counter with his hands in his pockets, head cocked quizzically to the side. You could use his jaw to open a can of corn.

"Hi," she manages, like he's any other customer and not . . .

whatever he is to her after all this time. Nothing, she tells herself firmly. He isn't anything. "Can I help you?"

"Holy shit," he says softly, his green eyes big as two vapid moons. "It *is* you."

Fiona frowns. "What?"

He shrugs, the muscles in his shoulders moving inside his expensive-looking white T-shirt. "I just—I thought maybe it was an urban legend or something. When they said you worked here."

"*What?*" Holy shit, she cannot believe this is happening. She would have thought that by now she'd be immune to this kind of deep, searing humiliation, like at some point her embarrassment impulse should have calloused over. Clearly, she was wrong. "Who the fuck is 'they'?"

"I—nobody." Sam shakes his head, sheepish. "Hi."

Fiona breathes. "Hi," she says again. For a moment they just stand there, facing off across the counter. She hasn't seen him in eight years, since the night of the cast party for his last season of *Birds*. Actually, it was the last full season of *Birds*, period, but nobody knew that at the time; it would be a few more months before the network finally lost its patience and pulled the plug on the whole operation. "Do you need something copied?" she asks.

"I—no." Sam looks confused. "What?"

Jesus Christ. "Why are you here?"

"I was looking for you," he tells her, and just for one second her heart stops dead inside her chest. "I wanted to talk to you about the reboot."

Oh. "Oh." Fiona wills herself not to deflate. Of course that's what he wants from her. She doesn't know how she didn't figure it out as soon as he walked in. Him showing up here sideswiped her somehow, turned her into the kind of naïve, slow-thinking bone-head she was back when she was seventeen. "Well, you could have saved yourself a trip," she announces, somehow managing to keep her voice even, "because there's nothing to talk about. I already told them I'm not going to do it."

"Yeah, I heard." Sam nods. "How are you?" he asks, after exactly one beat too long. "Sorry, I probably should have led with that."

"I'm fine."

"Yeah?" he asks, taking the cap off and running a hand through his thick, messy hair. "That's good. I know you kind of had a rough go there for a while."

Fiona barks a laugh. "A rough *go*?" Just like that she's suddenly furious: at her dad for being too out of it to run his own business and at Richie for being late to work again, at her own traitorous heart for the way it's banging around in her rib cage, slamming away against the inside of her chest like an animal trying to get free. At Jamie, always. At Sam most of all. She can feel the anger leaking out of her, bright red and orange. They ought to use it to print banners. "Is that what you heard I had?"

"Sorry," Sam repeats immediately—palms out, trepidation written all over his pretty face, like he's afraid she's going to lunge across the counter and rip his throat out. She's been arrested for assault on two separate occasions. "I didn't mean, like—"

"Hey, boss." That's Richie coming into the shop in cargo

shorts and a Bob Marley T-shirt, an enormous blue Slurpee in one hand. He once told Fiona that he drinks two of them every day, one in the morning and one to wind down before bed. "Everything okay?"

Fiona nods. "Yeah, Richie," she says, eyes still locked on Sam across the counter. "Everything's fine."

Richie hesitates for a moment, gaze darting back and forth between them, then nods and heads back into the workshop. "That your bodyguard?" Sam asks once he's gone.

"I guard my own body, thank you." Fiona feels herself sag a little, suddenly exhausted. She's always imagined this going differently. "Look," she finally says, "if you don't need something copied, then you're just loitering. And we have a policy about that."

Sam looks at the firmly worded sign on the door, then back at her. "Do you guys have a problem with loiterers?" he asks.

She raises her eyebrows. "Apparently so."

"Ohhhkay," he says, digging around in the back pocket of his jeans until he comes up with a crumpled CVS receipt." Can I get a copy of this, then?"

Fiona doesn't take it. "The minimum we do is ten at a time."

Sam rolls his eyes. "Fine," he agrees. "Ten copies."

She snatches the receipt from his outstretched hand, sneaking a look at it before she smooths it out against her thigh and lays it facedown on the glass. It's from this morning; he bought condoms and a hippie-brand energy bar and a VitaminWater in the hangover-buster flavor, thus confirming him as exactly the kind of person Fiona has always assumed he is. They stand there in silence while the machine whirs to life. When she glances up he's gazing back at her, curious. "You look different," he observes quietly.

Fiona shrugs at the copier, reflexively wondering if he means good different or bad different and telling herself it doesn't matter. "You look the same." It's a bald-faced lie, obviously. Sam was always cute, with dark hair and a crooked, bashful smile—she remembers watching him in the mirror in the makeup trailer right when the show first started, his eyes closed, his long lashes casting tiny shadows on his cheekbones—but he was barely out of his teens back then, with skinny ribs and acne the makeup girls used to cover with thick pancake every morning. Now he looks like a grown-ass man, all broad chest and tan forearms and a day's worth of beard that Fiona recognizes from the sleepy Saturday morning shots he posts to his Instagram stories sometimes.

Not that she looks at his Instagram stories.

Well. She certainly doesn't *follow* him on Instagram, that's for damn sure.

"Why don't you want to do it?" Sam asks as his copies pile up on the tray one after the other, a tidy stack. "The show, I mean."

"Why *do* you want to?"

"I asked you first."

Fiona sighs noisily, turning to face him. She knows that Pam, her old therapist, would remind her that it's not her responsibility to satisfy every random jabroni's curiosity about her personal life and mental wellness; still, she finds herself ticking the reasons off on her fingers. "I don't act anymore," she informs him. "I don't have any *interest* in acting anymore. And not for nothing, but Darcy Sinclair finally stopped waiting outside my house trying to get a photo of me taking a dump on the curb like an animal, or whatever the hell else she thought I was going to do next."

It's more than she meant to say—to anyone, but especially to Sam Fox, with his narrow hips and SAG card and perfectly capped teeth—but to her surprise it actually seems to register. "That must have sucked," he says softly. "The stuff with Darcy's website, I mean."

Fiona turns back to the copier, taking longer than necessary to pull the original off the glass. "It wasn't a big deal," she lies. "But I'm out."

"Hey, I hear you," Sam promises. "I guess I just thought it sounded kind of fun, that's all."

Fiona scoffs. "I think that is exactly the opposite of what it would be, actually."

"Oh, come on!" he protests. "We used to have a good time, right? You and me and Thandie and what's his name, the little ginger kid who played the cousin."

"Seriously?" She rolls her eyes. "His name is Max, and we worked with him for five years. God, you really are just as douchey as you look, huh?"

For a second Sam seems stung by that, which is surprising—she's never thought of him as an actual person capable of having his feelings hurt—but then he blinks and it's gone. "Douchier, probably," he admits with a crooked *aren't I charming* smile. "But I mean it. I think you should reconsider."

"I'll keep that in mind. Here," Fiona says, handing him the stack of copies across the counter. They're a little blurry, actually, now that she's looking. If her dad was here he'd make her redo them.

Sam doesn't care. "Keep 'em," he says, waving her off with one hand and pulling his wallet out with the other. "What do I owe you?"

Fiona rings him up, running his debit card through the ancient machine. It's weird to see his full name printed on the plastic, a strange reminder that this whole time he's just been out there in the world, charging things. Existing. As she's handing it back their fingers brush, just for a second. Fiona feels the zing of it all the way up her arm.

"Well," Sam says finally, tucking his wallet back into his jeans pocket and adjusting his dopey hat on his head. "I had to try, anyway. I'll let you get back to work."

"Yeah," Fiona agrees, though obviously it's not like anybody else is clamoring for her attention. Still, she doesn't want to encourage him. At least, she doesn't think she does. "I should probably . . . do that."

Sam smiles one more time, easy, generous as a newly crowned king. "It was good to see you, Fee."

He's gone before Fiona can decide if was good to see him too.

CHAPTER FOUR

Sam

So, okay, Sam thinks as he peels away from the curb outside the print shop. That's definitely not going to happen, then. Which is fine. He didn't even want it to. Who wants to play second banana in a reboot of a show they did half a lifetime ago, anyway? He's trying to move forward here, not back.

He spends the rest of the afternoon getting ready for his audition and trying not to think about Fiona. It was a total mindfuck, seeing her again after all this time. Which isn't to say she didn't look good; she looked sort of incredible, actually, dark eyes and sharp cheekbones and those long, tan limbs. She's put on some weight in a way that makes him think of girls from back home in Wisconsin—the dramatic curves of her body, the roundness of her ass in her jeans.

None of which actually matters, he reminds himself, turning back to his script. The audition is for a half-hour comedy pilot about a pair of newlyweds who have to move back in with the guy's parents after his startup collapses. It's cheesy as all hell and has at least two jokes Sam is definitely uncomfortable with, but it's a lead, so he preps for it with the same attention he's given to any of the other hundreds of auditions he's been on since he moved to LA fifteen years ago. He remembers his first day on set for *Birds of California*, the way his heart stuttered when he saw their names on the doors of their trailers: *Sam Fox. Jamie Hartley. Fiona St. James.*

Fuck, he should try to stop thinking about Fiona.

He runs through his lines, irons his button-down. Messes with his hair for a while. There's a tiny part of him that worries it's thinning, even though he's only thirty-one. "Hi," he says once he's finally satisfied, smiling his most charismatic smile into the mirror and hoping the casting director is more taken with him than some other people he could name. "I'm Sam Fox."

The audition goes decently, he thinks, though even after all this time he can still never really tell what they're thinking back there behind the folding table. He's hopeful, at least. He texts Erin from the car when he's finished to see if she wants to meet at their usual place and get drinks.

Can't, she texts back. Dinner with hipster glasses girl.

Sam sends her a series of crass emojis meant to communicate *Hope you get laid*, trying to ignore his own weird, sudden pang of loneliness. After all, if he really wanted company, there are at least a dozen other people he could text. But the thing about a lot of his friends here is that Sam knows they're going to want to talk about work—who booked what or what he's going to do now that the show is canceled—and he doesn't want to do that tonight.

He thinks about Fiona again, but that feels like a dangerous road to wander down, so instead he drinks two beers and watches some porn and passes out on the couch in his living room. When he wakes up, his phone is buzzing on the cushion beside his face, a picture of his brother Adam wearing a cheese hat displayed on the screen. The home page of the porn site is still up on his computer, a pop-up ad for some disconcerting animated game playing over and over.

"Did I wake you up?" Adam asks, when he answers. "It sounds like I woke you up."

"What?" Sam blinks, watching the cartoon boobs bounce for a moment without entirely meaning to. He shuts the screen of his laptop, then slides the whole operation under the couch. "No."

Adam doesn't buy it. "Isn't it like, seven p.m. there?"

"I wasn't asleep."

"Okay," Adam says. "Sorry again about your show, man."

"It's no big deal," Sam says automatically. Part of being the one who got out of their hometown means it's his job not to complain about his life here, to pretend that it's all industry parties and movie premieres and sticking his hands in the prints outside the Chinese Theatre. He doesn't tell his mom and brother about the directors who never follow up, or the Thanksgiving he spent eating Indian takeout by himself because Erin flew home to Corpus Christi and he was too proud to go to Russ's house. He definitely doesn't tell them about his credit card bills.

"You okay for money?" Adam asks now.

"I—what?" It takes Sam a second to realize he's asking because of the show getting canceled and not because he somehow read Sam's mind or saw his bank statement. "Yeah, of course." He clears his throat, rubbing a hand over his nap-dazed face. "How did it go today?"

"Fine," Adam reports. "Although Benson just left to go work in computer crimes because things were getting too complicated between her and Stabler."

"Well, shit," Sam says. His mom and brother are working their way through all seventy-nine seasons of *Law & Order: Special Victims Unit* while nurses drip poison into her veins with the intention of shrinking her tumor enough for her to have surgery. It makes Sam feel like he can't breathe when he thinks about it, so he tries not to, although more often than he'd like to admit he wakes up sweating through his sheets in the middle of the night, promising himself he's going to be a better son in the morning. "You think she'll come back?"

"You know," Adam says, "somehow I do."

Sam hauls himself up off the couch, filling a glass of water at the tap to wash the beer and sleep taste out of his mouth. "Speaking of comebacks," he says, "did I tell you they're going to reboot *Birds*?"

"Yeah, I got your text," Adam says. "It's a sure thing?"

"Well, no, not exactly," Sam admits. "I guess they're still waiting for Fiona to sign on the dotted line, or whatever."

"Oh, man," Adam says, and Sam can hear the grin in his voice. "Fiona St. James. I haven't thought about her since she did that photo shoot with the crocodile."

Sam drains his water in one long gulp. "I think it was a Gila monster."

"You'd know better than me, dude." Adam laughs.

Sam frowns. "What does that mean?"

"I mean, you're the one who knew her. And you guys had a little thing, didn't you?"

"Uh, nope," Sam says immediately. He has no idea why Adam thinks that. Shit, do *other* people think that? Does he have that reputation in this town, as one of the million quasi-famous dudes Fiona St. James boned on her Oregon Trail through the tabloids? "We definitely didn't."

Adam, for his part, seems utterly unconcerned. "That was a great poster," he muses. "My friend Kyle had it on his wall in high school, and all of us used to take turns—"

"Okay." Sam winces. "I get the idea." He bought the magazine in print back when it came out—everybody bought the magazine, even though the pictures are still, to the best of his knowledge, the first thing that comes up if you google Fiona's name—but it makes him feel vaguely ashamed now in a way he doesn't want to examine too closely. After all, it's not Sam's fault she completely lost her marbles and posed more or less naked with a bunch of reptiles.

"Anyway, it's probably not even going to happen," he says now, rubbing at the back of his head. He feels hungover, even though he didn't actually drink that much before he fell asleep. "The reboot, I mean." He doesn't know why he's telling this to Adam—they're not that close—except that for some reason he kind of wants to talk about Fiona a little more. "I went to see her, talked to her about it. She didn't want anything to do with me."

"Huh," Adam says. "Well, you probably dodged a bullet, right?"

"Yeah," Sam agrees, only it doesn't feel like he did, exactly. In fact, it kind of feels like he went in for a part he wanted and whiffed. "Probably."

He hangs up with his brother and gets another beer out of the refrigerator. He pulls up YouTube on his phone. He types Fiona's name into the search bar and is immediately presented with a list of public embarrassments so long and eclectic it makes the menu at the Cheesecake Factory look like an exercise in restraint:

Fiona St. James berates photographers outside hotel in Santa Monica
Fiona St. James shoplifting security footage
Fiona St. James drunk on Ellen *(full interview)*

Sam hesitates for a moment, his thumb hovering over the screen:

UNCENSORED Fiona St. James flashes paps from moving car!!!

Then he tosses the phone on the couch, which is where it stays until it buzzes a little while later with a text from Russ. Looks like the newlywed folx are going in a different direction, he reports. We'll get 'em next time!

Then, before Sam can answer: Any luck with Riley Bird?

Sam rubs a hand over the back of his head, debating. He remembers her hands in his hair all those years ago at the cast party.

He remembers the way the neon streak in her hair used to catch the lights on set. He hardly ever thinks about that time in his life anymore, but now it's like it's all coming back in bright, screaming Technicolor: the heat of the soundstage and the dense, chewy bagels at the craft services table and how deeply, sincerely thrilled he was just to get to be on TV. He remembers working a scene with Fiona during the second or third season of *Birds*—her character had called his to come pick her up at a party, and the two of them were sitting on the hood of a car talking obliquely about peer pressure. The whole thing was kind of corny both in retrospect and in the moment, but he remembers being surprised by how seriously she seemed to take it, how hard she was working to get it right. Usually when Sam found a line reading that clicked he repeated it over and over, take after take, but he noticed she played it differently every single time—putting the emphasis on different words, trying new things with her face and her body.

"And cut," the director called finally, pulling off her headphones. They had someone new that week, a woman in Doc Martens who'd made a couple of indie films out on the East Coast; Sam couldn't help but notice, as the days had gone by, that Jamie didn't seem to like her very much. She'd been kind of demanding so far, he guessed, though Jamie was demanding, too, so Sam didn't exactly think that was the problem. Still, "Is Susan chapping your ass as much as she's chapping mine?" he'd muttered in Sam's ear as they made their way down the hall earlier that day, and though actually Sam thought Susan was fine he'd laughed because he liked the feeling of Jamie trusting him with something, even if that something seemed faintly untoward.

Susan crossed the set to where he and Fiona were still sitting on the car, waiting to find out if they were finished. "Nice work, guys," she said, then turned to Fiona. "*You*," she continued, "are incredible."

Sam waited to feel jealous—he *did* feel jealous, actually, and annoyed and overlooked, but also, as he glanced over at Fiona's ducked, bashful head he mostly just felt kind of impressed by her, like possibly there was something for him to learn here. He wondered what she'd do when all this was over? Whatever it was, he thought he'd probably want to watch.

Now Sam looks down at his phone, at Russ's text still awaiting an answer. Didn't reach her yet, he types quickly, hitting send before he can talk himself out of it. Going to try again tomorrow.

It's weirdly, alarmingly easy for him to figure out where her house is. It makes Sam a little nervous for her, actually: the following morning he just calls up her old agency and flirts with the assistant for a while, and before he knows it he's plugging an address in the Valley into the search bar on his phone. The GPS chirps officiously away.

Still, when he pulls up to the curb, for a second he thinks maybe he was wrong, that this place must be some kind of decoy: the house is brick and one-story and modest, with a scrubby lawn and a purple gazing ball sitting on a pedestal to one side of the wide front window. Back when they knew each other Sam always imagined Fiona going home to a mansion in a gated community in Brentwood with a fountain in front, a thousand nannies and personal chefs and trainers running around. The car in the driveway is at least six or seven years old.

He unbuckles the bird-of-paradise from the passenger seat beside him, balancing it on one hip as he makes his way up the walk. He rings the bell, but nobody answers. He tries again, but the house stays dark. He's about to give up when a dog starts barking; half a second later, a pit bull with shoulders broad enough to play defense for the LA Rams and a head the size of a napa cabbage comes careening around the side of the house.

Sam almost drops the plant. "Oh, shit," he mutters, bracing himself for the impact. Leave it to Fiona St. James to have a terrifying guard dog on top of everything else. He thinks he has problems now, watch him try to book a movie with half his face ripped off and no fingers. He's going to have to learn all the words to the *Phantom of the* fucking *Opera.*

"Brando!" a woman's voice yells from the direction of the house next door. "Brando, no!" and suddenly there she is, stalking out of the backyard in cutoffs and a topknot. The dog drops to the ground immediately, rolling over and rubbing his back delightedly on the browning grass.

"It's you," Sam says, lifting his free hand in a wave.

Fiona stops short when she sees him, staring with her lips just slightly parted. In the second before she rearranges her expression into a scowl, he can tell she's not *entirely* unhappy he's here.

Mostly unhappy, sure.

But not entirely.

And Sam?

Sam can work with that.

"We've got to stop meeting like this," she manages after a moment. She's wearing a white tank top over a black sports bra, barefoot on the concrete. Sam is very, very careful to keep his eyes on her face.

"I was going to call," he says, "but I thought you might not pick up."

"That was very astute of you," she says. Then, peering over his shoulder with no small amount of horror: "Is that your car?"

Sam turns and follows her gaze to where the Tesla is gleaming, freshly washed, at the curb. ". . . Yes?"

Fiona opens her mouth to respond to that, then seems to consciously decide not to, nodding instead at the plant in his arms. "What is that?"

"Oh!" he says, holding it out in her direction. "It's a bird-of-paradise. My mom would kill me if she knew I came to somebody's house empty-handed, so. It's called a Wisconsin Hello. I mean, that's what my mom calls it. We're from Milwaukee. To be fair, it might mean something else on Urban Dictionary."

He's rambling. Fuck, he's *nervous*. Why is he nervous? He wasn't nervous yesterday. Fiona blinks, an expression he doesn't recognize flickering across her face. "You brought me a plant?" she asks quietly.

"I did," Sam admits.

"Fiona, honey?" someone calls from the backyard. "Who is it?"
Fiona's spine straightens. "Nobody!" she calls back.

"Ouch," Sam says, just as a woman in her seventies hobbles out into the front yard, ropes of paper towel threaded between her freshly painted toes. A teenage girl in silk pajamas follows at her heels.

"It doesn't sound like you're talking to—oh!" The older woman stops on the grass and abruptly rearranges herself at the sight of him, throwing her shoulders back and thrusting one hip out. "Well, hello there." She turns to Fiona. "Who's your guest?"

Fiona sighs theatrically. "This is Sam," she reports. "He's not staying."

"I brought her a plant," Sam offers. He smiles at the girl— Fiona's sister, he realizes suddenly, pulling her name from the foggiest depths of his memory in a flash of utter brilliance, if he does say so himself. "Claudia, right?"

Fiona whirls on him. "How do you know that?" she demands. "You couldn't remember Max, but you remember my little sister? What are you, some kind of perv?"

"Fiona," the woman chides mildly, holding out one manicured hand in a way that suggests she expects Sam to kiss it. "Estelle Halliday."

"Sam Fox," Sam says, pressing his lips to her knuckles.

"Oh, we know," Estelle says, as Fiona tsks in audible exasperation. "We're big fans of your show."

"It got shitcanned," Fiona reports bluntly.

Estelle's eyes widen. "Fiona!"

"Well, it did, didn't it?" She turns back to Sam. "That's why you came to the print shop yesterday. And that's why you're here."

"He came to the shop?" Claudia asks, her eyes wide.

Fiona yanks her hair roughly out of its giant bun, flipping her head forward and massaging her scalp for a moment before righting herself so quickly that Sam almost gets whiplash just watching her. "They want to reboot *Birds*," she announces.

Claudia and Estelle both startle, their expressions twin caricatures of shock sixty years apart. "They do?" Estelle asks softly.

"Why didn't you say something?" Claudia wants to know.

"Because I'm not going to do it. Which I already told him." She turns to Sam. "Am I wrong?" she asks, her voice rough and demanding. "Isn't that why you're at my house right now?"

Sam stares for a minute even though he's trying not to. Her hair is a long, curly lion's mane around her face, darkly golden— movie-star hair, he thinks. Her eyes glow like two hot coals. "I came to ask if you wanted to go to lunch," he hears himself say.

Fiona gapes at him. He can see her pulse ticking in the soft, vulnerable skin of her neck. "I can't," she tells him flatly, at the same time as Estelle says, "She'd love to."

Fiona glares at her. "I've got things to do," she protests. "I was literally just on my way out."

"What things?" Estelle asks.

"Costume shopping," Fiona replies immediately, looking relieved to have an answer. "For the show."

"Well, that seems like an activity you could do together." Estelle turns to Sam. "She's directing a play," she confides. "And acting in it! People don't realize this, but she's very talented."

"Estelle," Fiona says, "Jesus."

"Well, you are!"

"She is," Sam agrees. "And I'd love to."

"That's okay," Fiona says, holding a hand up. "I'm all set."

"Surely it would be useful to have someone else along?" Estelle says reasonably. "To carry heavy things?"

"I love carrying heavy things," Sam says, hoisting up the plant for emphasis. "In fact, I've been thinking about getting a job as a bellhop at the Beverly Hills Hotel." He raises his eyebrows. "You know, now that my show got shitcanned."

Fiona's mouth does something that might or might not be a fraction of a smile, and that's when Sam knows he's got her. "Fine," she announces, handing the plant off to her sister and brushing her palms off on the seat of her shorts. "Let's go."

CHAPTER FIVE

Fiona

"Okay," Fiona says half an hour later, rolling her eyes at him as she tips the base of an ugly table lamp upside down to check the price tag on the bottom. "Can you stop that, please?"

"Stop what?" Sam asks. They're standing in the housewares section of a Goodwill on the very outskirts of Hollywood, surrounded by other people's castoffs.

"Swanning around like that," Fiona says, setting the lamp back down on the shelf and crouching to examine a wobbly-looking end table. "Not all of us are trying to get asked for our autograph."

Sam frowns. "I'm not *swanning*," he protests, looking a little stung. "This is my normal walk."

"It's not just your walk," she says, straightening up again. "It's your whole——" She gestures at him vaguely. He's wearing dark jeans and a pair of expensive-looking lace-up boots that are too hot for LA, a chambray shirt rolled to his elbows. A pair of sunglasses that probably cost as much as her car dangle from the ostentatiously unbuttoned V of his collar. "Forget it."

"Also," Sam says as he follows her down the aisle past wall

décor, where half a dozen *Live Laugh Love* canvases teeter like cursed dominoes on a rickety metal shelf, "anyone who says they don't want to get asked for their autograph is lying. You don't do what we do if you don't want to get asked for your autograph."

"What *you* do," Fiona corrects him.

But Sam shakes his head. "Nice try," he says, draping a macramé wall hanging over his shoulders like a shawl. "Except for the part where *apparently* you're still secretly acting."

Fiona doesn't have an answer for that, but luckily Sam doesn't seem to expect one. He drops the wall hanging back where he found it and wanders over to office supplies, mostly empty boxes of #10 envelopes and discarded three-ring binders with the labels half scratched off. "Why do all Goodwills smell the same?" he wonders out loud.

"Human dander and broken dreams," Fiona says, glancing at him sidelong. "Have you *been* to a lot of Goodwills in your life?"

"Yes, actually." Sam shrugs, no hesitation in his voice at all. "Before I started booking print work, at least."

That surprises her. Fiona always figured Sam came from some kind of rich Midwestern dynasty, that his dad was in steel or oil or something and they had season tickets to the Green Bay Packers. "When was that?" she asks.

"I was ten," he says. "Or nine, maybe? I had the right look for back-to-school clothes."

"You still have the right look for back-to-school clothes."

"Thank you."

"What makes you think that was a compliment?"

"You said it in a complimentary tone of voice."

"Did I?"

"You did," he tells her confidently, and before Fiona can figure out how to reply, he lets out a sound that's halfway between a laugh and a bark. "Holy shit," he crows, disbelieving. "Look at this."

"What?" Fiona asks, full of dread. It's a crapshoot, shopping at Goodwill. One time she found a family of baby mice nestled cozily in the pocket of a crocheted cardigan she bought for *Arsenic and Old Lace*.

But when Sam turns around he's grinning. "Oh, nothing," he sings, holding up—for fuck's sake—a *Birds of California* pencil case, hot pink plastic with a yellow zipper and a garish cartoon of Fiona's own face emblazoned across the front, a bright green parrot sitting on her shoulder. "Just trying to figure out what I'm going to keep in this baby, that's all."

Fiona huffs a breath. "Give me that," she says. She grabs for it, but Sam yanks it away, holding it up over his head and switching it from hand to hand like they're playing keep-away on the playground in elementary school. He's a lot taller than she remembers; close up he smells like cologne and deodorant, and a tiny bit like sweat.

"I mean, the answer is weed and papers, obviously," he says thoughtfully, still holding the pencil case aloft like a flag from a country where they lived in some other lifetime. "But that feels almost too easy? Like, surely we can do better than that."

"Oh, you're very funny."

"Only ninety-nine cents," Sam reports happily. "A bargain at twice the price."

Fiona shakes her head, turning and pushing the cart in the direction of women's clothing. Honestly, let him have it. Better than letting him know she cares one way or the other, that the very idea of *Birds of California* paraphernalia still existing in the world—clogging up secondhand stores and landfills, moldering away in Rubbermaids in the basements of people's childhood homes and contributing to the rapid warming of the planet—makes her want to peel her skin off like wallpaper. "Is there *Heart Surgeon* swag?" she asks. "Branded catheters, et cetera?"

"Bedpans, maybe," Sam says, trotting along behind her. "I signed a licensing agreement. If there is I should probably try and get my hands on some. Collector's items."

Fiona hums. "Are you bummed about it?" she can't help but ask, slinging an A-line skirt and a ruffly blouse over the edge of the cart. "Your show, I mean?"

Sam shrugs. "Yeah, of course," he allows, pulling an ancient-looking trucker hat bearing the logo of the San Francisco 49ers from a basket and modeling it casually in a nearby mirror. "I liked the people I worked with. Plus it's hard not to feel responsible, you know? Nobody wants to be the reason a whole crew gets fired." Then he looks at her and immediately blanches. "I mean—"

Fiona smirks, though it's not like it doesn't smart a little. Still, she knows it's true. Jamie said as much to her, once she'd finally committed so many obscenities in so many public venues that the Family Network yanked *Birds* from the schedule. "Do you have any idea what you just did?" he demanded, his cheeks gone red and blotchy underneath a day's worth of beard. There was a tiny drop of spit at one corner of his mouth. "The number of hardworking people whose lives you just shat all over?" She was twenty years old at the time.

"You're going to get head lice," she says now, reaching out and plucking the cap off Sam's head and putting it back on the shelf before reconsidering at the last second and throwing it into the cart instead. She'll put it in the washer on sanitize. Claudia will like it. "Come on, let's go."

"Anyway," Sam says, trailing her up to the cash register, "I'm trying to look at it as an opportunity. You know, to do the kind of stuff I've always wanted to do."

"Shakespeare?" Fiona asks dryly.

"Porn," he deadpans, then turns and smiles broadly at the moon-eyed checkout girl.

"I'd like to purchase this excellent pencil case, please."

Fiona ducks her head to hide her grin.

"Are you hungry?" Sam asks her as he pushes the cart out into the parking lot, its bum wheel screaming bloody murder against the crooked asphalt. In the end Fiona found nearly everything she needs: a briefcase for Larry and matching Christmas outfits for the kids, a couple of ugly paintings for the living room set. Her mom taught her the trick of thrifting in expensive neighborhoods, which makes one useful thing her mom ever did. "We could go grab lunch."

Fiona hesitates. On the one hand, yes, she's always hungry, but on the other she doesn't want him to think . . . anything. "Where?" she asks, hedging.

Sam shrugs. "Pink's?"

Fiona snorts. "Why," she says, "so we can wait in line for an hour in the blazing sun and people can take pictures of us together and then everyone will assume I already said yes to the show, at which point I'll think to myself, *Gee, I might as well just do it?*"

Sam looks at her like she's unhinged. "I mean, I was suggesting it more because I like hot dogs," he says calmly. "But I agree that that would have been very clever of me."

Fiona gazes back at him for a long moment, suspicious. Tempted, and trying not to be. His eyes are very, very green.

"I know a place," she finally says.

She takes him to a diner on Pico Boulevard, an old-fashioned East Coast Greek situation with fraying Naugahyde booths and jukeboxes bolted to the wall at each table boasting such contemporary hits as "Where Have All the Cowboys Gone?" There's a full bar behind the counter, with a million different kinds of cocktail glasses hanging from an overhead rack.

"I always wonder who comes into places like this to get hammered," Sam says, squinting at the dusty bottles of crème de menthe and sambuca. "Like, I'll have two scrambled eggs and a Rusty Nail, please."

Their waitress appears just then, wearing sensible sneakers and a name tag that says KAREN, her hair in a graying bun at the back of her head. "Hi, Karen," Sam says with a smile, then proceeds to flirt with her until she's blushing like a teenager, hiding her pale mouth behind her notepad. Fiona rolls her eyes and orders a patty melt and french fries. Sam orders cold baked salmon on greens.

"Wait a second," Fiona says to him, holding a hand up. "Excuse me. What happened to 'I love hot dogs'?"

"Are you kidding?" Sam grins. "I haven't eaten a hot dog in like six years." He nudges his ankle against hers under the table, winking. "It was a good plan, though, right? The Pink's thing."

"Oh my god." Fiona shakes her head slightly, hoping she looks more annoyed than she actually is. "I'm leaving."

"You're not leaving. Karen," Sam says, utterly unfazed, "may we please also get one hot dog with the works?"

Karen smiles, doe-like. "You sure can, peaches."

"Can I ask you something?" Fiona asks once she's gone, sitting back in the booth and crossing her arms at him. "Why do you assume that every woman finds you charming?"

He shrugs. "Experience, mostly. Can I ask *you* something?"

"I would prefer that you didn't."

Sam ignores her. "You answered the phone, right?"

Fiona plucks a sour pickle from the dish on the table and takes a bite, then immediately realizes her mistake—it tastes like canned garlic and standing water, mushy and sad. "What?" she asks, once she's swallowed.

"When your agent called you about the show, you answered the phone. So there must be a tiny part of you that wants to have a career again."

"I have a career," Fiona reminds him.

"At a copy shop?" Sam looks dubious.

Oh, that annoys her. "It's my father's business," she snaps, temper sparking like flint against steel. "That he built with his two hands, and that paid for the house that I grew up in and my sister's braces and my stupid fucking acting lessons. It's not some random Kinko's."

Sam blinks. "No, I—sorry," he says quietly. "I didn't mean to—you know."

Fiona feels her shoulders drop. "It's fine," she says, a little embarrassed—wishing, not for the first time, that she was the kind of person who didn't get so worked up over every little thing. Pam, if she was here, would advise a deep breath. Instead Fiona finishes the rubbery, tepid pickle, then reaches for another one just for something to do.

"Are you really going to eat those?" Sam asks.

"Yes," she says immediately, crunching as loud as she can.

"Because I'm just saying, they've probably been sitting out here all day."

"Great," she says, and picks up a third. "Plenty of time for them to cure."

Sam takes a sip of his unsweetened iced tea, an expression on his face like *Have it your way, psycho*. "What about Thandie?" he asks.

Fiona doesn't choke, but it's a near thing. "Thandie?" she manages to repeat, eyes watering a little. She clears her throat. "Thandie . . . would probably not eat the free pickles, no."

Sam makes a face. "You guys were friends, weren't you?"

"We are friends," Fiona says automatically, though in truth she hasn't seen Thandie in almost five years. The last time they hung out in person, Fiona convinced her to go to a party the second-cutest member of a popular boy band was throwing in a suite at the Chateau; the next day pictures of Fiona's bleary face were everywhere, but Thandie had somehow managed to stay out of the camera's panoptic eye. "I know acting isn't a big deal for you, or whatever," Thandie said quietly, picking at a fray in her sweater as they drank iced lattes on the couch in her apartment that morning, "but it's serious for me. And not for nothing, Fiona, but the world tends to be a lot less forgiving of bullshit from people who look like me." Six months later Fiona sat on a couch in the common room at the hospital and watched as Thandie accepted an Academy Award for Best Supporting Actress; Fiona's never said it to anybody, but it's still the proudest moment of her life, and if getting the hell away from her is what Thandie needed to do to make it happen, then Fiona guesses she has nobody to blame but herself.

"Well," Sam says now, gazing at her across the table, "what does she say?"

Fiona snorts. "Thandie isn't going to do a *Birds of California* reboot in a million years," she promises flatly.

"Why not?"

"Because she's a serious actor!"

"I'm a serious actor," he counters, and Fiona throws her head back and laughs.

Sam's plush, pretty mouth drops open. "Fuck off!" He's laughing, too, though Fiona can't tell if she's imagining that he also looks just a tiny bit hurt. "I am!"

"You're something," she admits without thinking, and right away she feels herself blush. "I mean—"

But Sam is shaking his head. "Don't patronize me," he tells her, then gestures down at his general person. "Come on, Fee, do you really want me to hide this light under a bushel? Or are you just too good for TV?"

"I'm not too good for TV," she says honestly. "I'm not too good for acting, either. I like acting. I just didn't like . . . everything that came with it."

"Money?" Sam asks. "Fame? People bending over backward to meet your every need and desire?"

Fiona huffs a laugh. "Oh, is that your experience of it?"

"Sometimes," he says easily. "So when we were doing *Birds*, that was just, like, all torture for you?"

Fiona hesitates. She remembers running around the UBC lot with Thandie, the two of them eating craft services chocolate chip cookies and making dirty fortune-tellers from the pages of their scripts. She remembers nailing a scene in one take and knowing it was funny. She remembers Sam in the alley outside the wrap party that very last night, his warm, curious mouth pressed against hers, and finally she shakes her head.

"No," she admits. "Not all of it."

Karen returns with their food just then, and once Sam has done his little bit about how much he loves her and how she's his perfect woman, he turns back to Fiona. "So," he says, squeezing a lemon slice over his unadorned salmon, "what's *A Doll's House* about?"

"None of your business," she says pleasantly, and takes a bite of her patty melt.

"Oh, you want me to guess? Why didn't you say so?" Sam smiles. "It's about dolls that come alive in the night."

"Nailed it in one," she tells him, but Sam keeps going.

"It's about sex robots. It's about little girls doing evil spells. It's about shrinking down to get away from capitalism, like that Matt Damon movie."

Fiona sighs. "It's about a woman who has a bunch of stuff happen to her and suddenly realizes she isn't in charge of her own life or reputation," she tells him. "So she decides to do something about it."

"That was my next guess," Sam says. "Does she kill herself at the end?"

Fiona stares at him for a moment. "What the fuck is wrong with you?"

"I'm not saying I *want* her to kill herself," he says quickly. "I just feel like a lot of those stories end with women walking into the ocean with rocks in their pockets or putting their heads in the oven or something."

"I mean, you're not wrong," she admits, "but no. She leaves her husband and children and the play ends with the sound of the door shutting behind her."

Sam nods. "That," he says approvingly, "is kind of metal."

Fiona smiles; she can't help it. "For 1879?" she asks. "Yeah, I'd say it's pretty metal."

"Who do you play?"

Fiona reaches for a french fry, not quite meeting his gaze. "Nora," she reports, feeling oddly shy.

"Who's Nora?"

"The butler." She looks up then, catching Karen's eye as she bustles by with a pot of coffee in one hand. "Excuse me," she says sweetly. "Could we possibly get some more pickles?"

The sun is just starting to set when Sam drops her home, the palm trees darkly silhouetted against a sky streaked in pinks and blues and oranges. The air smells like star jasmine and smoke. Sometimes Fiona wishes she didn't love California so much, that she could pick up and pack her bags and start over in New York or Chicago, but then she looks around on nights like this and knows they'll bury her in this sherbet-colored desert. She'll wander the canyons and haunt the hills until the end of the breathing world.

"Last stop, cowgirl," Sam says as he pulls into the driveway, glancing at her sidelong. "This was . . ." He trails off. "You know."

"Not as *uniquely* horrible as I thought it would be," Fiona admits.

Sam grins. "Generically horrible, only."

"Exactly." Fiona makes a face. Sam makes one back, then holds her gaze, shifting his weight in the leather bucket seat. She can see the flecks of amber in his eyes. She's not sure if she's imagining that he's leaning in just a little bit closer, his gaze flicking down to her mouth for the barest of moments, but she's picturing it before she can stop herself: his hands and his tongue and his straight white teeth, the rasp of his day-old beard against her chin. It occurs to her to wish she hadn't eaten four sour pickles back at the diner. She hasn't kissed anyone in a long time.

Jesus Christ, what is she *thinking?*

Fiona straightens up as fast as if someone poked her in the back with a pencil. Right away, Sam straightens up, too. "So, listen," he says, rubbing a hand over the back of his neck, "you should think about the reboot."

Fiona feels her entire body drop, involuntary, like someone pulling the plug on a novelty pool float. Probably good, she reminds herself, to be clear about exactly what he's been after all day long. "I . . . will definitely not be doing that," she promises him brightly. "Take care of yourself, Sam."

"I—yeah," he says. Fiona has no idea what exactly she feels so disappointed about. "You too."

She takes a moment to gather herself once he's gone, standing outside the front door of the house as the taillights of his ridiculous, embarrassing car disappear around the corner. It occurs to her that being with Sam felt like being onstage—not like she was performing, exactly, but more like she was lost in something besides her normal life. Like she was someone else for a while. It wasn't the worst feeling in the world.

Inside the house her father is sitting in the same exact place where she left him this morning, the light from the TV flickering across his face. "Hey, Dad," she says gently, knocking on the door-frame like it's his bedroom, which honestly it might as well be. For a moment she remembers how he used to be back when she was a little kid, growing basil in big pots on the patio and making Special Scramble on Saturday mornings after her swim meets. "How was your day?"

He looks up—surprised, though Fiona isn't sure if it's because he didn't realize she was back or because he didn't realize she was gone to begin with. "Fine, honey."

"How about a shower before dinner?"

Her dad shakes his head, eyes on the screen. "I'm not hungry, sweetheart."

Fiona bites her tongue so hard she tastes iron. Sometimes she gets so mad at her mom for leaving that she almost can't breathe. Fiona deserved it; she knows that about herself. But Claudia didn't. "That's not really what I said, Dad." She forces herself to smile. "Come on, quick rinse."

Eventually her dad sighs and shuffles off toward the bathroom. Fiona resists the urge to stand outside the closed door and listen for the sound of the running water, but barely. Instead she heads out into the backyard, where Claudia is sitting on the patio read-ing some four-thousand-page fantasy book and rubbing one bare foot along Brando's bristly back. Claudia found Brando wander-ing crookedly down their street when she was twelve; he was flea-bitten and emaciated and had a giant scar on one side of his neck that suggested an extremely checkered past, but as soon as he saw Claudia he stopped, rolled over, and begged to be petted. Fiona's father is allergic to dogs, but Estelle isn't, and so Brando has lived with her ever since, although periodically Fiona comes into Claudia's room to wake her up for school in the morning and finds him curled into the shape of a doughnut at the bottom of her sister's bed.

"Oh hello," Claudia says now, marking her place with her index finger and peering at Fiona through a pair of cat-eye glasses with no lenses. "How was your date?"

Fiona comes up behind her and scoops Claudia's hair off her neck, liking the thick, silky weight of it in her hands. "It wasn't a date," she says, which is true, though there's still a tiny part of her that feels pleasantly dazed in the aftermath, like maybe he kissed her after all. He wants her to do the show, Fiona reminds herself firmly. That's all any of that was.

Claudia looks unconvinced. "Did you eat?" she asks.

"Yes," Fiona admits grudgingly.

"Date."

"Oh, right." Fiona tugs Claudia's hair lightly, dragging Claudia's head back to peer at her upside down. "Is that how it works at school?"

Claudia snorts. "Uh, no. Definitely not."

"Just for olds like me?"

"And Estelle," Claudia says. "Probably for Estelle, too."

"Nah," Fiona says, letting go of Claudia's hair. "Estelle is on the apps."

"Down to fuck," Claudia agrees, and follows Fiona back inside.

For dinner Fiona makes chicken quesadillas and microwaves

some broccoli with butter and salt, tucking a folded paper towel under the silverware beside Claudia's plate. She always makes Claudia sit at the table, even if she's the only one eating. "We're not animals," she says, when Claudia complains.

She's headed for the fridge to see if there's any sour cream left when she catches sight of her reflection in the glass of the microwave door, then frowns and lifts a hand to her earlobe. "Shit," she mutters. She drops to her knees on the floor, running her hands over the tile and coming up with a palmful of crumbs. "We should vacuum," she observes.

"What are you doing?" Claudia asks, peering down at her with consternation.

"I lost an earring." Fiona grimaces. "Mom's earring. The pearl."

Right away, Claudia scuttles down off her chair and crouches beside Fiona, her hair making a curtain around her face. "When was the last time you saw it?" she asks, peering under the table.

Fiona shakes her head. "This morning, maybe? I don't know." She retraces her steps, the patio and the living room and the front yard, but it's useless. The thing is probably in the pocket of some cigarette-smelling blazer at the East Hollywood Goodwill, or down the garbage disposal at the diner with leftover hash browns and the curly rinds of orange slices. "It's okay," she says finally, sitting back on her haunches, though it doesn't feel okay. "We're not going to find it."

"Probably not," Claudia agrees, and something about the way

she accepts the inevitability of disappointment makes Fiona feel about three inches tall.

"Come on," she says, scrambling inelegantly to her feet and holding out a hand. Their dad is still shut in his room. "Let's go get doughnuts."

Claudia grins.

They get in Fiona's car and head for the twenty-four-hour Krispy Kreme on Crenshaw, neon lights streaking by outside the glass. They started doing this after their mom left, Fiona waking her sister up at two or three in the morning and loading her into the car for the long haul across the city, both of them singing along to Stevie Nicks or Pat Benatar on K-Earth 101. Krispy Kreme has a drive-through but Claudia loved to stand outside the plate glass window on the side of the building and watch the doughnuts rolling by on the conveyor belt, and Fiona loved how much she loved it enough that she was willing to let Darcy's goons take her picture from time to time.

Tonight they stay in the car, Fiona taking the box from the girl at the window and handing it carefully across the gearshift to her sister. "Careful," she says, breathing in the warm smell of sugar and fry grease, the night air thick and soupy through the open window. "Still hot."

CHAPTER SIX

Sam

He's definitely too broke to be eating out more than once a day, so
when Erin calls to see if he wants to get dinner that night he tells
her to come to his place in WeHo for tacos instead. "By which you
mean, you want me to make tacos?" Erin asks.

Sam's mouth falls open at the unfairness of it. "I make decent
tacos!" he protests, which is true, but then when he realizes how
much the ingredients are going to cost he winds up just going to the
place they like and ordering half a dozen to go along with chips and
guac. Then, on second thought, he doubles back to get an order of
queso, even though he tries not to eat cheese. "It's fine," he says,
waving his hand magnanimously when Erin offers to Venmo him
for her half. "It'll all come out in the wash."

She eyes him from the couch, where she's flipping through
Martha Stewart Living, which comes to his house faithfully every
month addressed to the woman who lived here before him. "You're
cheerful," she observes.

"Yeah, I guess." Sam hadn't really thought about it. "How'd it
go with Hipster Glasses?"

"Oh, I don't know." Erin sets the magazine down and unwraps a taco. "Too hip, maybe. I don't think I quoted enough feminist theory to impress her."

"Impossible," Sam says, handing her a napkin. Erin is the most impressive person he knows. And sure, part of it is how killer she is at her job—back in the fall she broke open a huge thing with a pervy coach at a private school in the OC, and since then her career has been on fire, her byline in *The New Yorker* and *The Atlantic* and the *Los Angeles Times*—but mostly it's how she's just legitimately good at life, someone who sends actual paper birthday cards and speaks fluent Spanish and knows all the best stuff to get at Trader Joe's. He knows exactly which one of them scored the better end of the deal when he answered her Craigslist ad for a roommate all those years ago, and truthfully Sam has no idea why she still hangs out with him. He wants to be like her when he grows up. "I'm sure you quoted exactly the right amount of feminist theory."

"We'll see," Erin says, opening a tiny plastic ramekin of salsa. "What'd you do today?"

Sam grins. He's been saving the whole story to tell her in person, fully prepared to make Fiona sound extra fucking batshit for her benefit and amusement, but when he opens his mouth he's surprised to find that for some reason he doesn't actually want to do that at all.

"I—nothing, really," he lies, squeezing a lime wedge over his taco. "Drove around, felt sorry for myself. I did one of those quizzes to figure out my porn name, just in case it comes to that."

"And?"

"Ajax Dagger."

"That's a good one," Erin says approvingly. Sam hands her the extra chips.

He spends the next morning at the gym, getting his ass cheerfully handed to him by his trainer, Olivia. Sam loves his gym. He loves everything about it: The steam room. The spa. The juice bar. The regular bar. And sure, his membership costs almost as much as his rent every month, but he needs to look a certain way for his job, and it's not like he's about to stroll into a Planet Fitness and fight some sorority girl for the elliptical machines. Besides, it's a tax write-off. Or if it's not, it should be. Sam doesn't really keep track.

Russ calls as he's getting dressed in the locker room: "How'd it go with Riley Bird?" he wants to know.

That is . . . an interesting question, actually. Sam pulls his T-shirt over his head and thinks of the way she smiled at him across the table in the diner; he thinks of that heavy, loaded moment in the car. Then he thinks of the way she tucked and rolled out of his passenger seat like she was considering a career as a stunt double for the Mission Impossible franchise and concludes it's pretty unlikely she's going to suddenly change her mind about the whole thing. "Not super," he admits. "I tried."

"Try harder," Russ suggests. "You're a charming guy."

"That's what I told her," Sam says. "She didn't seem convinced."

"Better be a little more convincing."

"I—duly noted," Sam says, a little confused. It doesn't exactly sound like a suggestion. He tries not to wonder if Russ is pushing *Birds* because there isn't anything else promising in the pipeline, because his career is already over before it's even really begun. But that can't be right, can it? Russ would tell him. Besides, he's got another audition lined up at the end of the week. Everything is going to be fine.

"I'm taking Cara and the girls to Tulum on Thursday," Russ tells him as they're hanging up, "if you want to stop by and use the pool while we're gone." That's another reason why Sam doesn't want to fire Russ as his agent, if he's being totally honest: Russ has an extremely nice house that he's very generous about letting Sam hang out at. He likes to float around on all the different rafts.

Now he tucks his phone back into his pocket just as the valet brings his car around, sunlight glinting off the freshly waxed hood. Sam rolls the windows down, trying to soak in the wave of well-being that always crashes over him when he slides behind the wheel of the Tesla and not to think about the notice he got in the mail this morning from the company that handles his lease, PAST DUE stamped in red right there on the envelope for the mailman or anyone else to see.

It's fine, he reminds himself one more time. He just needs to chill.

He's about to pull into traffic when out of the corner of his eye he notices something catching the light on the floor of the passenger side: he reaches down and plucks a tiny gray pearl earring off the mat, no bigger than a sesame seed.

Sam frowns. The only other girl who's been in his car lately is

Erin, and he knows for a fact Erin would sooner walk directly into a volcano than wear pearls.

Which means it must be Fiona's.

And what kind of jerk-off would he be if he didn't bring it back?

He tries her house first, where her sister and the old lady neighbor are sitting in the backyard wearing matching turbans and playing what he's pretty sure is a bastardized version of canasta. A cheery instrumental rendition of "The Girl from Ipanema" pipes out of Claudia's phone. "Fiona's at rehearsal for her play," the neighbor—Estelle, Sam remembers—reports, looking genuinely disappointed not to have better news for him. "She'll be sorry she missed you."

"I mean," Sam says, "I don't know if I'd go *that* far."

That makes them smile. "She had a good time with you yesterday," Estelle tells him, taking a sip of her afternoon cocktail.

"Estelle," Claudia warns, but Estelle waves her off.

"Well, she did! Granted, she didn't *say* as much, but you know how your sister is better than anyone. And anyway, Sam's not going to tell her I said that, are you, Sam."

Sam shakes his head, weirdly pleased. "I had a good time with her, too," he admits.

"I would assume so."

Claudia shoots Estelle another look, then holds her hand out for the earring. "I can give it to her," she says, but Sam shakes his head, slipping it back into his pocket.

"I was hoping to see her in person, if that's okay." He checks his watch as if he might have somewhere to be, which he does not. "I could swing by her theater, maybe? I've got a little bit of time."

Claudia and Estelle confer for a moment—a quick, silent familial negotiation that he isn't sure how to interpret. Finally Claudia nods. "The drive is long as balls," she warns, digging her phone out of the pocket of her flowered caftan. "But I can give you the address."

"Thank you," he says, already regretting this a little. "I appreciate it."

"I hope so," Claudia says darkly. "She's going to murder us in our sleep."

"Oh, sweetheart, don't be silly," Estelle counters, patting Claudia fondly on the arm. "She's not going to wait that long."

He gets lost twice on the way to Fiona's theater, which is tucked away on a downtown side street. He passes the same guy pissing in the same alley three different times. At least, Sam *thinks* it's the same guy in the same alley. It's not like he pulls over to check.

Finally he finds a parking spot not too far from the address Claudia gave him, double-checking that his car is locked before pulling his baseball cap down over his eyes. He follows the handwritten signs down a flight of stairs and through a hallway that stinks like a urinal in a dive bar before quietly opening the door to the theater and stepping inside, catching it just before it shuts behind him so it doesn't make any noise.

He spots her right away, standing at center stage in leggings and a hoodie, her battered script clutched in one hand. "Hector," she's saying to an olive-skinned dude in a Hawaiian shirt, "you're going to cross upstage as you're—yup, exactly like that. Thank you. Hey, Georgie?" She motions for a cherubic mom-type to come closer. "Can we talk for a minute about what's happening between Krogstad and Mrs. Linde in these next few lines?"

Sam stands at the back of the house while they work through the scene, his hands shoved deep in the pockets of his Levi's. A thing about having done one-episode guest spots on basically every prime-time drama is that he's worked with a lot of directors, and he doesn't have to watch Fiona for more than couple of minutes before he realizes she's good. Like—*really* good, actually. He likes the way she talks to her actors, how he can tell she's really interested in what they have to say and isn't just moving them around like the whole theater is her own personal Barbie DreamHouse. In the second before he comes to his senses, he thinks it might be kind of cool to be in one of her plays.

Fuck, Sam really needs to book some actual work.

"Okay," Fiona says once she's satisfied, Converse squeaking as she turns and hops down off the stage. "Let's go ahead and take it from the top of the—" She catches sight of him across the theater just then, her dark eyes widening. Sam smiles. Fiona emphatically does not smile back. "Um. From the top of the scene," she finishes.

She makes him wait—which Sam guesses shouldn't surprise him—while they run the scene, while she gives notes, while they run it again. Finally she nods her approval. "Okay," she says, yanking the elastic from all that wild hair before gathering it up one more time. "Let's take five."

In the end she comes to him, though only once she's satisfied nobody else is paying attention. "Are you stalking me?" she asks, taking his arm and yanking him back out into the smelly hallway. Her grip is hard enough to bruise.

"I mean, no," Sam says. "But I do recognize that's what a stalker would say, so . . . yes?"

"Because I've had stalkers," Fiona informs him. "I've also been one, so. I'm just letting you know now that it's not going to work."

Sam feels it best not to engage with that line of conversation. "I googled this play," he says instead, gently extricating his arm from her death clench. "You didn't tell me Nora is the star."

Fiona laughs out loud. "Please look around at this venue, Samuel," she implores him. "I think it's *pretty* safe to say there are no stars at the Angel City Playhouse."

"But the lead," Sam presses, clearing his throat a little. Hearing her use his full name, even to make fun of him, made the inside of his body do something weird.

"I mean." Fiona shrugs. "I guess."

"So you're directing and starring?"

"Oh, yeah, I'm a regular Lin-Manuel Miranda."

"Don't flatter yourself," Sam says easily. "He's a writer, too."

Fiona makes a face. "You shouldn't be here," she hisses, jerking her head toward the theater door. "None of those people know who I am."

"Wait." Sam frowns. "Seriously? I thought you said you'd been doing this for like a year and a half."

Fiona shrugs. "Did any of those folks in there strike you as particularly avid viewers of the Family Network?"

Sam considers that. In fact, most of them looked like the kind of people who would proudly announce that they didn't own a television at all, and the rest suggested a strict diet of PBS and *Frasier* reruns. Still, a year and a half is a long time. "It's very Method of you," he says finally. "I admire your commitment to the work."

Fiona doesn't laugh. "Did you need something?" she asks.

"Yes, actually." Sam nods, fishing around in his pocket until he finds the tiny post. "You left this in my car," he tells her, holding it out. "You can thank me later for bringing it back to you."

Fiona breathes in. "I—shit," she says softly. She's quiet for a minute before holding her palm out; Sam drops the earring inside. "Thank you."

He nods. "I gotta say, you didn't strike me as a pearl earring kind of girl."

"I'm not," Fiona mutters, though he can't help but notice she slides it back on right away, double-checking to make sure it's secure in her earlobe. Checking a third time.

"You got it," he assures her. "I don't think it's going anywhere."

"Yeah."

Neither one of them says anything for a moment, the silence stretching on just a beat too long not to be awkward. Sam tries to think of a natural way to segue into a conversation about *Birds*—after all, that's what he supposedly came here to talk to her about, the only reason he drove all the way the fuck across the city—but to his utter shock, what comes out of his mouth is: "What are you doing tomorrow night?"

If Fiona is even one-millionth as surprised as he is, she doesn't show it: "Scalping tickets outside the Staples Center," she deadpans immediately. "Washing my hair. Cleaning the inside of the K-Cup machine."

Sam tilts his head to the side. "I didn't know that was a thing you had to clean."

"Most people don't," Fiona says.

"Sounds like a busy night."

"I'm a busy girl."

Sam nods slowly. "Well, Cinderella," he says, "in case you happen to get through all your chores. I'm meeting some friends for drinks around nine, if you want to come hang out."

"Where?" she asks with a smirk. "Like, the Chateau Marmont?"

"No, smartass," he says, though the club he names admittedly isn't that far off, in terms of vibe, and Fiona bursts out laughing.

"Look," she says once she's pulled herself together, and Sam isn't sure whether he's imagining that for a moment she looks almost fond of him. "I get why you want to do this reboot. Clearly you've got some pretty significant cartel debt, and I can respect that. But I'm not going to do it, no matter how many different ways you try to leverage whatever crush you think I had on you back when I was eighteen."

That gets Sam's attention. "You had a crush on me?" he asks.

"Oh my god," Fiona says, rolling her eyes so hard he thinks she can probably see her own brain. "We're not talking about this."

Sam smiles. "We're talking about it a little, though."

"We're not," Fiona assures him, but her cheeks are definitely getting pink.

"Okay." He thinks for a moment. "Listen, you don't have to do it," he promises. "The show."

"Oh, I know I don't."

"No, obviously, that's not what I—" Sam breaks off. "I just mean I won't bring it up again, that's all. But you should still come to drinks tomorrow."

Fiona shakes her head, just faintly. *"Why?"* she asks.

"Because I want to see you again," he tells her. "With no agenda. Is that so hard to believe?"

"Yes," she tells him immediately. "It is extremely hard to believe."

"Well, it's true." He takes a deep breath. "Fee. Come meet me tomorrow night."

Fiona makes a big show of sighing, this full-body situation like she's trying to make sure it reads all the way to the very back of a theater. They're standing close enough that when she shifts her weight his knee brushes hers, just for a second; Sam feels the contact all the way up his thigh.

"Fine," she says at last, rotating her neck like possibly she's gotten a cramp just from the physical strain of having to talk to him, "but only so you'll leave."

Sam nods seriously, biting the inside of his cheek to keep from grinning. He feels like he landed a part he didn't even know he was auditioning for, and he tells himself it's just because he's happy to have won. "Uh-huh."

"I mean it," Fiona warns him. "Don't say anything else."

He mimes zipping his lips and throwing away the key. *See you tomorrow*, he mouths, then holds up nine fingers in case somehow she's forgotten. Fiona groans.

Sam heads back out into the steamy pink twilight, where someone has let their dog—at least, Sam hopes it was a dog—drop a steaming dump beside his right front tire. It takes an hour and fifteen minutes to get home, with traffic. He hums along to the radio all the way there.

CHAPTER SEVEN

Fiona

"Is that what you're wearing?" Claudia asks the following night, standing in the doorway of Fiona's bedroom with her arms crossed.

"Uh, yup." Fiona looks at herself in the mirror. She'll be damned if she's about to get dressed up to meet Sam Fox of all fucking people so she's wearing her usual jeans and boots and tank top, a hair elastic looped snugly around one wrist. "Why?"

Claudia shrugs. "I just think maybe sometimes you don't realize the message you're sending, that's all."

"Oh?" Fiona eyes her in the mirror. "And what message is that, exactly?"

Claudia seems to know better than to answer. "Will you just let me do your hair, at least?" she asks, padding barefoot across the carpet. "I'll be quick."

Fiona sighs loudly. "I guess."

Claudia's smile is megawatt, which almost makes this ridiculous masochistic stroll into Mordor worth it in advance. "Thank you," is all she says.

She makes Fiona sit on the bed while she coaxes out the tangles with a wide-tooth comb, careful not to tug too much. Fiona closes her eyes, tilts her head back. She's always liked having her hair played with; she used to fall asleep in the makeup trailer on set sometimes, while the girls straightened and curled and teased and braided her into Riley Bird. Even all these years later it's the one form of physical contact that's never made her feel itchy or weird.

"There," Claudia says finally. Fiona opens her eyes, peering at herself in the mirror on the back of the closet door. Claudia's done something with the flat iron to smooth the frizz out; she looks nice, but not like she's auditioning for the role of a florist slash amateur detective on Hallmark Movies & Mysteries.

"Thanks," Fiona says, touching it tentatively.

"No problem," Claudia tells her. "You're pretty. Also, and I'm just going to make this pitch one more time, you should change your shirt. You're going dancing with the Heart Surgeon, not out to hunt vampires or scavenge canned goods during the zombie apocalypse."

"That's what you think." Fiona huffs out a breath. "I'm not trying to date him," she reminds her sister.

"Why not?" Claudia asks immediately. "You should date someone."

"Why?"

"Because you're lonely."

Fiona blinks, the baldness of it catching her up short. Back when she was in the hospital Pam was always trying to get her to make ridiculous pronouncements like that, to emote all the god-damn time: *I feel lonely. I feel angry. I feel betrayed.* Fiona could never quite get the words out, even though she liked Pam and wanted to do a good job at therapy. The whole thing made her *feel*, quite honestly, like a giant fucking chump.

She doesn't say anything to Claudia for a minute. Then: "You know what?" She shakes her head. "I'm not going to go. You need somebody to quiz you on your Spanish—"

"Estelle will quiz me," Claudia says immediately, then marches over to the window and shoves it open. "Estelle!" she yells, voice carrying across the backyard like a Klaxon. "Will you quiz me on my Spanish so that Fiona can go out?"

Estelle, who's reading her Kindle and vaping on her patio, thrusts one thumb into the air. "You bet I will, señorita!"

Fiona rolls her eyes.

"You realize it's okay for you to go have fun," Claudia says, flopping backward onto the pillows. She herself is wearing vintage JNCOs and a Backstreet Boys tank top, so Fiona doesn't actually know if she's in any position to be doling out fashion advice. "Nothing bad is going to happen."

"That sounds like the beginning of the zombie apocalypse to me."

Claudia doesn't laugh. "I'm serious," she says, tucking one tan arm behind her head and looking at Fiona speculatively. "I know you think this whole operation falls apart every time you leave the house, but it's okay for you to have a life if you want to. Dad is . . . you know. Dad. But Estelle is here. And I'm going to be leaving for college in a few months anyway."

Fiona gazes at her sister for a long moment. She was ten when

Claudia was born; she used to like to load her into the stroller and pop wheelies all up and down the crooked sidewalk outside the print shop. "Okay," she says finally, wiping her stupidly sweaty hands on the seat of her jeans, "I'm going."

"And your shirt?"

"Goodbye, Claudia!"

It takes exactly two seconds for Fiona to realize she's made a terrible mistake.

The club is an enormously obnoxious velvet rope situation in West Hollywood, the bass from the sound system palpable through the sidewalk and a long line snaking down the block. Fiona hesitates, raking her fingers through her hair and trying to decide on a strategy. She's not about to wait in that line, that's for sure, but she's also not about to announce herself to a bouncer, both because people who do that are douchebags and because she's not at all confident it would work. Shit, this is why she doesn't go out.

Well, this is one of a thousand reasons, at least.

She's about to bail—it probably wasn't a real invitation anyway; it's not like he's in there watching the entrance waiting for her to show up—when the guy at the front door catches sight of her. He's a lot smaller and less assuming than she thinks of bouncers as being, like maybe he sells high-speed internet during the day and this is his side hustle. "Oh," he says, unclipping the rope and waving her through, "shit, sorry. Go ahead."

Fiona glances over her shoulder to make sure he isn't talking to someone else. "Um," she says, "thanks."

Inside the club is dark and hot and noisy, the music vibrating belligerently up her spine. Fiona works her way through the crowd, past the bar and the DJ booth and a cluster of low leather couches until finally she spots Sam talking to a guy she thinks she recognizes from a time travel thing on cable. She watches them for a moment, Sam's eyes and mouth expressive as he listens to whatever the guy is saying. Fiona remembers this from when they used to work together, how much he seemed to like people and how easy it was for him to talk to them, from celebrity guest stars doing cameos to impress their nieces and nephews down to the lowest of PAs.

He catches sight of her over the guy's shoulder just then, his eyes widening in naked surprise. "Hey," he calls, sounding frankly shocked—though not, if Fiona had to guess, in a bad way. He's wearing white jeans and a short-sleeved shirt with an extremely loud paisley print; on any other human it would look ridiculous, and it looks ridiculous on Sam too, but the rest of him is so maddeningly, infuriatingly attractive that it almost doesn't matter. He hugs her hello, which is how she knows he's already drunk. "You came!"

"I came," she agrees grimly, trying to ignore the dorky way her stomach swoops at the contact, like something out of Riley Bird's teenage diary.

"I'm glad," he says. "You thirsty?"

Fiona nods.

He leads her over to the bar and introduces her to a dozen different people whose names she forgets the moment she hears them—actors and models and influencers, a singer in a girl group that Claudia likes. Just for a second, Fiona wishes she'd changed her shirt after all. Back when she was doing the show she used to love getting dressed up—hip local designers sending her a brand-new wardrobe every season, her closet overflowing with leather and denim and silk. She got rid of all of it once *Birds* got canceled, at first because she had it in her head that if she looked like shit all the time the paparazzi would stop taking pictures of her—which wasn't true, as it turned out—and later because she decided that if they were going to take pictures of her anyhow she wasn't going to let them know she cared what she looked like either way. And it worked. She did stop caring how she looked, for the most part.

Except that tonight, surrounded by beautiful girls in beautiful dresses—standing here next to Sam Fox—she cares a little bit.

Fiona drinks her wine, shifting her weight uncomfortably. She hasn't been in a crowd this size in five years. Her nerve endings feel raw and open, everything too loud and too bright and too *much*. She's trying to think of an inconspicuous way to bail when all at once Sam's palm lands on the small of her back. "Hey," he says, ducking his head so she can hear him. His hand is burning hot through her tank top. "You wanna dance?"

Fiona blinks, every sensation in her entire body concentrated in the place where he's touching her. "Are you serious?"

"I mean, I *was*, cupcake." Sam makes a face, looking just this side of bashful. "Why, is that stupid?"

Fiona shakes her head. She loves to dance, actually. It was one of the reasons she kept going to clubs even though she knew she'd wind up splashed all over Darcy's website, knew they'd say she was drunk or high even if all she ordered was water. Sometimes all the bullshit felt worth it for the chance to close her eyes and lose herself in some forgettable pop song, surrounded by a million people and alone in her own head.

Eventually it got to be too much, and she quit going out altogether. But shaking her hair in her bedroom with her sister just isn't the same.

"One song," she says now.

Sam grins, taking her hand and leading her out into the crush on the dance floor. Fiona can feel the calluses on his palms. They're from lifting free weights at his expensive gym, she reminds herself, not repairing ambulances or playing the cello or anything even a little bit respectable.

Still, she'd be lying if she said they were a thing she didn't like.

It's a fast one and she's worried he's going to look like a total boner but in fact he's a decent dancer, easy in his body and loose in his limbs. At least, Fiona thinks so; the dance floor is so crowded it's not like there's room to do a lot more than just hop up and down. Sam takes a flying elbow to the rib cage. Someone spills a drink on Fiona's boots. When they almost get separated by a group of drunk girls in matching crop tops Sam grabs her hand to keep her from drifting and then just doesn't let go, spinning her around so that her back is flush against him. Fiona breathes in. It doesn't mean anything, she tells herself, even as he's curling his hands around her waist and squeezing lightly, even as she presses herself back against his chest. More than that, she doesn't want it to. But she turns her head to look at him anyway, Sam Fox with his dimples and impeccable bone structure, his carefully tousled boy band hair. She finds him looking back at her, his gaze catching hers in the dark.

"Hey," he murmurs, his voice so quiet she can barely hear it over the sound of the music. Mostly she just sees his mouth move.

"Hey," she says, swallowing a little thickly. Her skin feels prickly and tight. Sam's face is so close that she could kiss him if she wanted, and for one reckless moment she's afraid she's just going to give in to the impulse and do it, can already feel the gentle bump of his nose against hers. With the music playing and his body behind her she thinks she wouldn't even care if it was here in front of all these people. She thinks she might not even care what anyone said.

That's when the song ends.

Right away Fiona takes a giant step away from him, her hands awkward and unfamiliar as a pair of Christmas hams. She's terrified he's going to take one look at her face and be able to tell exactly what she was thinking about, so she clears her throat and tucks her hair behind her ears, looking everywhere in the club but at him.

Sam, on the other hand, seems completely unbothered, and why shouldn't he be? He probably danced like that with half a dozen girls tonight alone. For all she knows he had sex with a Jenner sister in the bathroom right before she got here. "Want to get a drink?" he asks, and Fiona nods.

"Sure," she says, telling herself there's no reason to be disappointed about that. After all, she's the one who said only one dance.

She's following him through the teeming crowd toward the bar when a girl with long dark hair and full pink lips reaches out and puts a hand on Sam's arm. "There you are," she says, and Fiona thinks, *Of course.* "I was wondering what happened to you."

"Here I am," Sam agrees cheerfully. "Fiona, Kimmeree. Kimmeree, Fiona." He smiles. "Fiona and I used to work together."

"I remember," Kimmeree says, though it's unclear to Fiona if she remembers because she's been in Sam's life that long or because she once owned a *Birds of California* pencil case. "Nice to meet you."

"You too," Fiona says, smiling back. She can't tell if she's imagining that Sam looks a tiny bit surprised that she knows how to behave herself in social situations, like possibly he was expecting her to hiss and scratch like the feral cats that prowl the alleys around the theater. Whatever, so he has a very beautiful girlfriend. Fiona emphatically does not care.

"I'll get those drinks," is all he says.

Once he's gone Kimmeree turns to look at her, an expression on her face that suggests she too read on Twitter that Fiona was dead. "So," she says, "what are you . . . doing with yourself these days?"

Right away Fiona feels her spine straighten; it takes some effort, but she forces her shoulders to relax. It's a perfectly harmless question, she reminds herself. There's no reason to get defensive. "Laying low, mostly," she admits. "My dad has a business, so I'm working there for a while."

"Aw, that's so sweet!" Kimmeree chirps. She's wearing one of those dresses that's made entirely of spandex, so tight that it seems like you ought to be able to see the cartoon outline of everything she eats—assuming, of course, that she ever eats anything. Fiona feels like an American-made car.

Kimmeree puts a brightly manicured hand on her arm, leans in close. "Honestly," she says, "I have to tell you, I really admire you being out and about and everything. I think I'd die if all that, you know"—she waves a hand in a way that is ostensibly meant to indicate Fiona's entire life—"happened to me."

Fiona bites her tongue hard enough to taste iron. "And yet here I am," she says. "Stubbornly alive."

Sam comes back with a drink for Fiona then, though not one for Kimmeree, and Fiona is trying to decide what to make of that exactly when Kimmeree leans in close. "Wait," she says, ducking her head conspiratorially. "Fiona. Are you allowed to drink?"

Fiona tilts her head to the side, not understanding. "I . . . think so?" she says, though there's one insane moment where she thinks it's possible the law changed while she was being a hermit in her house and nobody told her. "I'm twenty-eight."

"No," Kimmeree says, wide-eyed. "I mean, weren't you in rehab?"

Fiona feels Sam react more than she sees it, the way his whole body gets very still like an animal smelling danger. She wills herself not to flinch. "Oh my god," she deadpans, putting a hand over her mouth. "You're right. Shit, I totally forgot."

Kimmeree's eyes narrow, uncertain. "Wait," she says again. "I don't—"

"No, I appreciate it," Fiona assures her seriously. "Thanks for looking out for me." She isn't even mad. Well, no, that's not true, she's totally mad, but more than that she just feels utterly, back-breakingly stupid. God, what did she think she was doing? Trying to be normal, trying to be a grown-up, trying to be the kind of person who could get a casual drink with—okay, fine, whatever—a hot guy she used to work with. She has no business being out like this. Everything Darcy Sinclair ever wrote about her was true.

Still, one good thing about the slow-motion natural disaster of the last decade of her life is that it's taught her just how easy it is to get up and walk away.

So that's what she does.

"Excuse me," Fiona says pleasantly, then sets her wineglass on the bar and turns on her heels and weaves her way through the thickly packed crowd toward the exit. She's made it all the way out onto the street before Sam calls her name.

Fiona ignores him, fishing her phone out of her purse. She Ubered here—she always Ubers if she thinks there's any chance she's going to have even one drink; the literal last thing she needs is to get herself arrested for a DUI on top of everything else—but the closest driver is finishing a ride six minutes away.

"Fiona!" Sam says again, catching up with her on the sidewalk. The hair around his face is a little sweaty, his eyes glassy and bright. "Where are you going?"

"I'm leaving."

"Why?"

Fiona hesitates. Her first instinct is to lie—*left my oven on* or *family emergency* or *Crohn's Disease flaring up again*—but in the end, what does she care? After all, she reminds herself firmly, it's just Sam. "Because I'm not having fun."

"Oh." He looks confused. "Really?"

She laughs. "Really," she tells him. "Why, is this literally the first time a girl has ever said that to you in your entire life?"

Sam considers that for a moment. "Yes, actually."

"Oh my god." Fiona looks down at her phone: four minutes to go. She can't wait to get home and change into her pajamas and tell Claudia being lonely is underrated—that, in fact, having tested out the alternative, she now feels even more secure in her plan to continue apace for the foreseeable future. Maybe she'll get a cat to make it official.

"Are you one of those girls who doesn't like other girls?" Sam asks. He looks pleased with himself for a moment, like he thinks he's figured something out about her. "Is that it?"

Fiona's temper spikes. "Fuck you," she says immediately. Three minutes, then two, then three again. "I'm one of those girls who doesn't like anyone."

"I mean, that's a fact."

That stings a little, even though all he's doing is agreeing with her. Fiona sets her jaw. "Okay," she says, waving shortly before turning to walk away. "Good night, Sam."

But Sam is persistent. "Come on, Fee," he urges, trotting after her like an animated sidekick in a Disney cartoon. "What are you even doing out here, waiting for the bus?"

Fiona cackles. "Is that your concept of how the world works?

Sorry I'm not cruising up to the valet every night in a ridiculous fucking weinermobile like some people I could name." She looks down at her phone again. "My Uber is going to be here in a minute."

"Cancel it," Sam says immediately.

"Why?"

"Because—because—" He breaks off, gazing at her in the light coming off the neon sign of the club. His eyelashes are long as a girl's. "Are you hungry?" he asks. "You want to go get food?"

Fiona shakes her head. She doesn't understand what his game is here—why he invited her out in the first place, why he cares either way if she stays or she goes. She fully expected him to give her the full-court press about the *Birds* thing tonight, as if by coming here she'd accepted a free vacation from a time-share company and would thus be required to sit through a lengthy and aggressive sales presentation, but in fact he hasn't said anything about it. She wonders if he's so drunk he forgot. It seems ill-advised to give him the chance to sober up enough to remember.

On the other hand: she's starving. She was too nervous to eat dinner, embarrassingly, and that bar wasn't exactly the kind of place to get loaded tots. And then there's the other thing, the way all her organs momentarily rearranged themselves when she looked up and saw him watching her from the back of the theater yesterday afternoon. The way she felt on the dance floor with his hands on her waist.

"Maybe," she allows.

Sam perks up visibly, like there's a dimmer switch attached to his belly button and somebody just twisted it up to full bright. Fiona has to resist the urge to roll her eyes. "Great!" he says. "Sushi? Or tapas? Or there's this really authentic Thai place I know—"

"Enough," Fiona says, canceling her ride before holding a hand out for his car keys. "I'm driving."

CHAPTER EIGHT

Sam

She takes him to In-N-Out, the two of them sitting outside on rubber-coated benches in the yellow light of the neon sign. The waffle weave digs into his ass. It's a warm night, the smell of car exhaust and fryer oil hanging densely in the air.

"Can I ask you something?" Fiona says, dragging a fry through a puddle of secret sauce. She ordered without looking at the menu, coming back to the table with a cardboard box full of cheeseburgers and fries; she also paid, which he appreciates, though he doesn't say that out loud. "How do you even know all those people?"

Sam takes a sip of his milkshake. "All those people, like, my friends?"

"Sure." Fiona looks dubious.

"They're industry people, mostly." He shrugs. "Kimmeree does something with social media."

"Of course she does."

Sam frowns. The truth is they're not actually his good friends, those guys back in the bar. Erin in particular hates that whole crowd; she heard who all was coming out tonight and bailed so hard and so fast Sam was surprised she didn't pull a muscle. They're a lot, he gets it. But he's also not about to sit here and let Fiona shit on a bunch of perfectly nice people she didn't even bother to talk to. "Look," he tells her, "whatever she said to you back there. She didn't mean anything by it."

"Didn't she?" Fiona huffs a laugh.

"No," Sam replies, "she didn't. She was trying to be friendly."

Fiona eyes him over her cheeseburger like he's too stupid to breathe air. "That is . . . emphatically not what was happening there."

"Fine," he admits, "maybe not. But—but—"

"But what, exactly?" Fiona raises her eyebrows, gestures with her chin toward the car. "Go back to the bar and hang out with her, if she's such a sweetheart. Honestly, I don't even know what you're doing out here eating french fries with me when your girlfriend is—"

"She's not my girlfriend."

"Okay," Fiona says, setting the rest of her burger down on its waxed paper envelope. "The person you have casual recreational sex with. Whatever."

"Isn't all sex recreational?" Sam points out.

"You know what I mean."

Sam doesn't, not really. "I'm not having any kind of sex with Kimmeree," he tells her, "not that it's any of your business. And I don't have a girlfriend, either, if that's the information you were trying to get."

That gets under her skin, which was the point. Sam watches

the temper flare in her dark, witchy eyes, like someone blowing on a campfire. He can almost see the sparks flying off her skin and out into the night. "It wasn't," is all she says.

"Okay." Sam shrugs, affecting carelessness. "Fine. I'm just saying, you don't have to go around hating everyone for fun. There are plenty of other ways to spend your time." He pops a fry into his mouth. "You could join an Ultimate Frisbee league, for example."

Fiona laughs, not nicely, and loud enough that a delivery driver glances over at them as he climbs back into his car with a giant bag of food. "First of all," she snaps, "I'd rather perform my own root canal. Second of all, I don't hate everyone for fun—I hate most people, because they deserve it. And third of all, I was in a psych hospital, not rehab. It's different."

That shocks him—not the information itself, necessarily, but the sound of her saying it. Sam is quiet for a moment before eventually he nods. "I wasn't going to ask."

"No, you were going to google it," she fires back. "Or maybe you already googled it, I don't know."

He did google it, actually, the day he went to see her at the copy shop, so he doesn't say anything. He tries to imagine her there, sitting in her sweatpants with the door locked playing checkers with the other patients. Everything he knows about psych hospitals he learned from watching movies and TV.

"I'm not embarrassed," she continues, her voice all brass and bluster. "Frankly, more people in this business should spend some quality time in a mental health facility."

"Hey, you won't hear me arguing," Sam says. Then, before he quite knows he's going to ask her: "What was it like?"

He fully expects her to tell him to mind his own business, but instead Fiona seems to stop and consider it, like possibly nobody's ever asked her to describe it before. "It was quiet," she finally says.

Sam nods. The sound of her voice is almost nostalgic, like his mom when she talks about going out to the bars with her girlfriends at UW-Madison in the eighties. "Seems about right."

"Everybody expected me to fight it," she continues. She's gazing across the patio at the cars whizzing by on the busy street, their headlights gleaming in the dark. "But, like, why would I have fought it? I was messed up, obviously. I never said I wasn't messed up. I wanted to be, like, *less* messed up, so I went to the place and I did the fucking thing, and still for the rest of my life nobody is ever going to let me——" She breaks off, looking almost startled to realize he's still listening. She shakes her head. "Forget it."

Sam gazes at her across the table, her jaw set and her expression haughty. She looks like a queen facing down a losing war. It's the most she's said about her past—the most she's said at once, period—since he walked into the copy shop the other morning. Just for a moment, it occurs to him to wonder what else she might be keeping to herself.

"People are taking our picture," she announces suddenly, nodding across the patio at a couple of teenage girls in babydoll dresses faking the world's least-convincing selfie; they look away when he glances over, muffling giggles behind cupped hands.

Sam shrugs. "I hadn't noticed," he says, which is bullshit, and he and Fiona both know it. The truth is he's got a sixth sense for people looking at him, and he never stops worrying that one day they won't care enough to do it anymore. Sometimes it feels like he's got a perpetual leaderboard in his head: Does he have fewer Instagram mentions than he did a couple months ago? Did fewer girls check him out at the gym? How many search results come up when you google his name? *Isn't that exhausting?* Erin asked him once, and the answer is yes, of course it is, but also he doesn't know how he'd possibly stop. "Quick, you better do something weird for the camera."

"Gotta preserve that personal brand," Fiona agrees. "Any thoughts?"

"Could scale the side of the building and perform the first act of *1776* as a one-woman show, maybe."

"Slather a bunch of animal sauce on my face like a mud mask and lie down by the dumpsters so the raccoons can lick it off."

"Take my car," he suggests, "and I'll start screaming about how you stole it."

Fiona smiles. One of the selfie girls lights up a cigarette, the match flaring like an old-fashioned camera bulb. "Do you still smoke?" Fiona asks him.

"Huh?" Sam frowns. "I never smoked."

Fiona frowns back. "Yes you did."

"I definitely didn't."

"At the wrap party, you told me you did."

"What wrap party?"

Fiona makes a face. "You know which one," she accuses. "The last one."

"Refresh my memory."

"The one where we—" Fiona gestures vaguely with her cup, tipping it back and forth between them. "You know."

"The one where we what, exactly?" Sam tilts his face to the side. He's fucking with her, obviously. He just wants to see if she'll say it. He remembers standing outside in the alley beside her, the cigarette burning down between his fingers and the safety light catching the neon streak in her hair.

Fiona shakes her head, popping the last fry into her mouth and gathering up their garbage. "Okay, you know what?" she says. "Fuck you."

"I'm kidding, I'm kidding. I remember." He smiles. "No reason to get defensive just because I was your first kiss."

Fiona scoffs. "Oh, is *that* what you think?"

Sam raises his eyebrows. "Was I not?"

"I was nineteen, asshole."

"No shame in being a late bloomer." Sam grins. "Who *was* your first kiss, then?" he asks, surprised to find he's actually curious. His first kiss was his neighbor Mallory back in Wisconsin, which he would tell Fiona if she seemed at all interested, which she does not. She did something different with her hair tonight, he can't help but notice. When she walked into the bar he did an actual double take—her tan shoulders and the sharp cliffs of her collarbone, the hourglass curve of her body—then purposely talked to his friend Anto for an extra two minutes before he went over to her so that he wouldn't look eager and pathetic and like he was waiting for her to show up, which he had been. His mom would slap his face if she knew that.

Fiona stuffs the last of their trash into the paper bag, standing up and waving to the girls across the patio. "Come on," is all she says.

The grease and the sugar went a long way toward sobering him up, but Fiona insists on driving him home anyway, leaning hard on the gas as they cruise down Fountain in the balmy purple night. Sam keeps glancing over at her, her face half-light and half-shadow in the pale green glow of the dashboard. Her cheekbones are very sharp.

"What?" she asks, the third time he does it.

"Nothing," he says, fishing his phone out of his pocket and scrolling industriously. Fiona hums a quiet sound of disbelief in reply.

"Here we are, sweet pea," she says when she pulls up to the curb underneath the massive jacaranda tree outside his building. Back in Milwaukee, Sam imagined all apartments in LA looked like this, a two-story U-shaped stucco situation with a courtyard at its center, a fountain burbling quietly away. Then he got here and spent ten years living in a series of particleboard dumps. "I'm going to call a car."

As she reaches for her purse on the dashboard, Sam gets a

whiff of her hair—vanilla and sandalwood. "Do you want to come in?" he hears himself ask.

Fiona laughs out loud. "No."

Sam rolls his eyes. It's not like he's dying for her to take him up on the offer or anything, but he doesn't know what there is to sound *quite* so incredulous about. "What do you think, I'm going to put a move on you?" he asks, leaning back against the passenger side window. "I'm not going to put a move on you."

"Oh, right," Fiona says, "you just want me to come in so you can show me your record collection."

"I don't have a record collection," he says. Then, before he can think better of it: "Do you *want* me to put a move on you?"

Fiona laughs again. "You got me," she says with a twist of her lips. "It was literally all I could think about on the ride over here."

Sam lifts an eyebrow. "Really?" he asks, though of course he knows she's just giving him shit. "What did you think?"

"I—" That flusters her, Sam can tell, which was the point, but it has the unintended consequence of flustering him a little, too. He imagines it in high definition before he can stop himself: his hands on the ladder of her rib cage, her soft-looking mouth on his jaw. Neither one of them says anything for a full second too long.

Fiona pulls it together first. "I *think* I probably should have made you get an STD test before I even got in the car," she says finally, but it's weak as far as insults go, and before he can answer she's sighing theatrically, opening the door, and climbing out into the warm, humid night.

"Fine," she announces imperiously, "one drink."

Sam smiles.

Sam's apartment is on the second floor, up an outdoor staircase laid with painted terra-cotta tile in reds and greens and yellows. Bright pink snapdragons vine along the wrought iron railing lining the catwalk. He moved in here as soon as *The Heart Surgeon* pilot got picked up, the same week he leased the Tesla. A couple of years in this place, he thought, then a house with a view in Laurel Canyon, the ghost of Mama Cass wandering around humming to herself early in the mornings. Then—once he finally broke out in movies like Russ keeps saying he's going to—a mansion in the Palisades, next door to Kurt Russell and Goldie Hawn.

That was the plan, anyway.

For now he'll be lucky if he can pay next month's rent.

Sam unlocks the heavy wooden door and flicks on the lights in the foyer, heading straight for the bar cart in the living room. He grabs two glasses and doubles back toward the kitchen for ice. "I have tequila," he calls over his shoulder. He feels nervous all of a sudden, though he isn't entirely sure why. "You want a lime?"

"Um, sure," Fiona calls back, though he gets the impression she isn't really listening. Sure enough, a moment later: "This is your place?" she asks, the surprise audible in her voice. "This is . . . nice."

Sam raises his eyebrows at the freezer. "Why, because you were expecting me to live in a cardboard box on the side of the freeway?"

"I mean, yeah," she admits. "Kind of."

"Thanks a lot," Sam says, though he isn't actually offended. He'd never bought real furniture before and had no idea what he was doing, so he hired the decorator at West Elm to pick it all out for him. She did a pretty good job, lots of wood and leather and a big modern armchair that makes him feel a little bit like Dr. Evil whenever he sits in it. There's a Gibson Les Paul signed by Van Morrison hanging on the wall above the couch.

When he comes back into the living room Fiona is standing in front of his bookcase; she's scooped her hair up into a knot on top of her head, the pale nape of her neck exposed. "You're a Sarah Waters fan?" she asks. She's standing on her tiptoes to peer at the top shelf, the muscles in her calves flexing. "Seriously?"

Sam reaches for the bottle. "Who?" he asks.

Fiona holds up a paperback he doesn't even think he's ever seen before, and he shakes his head. "My old roommate, Erin," he explains. "She did a whole Marie Kondo thing when we were moving out of our last apartment. I wound up with a lot of her stuff."

"Aha." Fiona nods. "You know, somehow I didn't take you for a connoisseur of erotic lesbian historical noir."

That gets his attention. "I am actually . . . very interested in at least a couple of the words you just said."

Fiona makes a face. "Uh-huh," she says, turning back to the bookshelves, "see, now *that's* more about what I expected from you, Sam Fox."

"Hey now." Sam presses the icy glass against her back, right in between her shoulder blades; Fiona gasps quietly. "I read."

"Oh yeah?" she asks, plucking the tequila from his outstretched hand and taking a sip. "Thank you. What's your favorite book, like, *The Alchemist*?"

"Shut up." Sam blanches. "How did you know that?"

Fiona bursts out laughing. "Oh my god, no it's not."

Okay, now he's a little bit offended. "What's wrong with *The Alchemist*?" he demands.

"I mean, nothing." Fiona shrugs, taking her glass and settling herself down on one side of the couch, crossing one long leg over the other. "It's just the favorite book of every man who's only read one book."

Sam shakes his head. "You really think you know everything there is to know about me, don't you."

"Of course not," she deadpans immediately. "The final ten percent is strictly conjecture."

"Cute." Sam sits down beside her, careful to leave a foot of space between them. "Okay then, princess. What's *your* favorite book?"

"Oh, I don't know how to read."

Sam laughs. "Unsurprising, really."

"I know, right?" Fiona runs her thumb around the rim of her glass, not quite meeting his gaze. "No, um. It's *Weetzie Bat*."

Sam shakes his head. "What now?"

"I mean, it's dumb," Fiona says, though from the guarded look on her face he can tell she doesn't actually think that. "It's about a girl who lives in LA in the eighties and is, like, amazingly, heart-breakingly cool. Back when we were doing *Birds* I used to keep a paperback of it jammed down the back of my jeans like a gun, for good luck or something. That's how bad I wanted to be her." She takes another sip of her tequila, waving her hand in front of her face like the idea is a visible cloud of stupidity she can fan away. "Anyway. Spoiler alert. It turns out I'm just me."

Sam shrugs, bumping his knee against hers. Her jeans are the kind with on-purpose holes in them, and patches of soft, tan skin are showing through. "You're not so bad, Fiona St. James."

"Well." Fiona smiles at that. "I'm no Weetzie Bat."

They're quiet for a moment, drinking their tequila. The silence feels electric and keen. Sam thinks, very clearly, *Fuck it*, and as soon as the words pop into his head it's like his hand is moving of its own volition from where it's resting on his own thigh over to Fiona's. His thumb slips inside a fray in the denim at her knee to rub at the hard cap of bone there, drawing slow circles on her smooth, warm skin.

Fiona's breath hitches. She looks down and watches his thumb move for a moment, the rise and fall of her chest visible inside her tank top. "I thought you weren't going to put a move on me," she reminds him, raising one thick eyebrow. She's still looking down at her lap.

Sam nods seriously. "I'm not putting a move on you," he promises, then ducks his head and kisses her.

Fiona gasps against his mouth, the smell of alcohol and lime sharp in the air as her wrist jerks and tequila sloshes out of her glass. He feels like the odds are fifty-fifty he read this all wrong and she punches him in the face, but instead she kisses him back right away, eager, like she was waiting for him to cop on all night long. Sam hums a low, pleased sound. He takes her glass and sets it on the coffee table, then reaches for her hand and licks the inside of her wrist where the tequila is still dripping down it. She tastes like limes and salt.

Fiona swallows hard. "Okay," she murmurs—more to herself than to him, Sam thinks. She touches her face, her neck, her collarbone. "I—um. Okay."

Sam smiles. If he'd known this was what it would take to get her to quit looking at him like he's a total fucking fool, he would have done it way before now. "Do you want me to stop?"

Fiona shakes her head. "No," she admits, so he kisses her again, harder and longer and deeper this time, then nudges her backward until she's lying against the throw pillows, her hair falling out of its knot and fanning out in a corona around her face. Sam makes a gentle fist, his fingers catching in the tangles as his other hand migrates up from her hip to her waist to her ribs, tracing the underwire of her bra and circling her nipple until he can feel it tighten up through both layers of fabric. Fiona whimpers.

"That okay?" he mutters, and she nods.

Sam backs off long enough to ruck her shirt up a little, ducking his head and trailing his mouth down over her stomach. It's been a long time since he did this with a person who wasn't actively trying to make a career at least in part out of counting macros, and he likes the soft curves of her body, the soap-sweat smell of her skin. "You taste good," he mutters, and Fiona makes a sound that might be a scoff but she's also arching up into it, reaching down and sifting her hands through his hair. She tugs once, not particularly gently, and Sam groans against her hip.

The sound of it seems to bring her back to herself. "Come up here," she orders, yanking at his shirt, working the tiny buttons through their holes and pushing the fabric off his shoulders. She rakes her nails lightly over the back of his neck, and Sam shivers. He pulls her tank top over her head and reaches behind her to work the clasp on her bra, pulling the straps down and catching her nipple in his mouth; Fiona closes her eyes and lets him suck for a minute before she tugs at his shoulders, pulling him up so they're fused chest to chest.

Sam's been hard since basically the first second he kissed her and when she opens up her hips to make space for him he growls into her neck, grinding himself mindlessly against her like he's thirteen and not thirty-one. Fiona hooks one leg around his to keep him close. He's only ever done cocaine a couple of times but this is what it felt like, his entire body buzzing like he swallowed a handful of stars or his bones are made of neon. She's chasing his hips with hers, gasping, and all at once Sam's—shit, Sam's pretty sure she's close.

He lifts himself up long enough to work one hand down in between them—if he's going to get her off he's damn well going to do it properly—but as soon as he reaches for the button on her jeans she freezes.

"Okay," she says—pulling away, boosting herself up onto her elbows. "Okay, okay, now I want you to stop."

Sam stops. "What?" For a second he thinks she's kidding,

but one look at her face has him sitting up so fast he gets light-headed, or maybe he would have been light-headed either way. Multicolored spots explode in front of his eyes. "Sorry," he says. "I—yeah, of course, sorry."

"No, it's not—" Fiona breaks off, touching her mouth like she's checking to make sure it's still there. "*I'm* sorry, I just—" She looks around for a moment, pulling her knees up and scrubbing both hands through her hair. "I shouldn't have—"

"No no no, you don't have to explain anything," he blurts, but he's surprised by how badly he wants her to. All at once he wants to know everything there is to know about her, her birthday and her middle name and the story behind the scar on the underside of her upper arm. He'd think it was the booze, except he's not actually even a little bit drunk anymore. He *likes* her. He likes her *so much*. And he's been trying not to think it and trying not to think it since that very first day at the copy shop, but here it is, sitting nakedly in the middle of the room for anyone to see.

"I'm sorry," Fiona says again. She's looking around the living room, presumably for her clothes; Sam plucks her bra off the back of the couch and hands it over, and she offers him half a smile. "Thanks."

"Yeah, of course." Sam nods, glancing politely away while she does up the hooks and pulls her shirt on, only then once she's dressed she leans over and kisses him *again*, slow and wet and a little bit dirty, and okay, now he really has no idea what the fuck is going on. "Fee," he starts, voice cracking a little. He's still completely, 100 percent hard. "Can you just—"

Fiona shakes her head. "I should go."

Something about the tone in her voice gives Sam the distinct impression he's never going to see her again after tonight, the idea of which makes him weirdly panicky, considering the fact that until the other day he hadn't thought about her in years. "What if you didn't?" he blurts.

That stops her. She looks over at him, raising her eyebrows. "What if—?"

"I'm serious," he says, scrambling shirtless up off the sofa, then immediately feels like a massive tool. "I mean, look, I'm not trying to be some creepy weirdo who can't take a hint, so obviously go if you want to go, but." He shrugs. "What if you stayed?"

"Sam—"

"We can just sleep," he promises, which is the kind of earnest, stupid Nicholas Sparks bullshit she is absolutely never going to let him hear the end of; he's holding up a hand to cut her off at the pass when she nods.

"Okay," she says.

Sam blinks at her. "Seriously?" That is . . . not what he was expecting her to say. If she'd said good night, gone outside, and set his house on *fire*, he would not be more surprised. "You want to stay?"

Fiona's eyes narrow. "Do you not *want* me to stay?"

"Of course I want you to stay," he says, and for once he honestly doesn't even give a crap about how eager it sounds. "That's why I asked."

"I'm not going to have sex with you," she reminds him. "This isn't some cute thing where I'm playing hard to get but I secretly want you to convince me to—"

"Fiona," he interrupts, because he likes to think that fundamentally he's not a piece of shit, "I know."

She studies him hard for another long second, like she's looking for the catch, and he doesn't know what she sees in his face, but it must satisfy her, because she nods again. "Okay," she says, sounding more sure about it this time. "I'll stay."

Sam feels his whole body relax. It's the feeling of swerving just in time to avoid hitting another car or making it to your seat just before the plane door closes, the flight attendant floating by to offer you a drink. "Okay," he echoes, trying not to smile. "Good."

Fiona relaxes, too, her shoulders dropping as she perches on the arm of the sofa. "We have to watch serial killer documentaries," she informs him. "That's what I watch to fall asleep."

Sam laughs, then realizes she's not kidding. "Wait," he says, "really?"

Fiona frowns. "Look, I can go," she says immediately, gesturing toward the door. "You're the one who—"

"No no no," Sam says again, holding both hands up in surrender. "Have it your way. You're missing out, though. Usually when girls sleep over I read to them by candlelight from *The Alchemist*."

Fiona laughs.

She pads down the hallway behind him, hovering barefoot in the doorway as he smooths the blankets over his unmade bed. Once they're in he turns off the light and opens up his laptop, then realizes as the screen blinks to life that he hasn't used it since the other night: sure enough, the cartoon boobs from the porn site are still bouncing merrily away. "Friend of yours?" Fiona asks, her voice completely even.

"I read it for the articles," he shoots back, clicking over to Netflix. "So, is one serial killer documentary as good as another? Or do you have, like, a greatest hits list you like to work from?"

Fiona smiles magnanimously. "You can pick."

In the end they watch some grisly fucking thing about the Mansons—a cheesy sixties rock score played over shot after shot of Sharon Tate's yellow hair and round, pregnant belly. Sam tries not to flinch. He likes a slasher flick as much as the next guy, but true crime has always weirded him out—the luridness of it, he guesses, low-end producers making money off the worst day of other people's lives.

Also, it always makes him a little nervous he's about to get serial murdered.

Still, he likes having Fiona propped up on one elbow beside him, the ends of her long hair just brushing his arm. It's not like he's *trying* to look or anything, but the collar of her tank top gapes open a little so he can see the tops of her breasts out of the corner of his eye, a handful of freckles scattered across her chest like glitter. He can feel the heat radiating off her skin. Something about the whole setup has Sam afraid to move too much, like how his mom always made Adam and him hold still when deer showed up in their yard while they were playing football. He doesn't want to scare her away.

"Okay," he says finally, grimacing as the narrator reports the findings of Sharon Tate's autopsy in excruciatingly minute detail. "Can we turn this off, please?"

Fiona sighs loudly, flopping over onto her back. "I guess," she agrees. "But if I wind up lying awake all night it's your fault."

Sam looks at her pointedly. "I might say the same thing to you, cutie-pie."

In any case, she's passed out what feels like two seconds later— hogging all the blankets, her chilly feet brushing his underneath the sheets. Sam looks over at her, squinting to try and see her in the darkness. The sound of her breathing is the last thing he hears before he falls asleep.

CHAPTER NINE

Fiona

The first thing Fiona registers when she wakes up the following morning is how nice the sheets are, crisp white cotton percale with what must be a thread count in the thousands.

The second thing she registers is that she's lying in Sam Fox's bed.

With Sam Fox.

Shit.

He's still sleeping, thank fuck, sacked out on the mattress beside her with one tanned, muscled arm slung over his face—lean and bare-chested, the sun streaming through the trees outside his bedroom window casting patterns of shadow and light across his smooth, unblemished skin.

Fiona pushes the covers back and sits up as quietly as possible so she doesn't wake him, lifting a careful hand to her mouth. Her lips feel swollen and itchy, bruised in a good way. Fiona shivers. She hasn't kissed anyone like that in—she doesn't know if she's *ever* kissed anyone like that, actually. Kissing Sam felt like how she imagines it would have been to make out in someone's car in high school: like she physically couldn't get enough of him, like all this time there was a secret string of explosives rigged inside her body and he methodically set about tripping every single one. She curls her toes against the plush shag of the area rug and lets herself stare at him for a minute, the jut of his hip bones and the trail of dark hair beneath his navel and his stupid perfect pectoral muscles, the kind you only get if you're a goober who goes to the gym every day and is obsessed with his own physique.

Oh, god, this is going to be so awkward.

Fiona tiptoes down the hallway into the living area, where her jacket is slung over the back of one of the leather barstools and her purse is slouched on a woven bench near the door. She slings the bag over her shoulder, then breathes a sigh of relief at having successfully avoided the cringiest non-postcoital morning after in recorded history and grabs her shoe off the hardwood floor of the foyer.

That's shoe, singular.

Because its mate? Is nowhere to be found.

Fiona frowns, turning in a slow circle and scanning the living room. Sam was right, last night—she *was* surprised by how nice this place is, not just the apartment itself but the physical items inside it: the deep, cognac-colored couch and the antique pharmacist's lamp beside the armchair, the block-printed throw pillows in geometric blues and greens. On the bookshelf is a black-and-white photo of a long-haired woman Fiona assumes is Sam's mother holding a fat, bald baby, her head thrown back laughing; there's a tall, proud palm tree in a big terra-cotta pot by the doors that lead to the balcony, and by all appearances it is alive.

Fiona checks fruitlessly under the coffee table and behind the door in the tiny black-and-white bathroom, then circles back to the kitchen and starts the search again. What the fuck? Like, quite seriously, did a coyote sneak in here while she was sleeping and run off with it? It's a *shoe*. She's on her hands and knees peering under the sofa when she hears the sound of someone clearing his voice behind her. "Uh," Sam says, his voice low and a little bit hoarse. "Morning."

Fiona winces, squeezing her eyes shut for a moment before straightening up and looking at him. "Oh," she says, tucking her tangled hair behind her ears. "Hey."

"Whatcha doing?" he asks, reaching up to scratch his naked shoulder. He hasn't bothered putting pants on, the outline of his cock fully visible through his dark gray boxer briefs.

Fiona clears her throat, trying not to stare. "Did you hide my shoe?" she asks.

Sam snorts. "What?"

"My shoe," she says again, feeling the slightest bit hysterical. "I was wearing two when I got here, obviously, but now . . ." She gestures at her orphaned boot. "Did you hide it?"

Sam looks at her like she's insane. "Why would I hide your—?" He breaks off. "What, like, to keep you here?"

"I—" Fiona feels her cheeks flame. It sounds absurd, now that she hears it out loud. "No, of course not. I just—"

"No?" Sam definitely isn't buying it; the corners of his plush mouth twitch in barely concealed amusement. "That's not what you were accusing me of just now? Being so desperate for more face time with you that I snuck out here in the middle of the night and absconded with your—" He stops himself mid-sentence, lifting one perfect eyebrow. "That one?" he asks, gesturing with his chin in the direction of the armchair in the corner, where the missing boot is lying on its side like a wounded soldier.

"Oh." Fiona nods. She remembers now, toeing it off mid-makeout—distracted by Sam's hot mouth moving down her neck, his fingertips playing over her body like a piano. "Thank you."

"You're welcome," he says, scooping it up off the rug and holding it out in her direction with a smile. It's a real one, open and fond, and Fiona's stomach swoops dangerously. When she reaches for the boot he holds on an extra second, tugging gently. She feels the pull right between her legs. "You want me to go back to bed so you can finish sneaking out of my house?"

"I wasn't sneaking *out*," she protests. "I was just trying to save us both from wanting to kill ourselves, that's all."

"Thoughtful." Sam rubs the crown of his head, his dark hair sticking up in every direction. "Do you want to kill yourself right now?" he asks.

Fiona considers that for a moment. In *fact* what she kind of wants to do is push him back onto that boat of a leather couch and climb on top of him, but she'd sooner shove this boot down her throat than tell him that. ". . . No?" she asks, then completely fails to follow it up in any meaningful way.

"No?" Sam smirks. "Tell you what," he says. "You stay there and consider your own suicidality. I'll make breakfast."

"You don't know how to make breakfast," she accuses, following him back into the kitchen. She's still holding the boot.

Sam opens the fridge and pulls out a dozen eggs and a bright yellow tub of Earth Balance. "Can I ask you a question?" he says. "What is it about me that makes you feel compelled to heckle me one hundred percent of the time?"

That stops her. "I—" she starts, then breaks off and tries again. "I—"

Sam raises his eyebrows. "You?"

Fiona drops her shoe on the floor, pops up onto her tiptoes, and kisses him.

Sam lets out a quiet *oof* sound and kisses her back, his hands coming up to cup her face. His chest is burning-hot through her tank top. Fiona sifts her hands through his hair and bites at his bottom lip, at his tongue, at the shadow of scruff along his jawline. She reaches down to squeeze his ass, and he groans.

"I like you," she admits quietly, her voice muffled against his shoulder. When she kisses his neck she tastes salt. "That's why I heckle you all the time."

Sam laughs out loud, the sensation of it rumbling pleasantly down her legs. "How old are you, twelve?"

"Basically," she admits.

Sam nods like that tracks. "Well," he says, reaching up under her tank top and tugging at her nipple through the fabric of her bra, making her gasp. "Grow up."

He boosts her onto the counter, then hooks his hands behind her knees and spreads her legs apart, stepping between them. Fiona winds her arms around his neck. She rocks herself against him, she can't help it, like he's a scratching post and she's got an itch.

"Fiona," Sam murmurs against her mouth. He's hard, the length of him thick and hot and urgent even through three layers of clothing. "Come back to bed with me."

Fiona hesitates. She wants to. Fuck, she wants to. And it's not like she isn't already imagining it—his fingers and his cock and his wet, clever tongue, those soft white sheets against her skin—but she can't help but feel like she'd be giving something up in the process. Something she isn't quite ready to lose.

"Tell you what," she says, kissing him one more time before nudging him away and hopping down off the counter. "Let's go out."

"Okay." Sam's lips twitch, uncertain. "But that is . . . not the same thing as bed."

"You're right," she says, reaching for his hand and lacing their fingers together. She can see the question on his face—*Is this a no for now, or is this a no forever?*—and she wants to tell him it's just a no for now, but she doesn't know how to say the words. "But also, waffles."

Sam looks at her for another long moment, then nods. "Yeah," he says, still a little breathless. "I've got an audition, but after that."

"An audition?" That makes her smile. She leans back against the fridge, raises her chin. "What for?"

Sam loops her arm around his waist, steps closer. "None of your business."

"Oh, you want me to guess?" Fiona mimics. "Why didn't you just say so?" She thinks for a moment, stroking an imaginary beard. "Hot male nanny on an intergenerational dramedy," she suggests. "Hot client on a legal procedural. Hot corpse on a minor CSI franchise."

"Aw, honey." Sam gazes at her through his eyelashes. "You think I'm a hot corpse?"

"I think you're the kind of person they *cast* as a hot corpse," she corrects.

"Understood," he says seriously, and kisses her again. "Anyway. Want to tag along? We can go get waffles after. Or, rather, you can get waffles and I can get a sensible yet tasty grain bowl."

Fiona thinks about it. She can see the flecks of gold in his eyes from the sunlight coming in through the window above the sink. There's a feeling in her chest she doesn't entirely recognize, and it takes her a moment to realize it's happiness. "Okay," she says, her smile slow and not entirely voluntary. "Yes."

Outside it's a vintage postcard kind of morning, blue sky and not too hot yet, the air with that sandy desert bite. They stop by Coffee Bean for iced lattes and Sam puts Otis Redding on the stereo. Fiona opens her mouth to make fun of him—it's just a reflex at this point; she actually loves Otis Redding—then closes it again. She trails her fingers through the breeze outside the window and hums along.

"Oh, PS," Sam says, as they creep along Cahuenga in the direction of the 101, "not to be a weirdo, but this thing is on the UBC lot. Just to like, give you a heads-up."

"Oh." Fiona blinks. UBC is the parent company of the Family Network; the UBC lot is where they filmed *Birds*. Fiona hasn't been anywhere near it in years and the thought of going back there fills her with an immediate, visceral panic, a hundred centipedes scuttling around inside her body. It was stupid of her not to ask. "Okay."

"Sorry," he says, glancing at her across the gearshift, "is that—"

"No," she says quickly. "No, it's fine."

The UBC lot is an old-fashioned studio campus with an art deco sensibility, the newer buildings tarted up in glass and steel. She's fully expecting the sight of it to freak her out in an deep and unbearable way and she can tell Sam is expecting it, too, the way he keeps looking over at her like he thinks she's about to jump out of the car, rip all her clothes off, and start moonwalking naked across the concrete while reciting the Pledge of Allegiance in pig latin. "I'm fine," she informs him. "How are you, are you nervous?"

"Nah." Sam shakes his head.

"Just that cool, huh?"

"Just that cool." He pulls into a spot in the visitor lot and slaps his parking pass on the dashboard, checks his teeth in the rearview mirror, then turns to look at her. "You gonna kiss me for luck, or what?"

Fiona considers that. "Yes," she decides, then grabs him by the scruff of his neck and lays one on him.

Sam winks. "We call that a Kenosha send-off," he tells her, touching a hand to an imaginary cap before opening the driver's side door. "See you later, doll."

"Oh my god, you absolute *turd*!" Fiona calls after him, but she's laughing. She hopes they cast him as the hot murder suspect whose alibi checks out after the second commercial break, or whatever the fuck he's auditioning for in there.

Once he's gone she scrolls her phone for a while, but it's too nice to spend an hour sitting alone in the passenger seat of this farcical car, so she glances around to make sure nobody with a camera is lurking at the edges of the parking lot, then gets out and climbs up onto the hood. She leans back against the warm metal and closes her eyes, letting the sunshine make patterns on the insides of her eyelids. She's thinking about ordering a ham and cheese omelet at breakfast. She's thinking about changing the blocking of the final scene in the play. She's thinking about saying screw it and telling Sam to take her back to his apartment when someone calls her name across the parking lot.

Fiona opens her eyes, scrambling upright like an instinct. Feeling her entire body go cold.

"Um," she says, instinctively rearranging her face into a mask of cheery, girlish, Riley Bird surprise. "Hi, Jamie."

CHAPTER TEN

Sam

The audition is for Hot Rookie Fireman with a Tragic Military Past, and it actually goes amazingly, mind-bendingly well. Sam is shocked, honestly; it's rare that he can feel himself nailing something in real time, slipping seamlessly into a character like he imagines legitimate actors do. He thinks of telling Fiona she's his good luck charm, then imagines listening to her fake barfing sounds all the way to breakfast and thinks better of it.

He says his thank-yous—"You'll definitely be hearing from us," the casting director says with a smile, and Sam manages not to fist pump until he gets out of the room—and heads out to the parking lot, where he finds Fiona perched on the hood of the Tesla, shooting the shit with Jamie Hartley.

"Hey!" he calls, pleased. It's a good day. "What is this, a reunion?"

"Uh-oh." Jamie grins, lopsided and familiar. "Can't be using that word yet." He looks exactly the same as he did when he played their dad on *Birds of California*, that extremely well-preserved look that all the network guys out here have. "Hey, Fee, he said it, not me."

Fiona smiles. "I will be sure to keep that in mind."

"You do that," Jamie says, slinging an arm around Sam's shoulders and squeezing. He smells like a redwood forest. "Man, this is a surprise. How you doing, kid?"

"I'm good," Sam says, ducking his head a little shyly. Back when he was still on *Birds* Jamie used to take him out for burgers at the end of every season and ask him what kinds of projects he wanted to work on, what his favorite movies were. Even back then Sam knew it was corny how much he looked forward to it, but he always looked forward to it anyway. When he heard about Jamie's development deal at HBO he wondered if maybe there was a chance he'd get a call.

"I love this," Jamie says now, letting him go and clapping him on the back. "The whole gang back together."

"Except for Max," Sam says, for Fiona's benefit. "Can't forget about Max."

Jamie frowns. "Which one was Max?" he asks.

"Oh, come on!" Sam chides. "Little redheaded kid who played the cousin, you remember."

"Of course I remember," Jamie says. "I called and talked him into coming aboard the other day." He turns to Fiona. "Did Thandie tell you she signed on?"

"I—" Fiona breaks off, the disbelief written all over her face. "Thandie?" she asks. "Really?"

"I know," Jamie says with a self-deprecating laugh. "I was surprised, too. I thought she'd be too busy with Soderbergh and Fincher to be hanging around with schmucks like us. But she said it was such an important part of her life that she'd come in and do a couple of episodes for old times' sake."

"That's big of her," Fiona mutters under her breath—or Sam thinks that's what she says, at least. Jamie doesn't seem to hear.

"Anyway, I've gotta get going," he says. "Got a meeting inside. But it was good to see you guys." He winks. "Nice that you still hang out."

He hugs both of them goodbye and lopes off across the parking lot in his leather jacket like Ben Affleck about to drill a nuclear missile into an asteroid. "I love that guy," Sam says once he's gone. Fiona is already back in the car, buckled neatly into the passenger seat with her hands folded in her lap. "Don't you love that guy?"

Fiona doesn't answer. "Did you plan that?" she asks. She isn't looking at him, instead staring straight out the windshield at Jamie's receding back.

Sam stares at her blankly. "Plan what?"

"Running into him."

"What? No." He shakes his head. Her tone is completely different than it was a minute ago, and when he looks at her a little more carefully he notices her body language is, too. She was *acting*, he realizes suddenly, and he's immediately and bizarrely impressed with her chops all over again. She's better than he is, that's for sure. He wants to march her back inside the studio and tell them, *This is the girl you should hire.* "I had no idea he was here."

"Okay," Fiona says, and it's obvious she thinks he's full of shit. "Because I'm just saying, he sure didn't seem that surprised to see us together."

That irritates him, even as he feels a little bit guilty; he thinks of the way Jamie winked at him, like they were in on something together. Still: "Really?" Sam can't resist saying. "He literally said, 'This is a surprise.'"

Fiona's eyes narrow. "Are you making fun of me right now?"

"No," Sam says as they pull out of the parking lot. "Of course not."

"Can you blame me for being a little bit paranoid? You're crawling all over me trying to get me to do this revival, and then suddenly—"

"Oh, is that what you'd call what happened in my apartment this morning?" he interrupts. And he knows, he *knows* he's going to regret it, but it's out before he can stop himself: "*Me* crawling all over *you*?"

Fiona's mouth gets very thin. "Okay," she says quietly. Sam can practically see her nailing the *No Trespassing* sign back up over her door. "You know what, that's fine, we don't have to talk about this anymore."

Sam sighs. "Fiona—"

"I said it's fine, Sam."

"Fine." They're quiet for a couple of minutes, both of them stewing, until all at once Sam realizes he doesn't actually know where he's going. "Do you still want breakfast?" he asks her. He can hear in his own voice that it sounds like he wants her to say no.

Fiona hears it, too, or maybe she really just doesn't want to be around him any longer than she has to. "I should get back," she says. "I can get an Uber, if you want to just drop me somewhere."

"Don't be ridiculous," Sam says crabbily. "I'll take you home."

They don't talk the entire ride back to her dad's house, Fiona staring out the passenger side window through a pair of sunglasses she dug out of her enormous handbag. Sam keeps glancing over, but her face is inscrutable, a mask.

"Look," she says, when he finally pulls into her driveway. She unbuckled her seat belt halfway up the block in preparation; frankly, he's surprised she's saying anything to him at all. "It was good to catch up. Hope they call you back for your thing."

"Okay. Thanks." Sam frowns. He thinks he should leave it alone, but he doesn't want to. "Fiona," he says quietly. "Can you tell me what happened just now?"

"What?" Fiona shakes her head, feigning ignorance. "Nothing. This was fun."

It definitely doesn't feel like nothing, but honestly, Sam is too irritated to press her about it. If she wants to act crazy and irrational, let her act crazy and irrational—that's her business. It's not like nobody warned him about her. "Okay," he says. "See you around."

"Yup."

Sam watches her cross the lawn and let herself into the front door of her house, her shoulders hunched and fingers twitching. He thinks she might look back, but she doesn't. He sits there for a moment longer once she's inside, feeling like a total boner. Then he steps on the gas and drives away.

Adam calls that night while Sam's eating plain quinoa out of the pot to atone for the burger, watching *Wheel of Fortune* on Hulu. "I'm going to tell you something," Adam says, "but I don't want you to freak out."

That's a terrible fucking way to get someone not to freak out, Sam thinks, fear already blooming in his chest. "What?"

"Mom's okay," Adam tells him, "but she had a little bit of a fall."

Sam sets the pot on the coffee table. "What do you mean, *a little bit of a fall?*"

"She fainted in the parking lot after her doctor's appointment."

"Put her on the phone."

"Sammy, I'm serious, she's okay—"

"Put her on."

There's a rustling sound, and Adam is saying something Sam can't make out. They still use the landline back at home. "I'm fine," his mom says when she gets on. "I was flustered, that's all. I saw a handsome doctor and just swooned away."

"That's not funny."

"Of course it's not," she agrees. "How are you?"

Who cares how I am, Sam thinks. He feels like he's about to cry. "I'm fine," he says. "How do you feel now?"

"Well, honey, I have cancer."

He makes a choked, phlegmy sound, halfway between a laugh and a sob. He wants to go home and sit at the kitchen table and ask her how to fix all his problems, up to and including *My mom is sick*. He wants to tell her about Fiona, bizarrely, though he has no idea what he'd say.

Instead he swallows hard. "I love you," he tells her finally. "Put Adam back on."

"I told you," Adam says a moment later.

"Should I come home?" Sam asks.

"Can you afford to come home?" Adam replies, which is not *Of course not, don't worry about it, there's plenty of time*.

"Of course I can," he lies. "Why do you keep talking to me like I'm broke?"

"I don't know," Adam says. "I don't think you need to come, though. I'll text you if anything changes."

Sam hangs up and looks around at his ridiculous apartment, his expensive chair and douchey midcentury lamps and the signed Van Morrison guitar he bought when *The Heart Surgeon* first got a full-season order. He doesn't even play the guitar. He doesn't even like Van Morrison! He just bought it because he thought it was cool and that girls would want to talk about it when he brought them back here, which they generally do, although Fiona didn't say anything about it either way.

Fuck, he doesn't want to be thinking about Fiona right now.

He gets a beer from the fridge and dicks around on his computer for a while, trying to figure out how to list shit on eBay, then getting frustrated five minutes in and giving up. He has no idea why he's so surprised that in the end she was exactly how all the memes made her out to be: moody and irrational and defensive, basically accusing him of messing around with her just to get her to do the reboot.

You were *messing around with her to get her do the reboot*, a tiny voice in his head reminds him, and he feels like the biggest jackass who ever lived.

That was why he went to see her at the print shop, maybe. But it wasn't why he invited her out last night.

And it definitely wasn't why he asked her to stay.

It doesn't matter, Sam reminds himself, getting up and wandering into the kitchen. *It's over now.* He opens a beer, drinking it down in three long, cold gulps without particularly tasting it. Reaches for another.

The next thing he knows it's morning, and Erin is banging on the door of his apartment. His mouth tastes like it's full of jockstraps. His head pounds. "Easy," he says, swinging the door open.

Erin wrinkles her nose. "It smells like farts in here," she says.

Sam scrubs a hand over his face. "Did you want something?"

"Don't freak," she says, and comes inside.

It's the second time in twelve hours someone has led that way, and Sam doesn't appreciate it one bit. He needs coffee. He needs water, and a bacon egg and cheese sandwich, and a starring role in an action-adventure blockbuster directed by Steven Spielberg. "Why would I freak?"

Erin holds out her phone, shoving the screen right up to his face. Sam blinks, focusing on the home page of a hugely popular gossip website—the same one that had such a boner for Fiona a few years ago, back when she was acting like a public nuisance all the time.

"*Love* Birds?" the headline reads, right above—oh, shit— four different pictures of Fiona and Sam leaving his apartment yesterday morning, his hand laced casually through hers. *Everything old is new again! Looks like things are heating up between these former costars. Rumor has it a revival of beloved Family Network megahit* Birds of California *is in the works—assuming, of course, that Fiona St. James can keep from flying (see what we did there?) off the handle. See a slideshow of her most shocking public meltdowns below!*

"Fuck me," Sam says, shuffling through the living room and collapsing onto the sofa, his arms and legs prickly and hot. He's got plenty of experience with gossip sites—there was a thing with him and Taylor Swift a couple of years ago, and he once wound up wrongfully implicated as a branch on the herpes tree of a catcher on the San Diego Padres. Still, something about this particular occurrence makes him feel like he's gotten caught with his dick out— not because they got a picture of him leaving his apartment with a woman, he realizes slowly, but because that woman was Fiona St. James, who once smashed the front window of a luxe Beverly Hills eatery with a child's pogo stick, which she had previously stolen. And yeah, he was half hoping somebody might snap a shot of them out at lunch the other day, but this is different. After all, it's one thing to be hanging out with her in the name of trying to get her to do *Birds of California*. It's another to just . . . be hanging out with her. It doesn't exactly scream *dashing, high-end leading man for hire*.

You invited her out in the first place, he reminds himself. *You're the one who asked her back to your house.*

Still, he'd be lying if he said he wasn't kind of regretting it now.

"*How* did you not mention this?" Erin asks, sitting down in the Dr. Evil chair and swiveling around like a delighted kid. "You're just, like, out here casually boning Riley Bird, not saying anything about it? Very gentlemanly of you, I must admit."

"We're not boning," Sam says, raking his hands through his hair. "It's . . . a weird situation."

"I'll say," Erin agrees cheerfully. "Look on the bright side, though: this is way more interesting than your show being canceled. People have probably forgotten all about that."

"Fuck you," Sam says, but there's no heat behind it. He knows it makes him an asshole to be embarrassed about this, on top of which he's pretty sure that however invaded he's feeling right now, Fiona's probably got it worse. He remembers that first day in the print shop, how she told him the press had finally left her alone. "I should call her." He reaches for his phone, knowing even as he's dialing that she isn't going to answer. Sure enough, it doesn't even seem to be on. He hangs up without leaving a message, both because he doesn't think it would make a difference and because he feels weird about saying anything sincere with Erin sitting right here, looking at him with that expression on her face that girls get when they think they know something.

"Go take a shower," she says once he's hung up. "I'll buy you some disgusting wrap with egg whites." Then, as he's padding across the living room: "And open a window, would you? It smells like a tar pit." Sam flips her off before he shuts the bathroom door.

CHAPTER ELEVEN

Fiona

❦

Claudia's the one who tells her about the pictures. Part of the agreement Fiona made with Pam back when she was in treatment was that she had to stop looking at Darcy's website, and she has, for the most part. But Claudia still has a Google Alert set for Fiona's name, meticulously scanning the horizon for any sign of trouble like the guys on the Wall in *Game of Thrones*.

"It doesn't say anything bad, really," Claudia promises, leaning against the kitchen counter. Brando hovers in the hallway, like a pinch hitter waiting to see if he's about to get called off the bench. "I just thought you'd want to know."

Claudia is right: objectively the photos aren't that bad. After all, Fiona is fully clothed, in command of all her faculties, and not actively berating any innocent bystanders, which means by Darcy's standards they're basically the watercolor illustrations from a child's book of nursery rhymes. Still, *Us* has picked them up, and so have half a dozen other websites, and seeing herself looking so dopey and unguarded—the openness of her expression, the gooney way she's smiling at Sam—makes Fiona feel like someone has stuck their dirty hands inside her chest cavity, getting smudge marks on all her organs.

Of course, it's possible it's not just Darcy that's making her feel that way. Everything is jangled up inside her: Sam, Jamie, *Birds*. It's like all the shit she spent the last five years trying to smooth over is all mixed-up again, and she can feel the urge building inside her to do something reckless: to hurt someone, to hurt herself. Last time she felt like this she wound up floating naked in the pool at a JW Marriott in Playa del Carmen with very little memory of how she got there, but she doesn't do that kind of thing anymore, so instead she goes to work and fixes spaghetti for her sister and lies in bed listening to LeBron James read a guided meditation on her phone.

She's trying. She's trying so hard.

Finally she gives up and throws one arm over her face, slipping the fingers of her other hand down into the waistband of her boxers. She thinks of Sam's touch on her hips and her thighs and her stomach; she thinks of his warm, clever mouth on her breasts. It's not enough—none of it feels like enough—but it gets the job done, and when she's finished she curls onto her side and falls into a restless, edgy sleep.

She gasps awake less than an hour later, soaked in her own sharp, panicky sweat: "Fuck," she mutters when her heart stops pounding, sinking back against the damp, clammy sheets. She hardly ever gets nightmares anymore, but when she does they're always vicious and embarrassingly unsubtle: suddenly realizing she's locked inside her trailer on the UBC lot, or Jamie banging on the door of her dad's house demanding to know where she's been. Fiona scrubs a hand through her hair, reaching for the remote and flipping on *Evil Among Us*, but even after an episode and a half of grisly murder she still feels like all her nerve endings are jangling around inside her body, so she gets up and heads into the kitchen to make herself a sandwich.

She doesn't bother to turn on a light as she grabs a plate from the cupboard and some turkey from the fridge, slapping some mayo on a slice of bread and willing herself to calm down. Pam used to say that focusing on a concrete task was a good way to get herself under control, but instead the longer she stands here the more it starts to feel like she's about to blast off to the moon, breath ragged and heart stuttering. When she tries to cut the sandwich in half she looks down and realizes she can't feel her hands.

Fiona swears under her breath, panic and rage roiling up inside her in equal measure. The knife clatters loudly into the sink. She thinks about the details of her time on *Birds* as infrequently as possible, but all at once she remembers sitting on set one night maybe halfway through filming on the second season, which everyone kept saying was even better than the first: they were getting quasi-famous all of a sudden, recognized in public and invited to parties and premieres. They'd been on the cover of *Entertainment Weekly* a few weeks earlier, Sam's arm slung around her shoulders, Thandie's head thrown back as she laughed.

She was on the floor with her ankles crossed paging through *The Long Hot Summer*, which Estelle had recommended, when a tall, broad shadow fell across the page. "Catching up on your reading?" a deep voice said. She looked up and realized with a start that Jamie was looming above her, his hands tucked in his jacket pockets and his hair curling down over his collar. "Anything good?"

Fiona held up the slim paperback so he could see the cover. "It's kind of . . . turgid."

Jamie laughed out loud. "I did it in college," he told her, "a million years ago. I should read it again." He leaned against the wall with his arms crossed, looking down at her curiously. "You're here late," he observed. "You're done for the day, aren't you? Somebody picking you up?"

Fiona shook her head. "Thandie's going to take me when she's done," she said, hoping that didn't sound pathetic. She'd gotten her license a few months earlier; her dad kept saying they were going to go car shopping, though now that he'd lost interest in so much as running to Ralphs for groceries, she sort of doubted that it was something they were going to get to anytime soon. Her mom had moved out three weeks ago.

Now Jamie glanced over at the set, where the lighting guys were readjusting for what seemed like the twentieth time, and rolled his eyes. "Thandie's going to be here for hours," he predicted, nudging her in the shoulder with his denim-covered knee. "Come on. I can take you."

Fiona shook her head. Even back then she always hated asking for favors from people, the itchy feeling of being in someone else's debt. "You don't have to do that," she said. "I'm fine."

But Jamie waved her off. "I want to," he said, "seriously. Go get your stuff."

She said a quick goodbye to Thandie, then followed Jamie down the long, cavernous hallways of the studio building and out into the darkened parking lot. It was wildfire season, and a smoky haze was just palpable in the air. As he turned the key in the ignition of his massive SUV, the radio turned on, a country station clanging away at top volume. Fiona laughed out loud in the moment before she remembered he was technically her boss.

"Sorry," she said, clapping a hand over her mouth.

Jamie fixed her with a look as he waved to the parking attendant. "Go ahead," he said wryly. "Have a giggle, go tell all your cool young Hollywood scenester friends. It's my secret shame."

"I mean, I'm not going to pretend this isn't embarrassing," Fiona said with a grin.

"The old stuff isn't!" he protested. "The beer, God, trucks stuff—yeah, I'll grant you that."

"And you're not here for the beer, God, trucks stuff?"

Jamie sighed. "I will be honest with you, Fiona," he admitted, "I kind of like the beer, God, trucks stuff, too."

"Uh-huh." Fiona settled back into the passenger seat. She hadn't spent a ton of time alone with Jamie since the show had started filming the year before; he intimidated her sometimes, with his insistence on perfection and occasionally stormy temper, though tonight he was in good spirits, drumming lightly on the wheel as they cruised toward the Valley.

"How you doing, St. James?" he asked once they were on the highway, the orange safety lights making patterns on the dashboard and the asphalt humming underneath the tires. "You good?"

"I'm good," she echoed reflexively. "No complaints."

Jamie lifted an eyebrow. "Why do I feel like you're bullshitting me right now?"

Fiona smiled. Nobody ever called her out like that, with the possible exception of Thandie. "My parents are going through a thing," she admitted, waving a hand in the hopes that it would seem like less of a big deal than it felt like. "But it'll blow over. It always does."

Jamie nodded. "I'm sure it will," he said. "But if it doesn't, you can talk to me about it. I know you're a big tough TV star and I'm a hundred fucking years old, but still."

Fiona huffed a laugh. "You're not *that* old," she said.

Jamie tilted his head to the side. "No," he agreed with a wry smile, the corners of his eyes crinkling up. "I guess I'm not *that* old."

They were quiet for a moment, just the croon of the radio and the rumble of the engine. Fiona glanced at him out of the corner of her eye. The makeup ladies were always going on about how hot Jamie was, that he looked like a young Harrison Ford in his sunglasses and leather jacket. Fiona had never really gotten the reference, though when she glanced over at him now she thought she kind of knew what they meant: his broad shoulders and stubble, his hands splayed out on the wheel. The windows of the SUV were tinted, but Fiona imagined people in other cars could see inside anyway. *That's Jamie Hartley*, she imagined them saying. *That's Fiona St. James.*

"You did a nice job in that scene with Sam today," he told her, reaching out and turning the music down. "You like working with him?"

Fiona glanced across the gearshift, trying to gauge why he was asking. She worried that it showed sometimes, her crush on Sam; occasionally she looked at fanpages for him on the internet, and she knew his astrological sign was Pisces and his favorite ice cream flavor was rocky road. "It's fine," she said. "He's a good scene partner." This wasn't strictly true: in fact, Sam forgot his lines half the time and relied a full click too heavily on the fact that most people found him winning. Still, Fiona thought it was possible that the way she felt about him made her own work better, even if she lived in perpetual fear that one of these days someone was going to point out that she was giving their brother/sister scenes a weird, Folgers-commercial incest vibe.

Jamie snorted. "That's very diplomatic of you, considering everybody knows you're carrying him."

Fiona wasn't sure what to say to that, torn between knee-jerk loyalty to Sam and guilty pleasure at being the teacher's pet. "We all carry each other, right?" she replied finally. "That's the *Birds of California* way?"

"That's the *Birds of California* way." Jamie smirked. "He likes you, though."

Fiona made a soft, surprised noise before she could stop herself. "I mean," she said, glancing out the window so Jamie wouldn't see her face, "I don't know about *that*."

"Why wouldn't he?" Jamie asked. "You're spectacular."

He said it as an empirical fact, the sun coming up in the morning or the traffic on the 101. Her whole body prickled with pleasure and curiosity, but by the time she looked over at him Jamie had already moved on—talking about plots he had in mind for the rest of the season, a pilot he was working on. "What do you want to do, huh?" he asked. "Once we finish our six seasons and a movie, I mean."

Fiona considered that. She thought of the play she'd been reading today—the way she'd been able to picture the set in her mind, imagine the actors moving around in the space. How they'd sound. The costumes they'd be wearing. "I don't know," she said. "Theater, maybe?"

"Really?" Jamie raised his eyebrows.

Fiona frowned, instantly regretting her answer. Ugh, she should have said something else: art films, or Michael Bay movies. She didn't know what would be impressive to him, and as much as she hated to admit it, she wanted to be impressive. "What's wrong with theater?" she asked.

"No, nothing," he promised quickly. "Theater is great, for a certain kind of performer." He shrugged. "I just think you're probably destined for greater things, that's all."

Fiona smiled a little uncertainly. It was a compliment, wasn't it? After all, he'd literally just told her she was spectacular. Still, there was something about the way he said it that rubbed her the wrong way—like she was Riley Bird and he was her wise-but-cool father, like maybe he knew her better than she knew her own self.

Then again, he'd been in this business a hell of a lot longer than she had. Probably he *did* know better.

Jamie made a face just then, like possibly he could read her mind. "Scratch that," he said, his fingertips landing briefly on her arm by way of apology. "I'm being an asshole. You're a grown woman. You know your own mind."

Did she? Fiona wondered, forgiving him instantly. Sometimes she felt grown-up, like the kind of person who could walk red carpets without giggling at the absurdity of it and talk eloquently in interviews with magazines and TV hosts. And sometimes she felt like the same dopey little kid she'd always been, frizzy-haired and noisy and awkward around guys. "No," she said. "I appreciate it. I can use all the help I can get."

"I'm always here for it," Jamie promised, glancing over his shoulder before signaling for the exit. "You're special, Fee. I knew that as soon as I saw you in that audition room with that neon streak in your hair. The second you walked in I thought, *Holy shit, that's my girl.* None of those other guys in there knew their ass from their elbow. But right from the beginning, you were different." He reached over and squeezed her knee, just quick, before letting go and putting both hands back on the steering wheel. "Even back then, you were a fucking adult."

Fiona smiled. She knew it was just Jamie being Jamie—he was generous with feedback like that, everybody's big brother and best friend; just this morning he'd told Sam he was a prince among men—but there was a part of her that felt like maybe this was different. That maybe he actually *saw* her, the two of them sitting here in the dark.

"This is me," she said when they pulled up in front of her parents' house a few minutes later. She felt suddenly embarrassed by the unremarkable smallness of it, thinking of the party he'd thrown at his place when the show first got picked up: his land and his pool and his collection of vintage arcade games on the lower level, how glamorous it had all felt. This was just a regular house where she lived with her parents. Her *parent*, she amended to herself. Just the one, now. "Thanks again for the ride."

"Yeah, no problem," Jamie said, waving her off. "I can drive you whenever."

"Oh, you don't have to do that," she said. She didn't want to be, like, a charity case, some sad orphan he felt like he had to look out for.

But Jamie didn't seem to be thinking of her that way at all. "Let's see how it goes," he hedged. "We'll work something out. And in the meantime, take care of yourself, will you? We need you." He grinned. "*I* need you."

Fiona smiled at that, gulping down the sudden lump at the back of her throat. For one crazy second she almost blurted it all out: *I think my dad is having some kind of serious mental health situation. My sister is wetting the bed again even though she's seven years old. Somebody took pictures of me in a bikini at the beach a few weeks ago and now they're all up on Reddit, with a bunch of creepy old guys in their basements saying what they want to do to me. And I don't actually think I like being quasi-famous that much at all.*

Instead she rolled her eyes, like he was silly for worrying. She was an adult, right? He'd just said it himself. She could handle it. "I will," she promised easily. "I always do."

Jamie hugged her goodbye across the gearshift, sturdy and solid. Fiona closed her eyes and held on.

"Fiona, honey?"

Fiona blinks and comes back to herself, the night air cool on her flushed, sweaty face. All at once she realizes she's outside in the yard. She doesn't remember opening the slider or stepping out onto the patio, but she must have, because here she is with bits of broken plate and scattered sandwich all around her; here's Estelle peering at her worriedly from the other end of the grass.

"Fiona, honey," Estelle says again, in a voice that makes Fiona wonder exactly how long Estelle has been trying to get her attention, "are you all right?"

Fiona's skin prickles with shame. It's not the first time she's had an episode like this—hell, the whole year after the show got canceled was basically one long and continuous episode like this—but enough time has passed since they were a regular occurrence that she'd started to believe maybe they were a thing of the past, faded out of her life along with the neon streak in her hair.

"I'm fine," she promises Estelle now, smiling across the yard in the darkness in a way she hopes looks convincingly sane. Her official diagnosis from Pam was post-traumatic stress disorder, which Fiona found profoundly embarrassing—she was on a *television* show, for fuck's sake; she didn't serve two combat tours in Iraq—and to this day she thinks it's ridiculous and implausible enough that she's never actually said it out loud. Still, every once in a while she'll watch a movie or read a news story about some poor ex-military guy completely coming apart at the seams in the supermarket over how many flavors of Triscuits there are and think: *You know what, dude? I get it.*

"I'm fine," she says again, still smiling. "I just . . ." Just *what*, exactly? What would be a valid explanation for smashing dishes on one's patio at two a.m.? "Boy troubles, that's all."

Estelle brightens at that, which Fiona thought she might. "Ah," she says sagely. "Well, in that case, I've got some glassware I've been meaning to get rid of, if you're interested."

Fiona laughs, surreptitiously tucking her still-shaking hands into the pockets of her shorts. "Thanks," she says, "but I think I've just about gotten it out of my system."

"Whatever you say, sweetheart." Estelle blows her a kiss. "Just make sure you're careful when you clean that glass up, will you?" She looks at Fiona for another minute, then turns toward her own backyard. "I don't want you to get hurt."

The next day is worse, if that's possible. She spills an iced coffee all over a finished batch of fundraising mailers for the Humane Society, then prints four hundred flyers from the wrong computer file and has to dump them all into the trash. When she glances at her phone she's got an email from Thandie, who saw the pictures in some European tabloid: You and Sam??? she wants to know, her surprise palpable from six thousand miles away. I require full details immediately, please and thank you.

Fiona cringes. It's the first email Thandie has sent her in ages, and there's a part of her that wants to fold like a house of cards and tell her everything, about Sam's deep laugh and the warm planes of his body and the embarrassing thing her stomach did every time he said her name. But she can just imagine how it will look to someone like Thandie, who's been quietly seeing an entertainment lawyer for the better part of two years without them ever having been photographed together: like a fame grab, some pathetic gambit to try and get back into the headlines. Desperate.

Thandie's your friend, though, reminds a reasonable-sounding voice in Fiona's head that sounds suspiciously like Pam. *Why would she ever think that about you?*

Fiona frowns, yanking idly at the ends of her hair for a moment. Debating. *It scared me,* she imagines telling Thandie, *how much I liked him. But in the end it didn't matter either way.*

Total nothingburger, she writes back finally, throwing in a French fry emoji for good measure. We hung out for like twenty minutes and all he wanted to talk about was his upcoming appearance as a guest judge on *Cake Pop Wars.* If I ever do try to date again, remind me to steer clear of anyone with a more involved skincare routine than the beauty editor of Goop.

Also! she types, hoping she sounds like the thought has just occurred to her and not like she's been stewing over it for the better part of two days. Is it true you told Jamie Hartley you'd do the *Birds* thing?

The rest of the morning is pretty much a wash. She's considering knocking off altogether and taking herself to a movie when the chimes above the door sound and a middle-aged woman saunters in with a hundred-dollar blowout and the kind of flattened, swollen lips that suggest she had fat from elsewhere on her body injected into her face at some point in the recent past. "Picking up invitations," she announces. "Last name Taylor."

This time, Fiona manages to get her rung up before it happens. "Oh my god," the woman exclaims, dropping the keys to her Mercedes onto the counter with a noisy clatter. "Aren't you Riley Bird?" Then, without waiting for Fiona to answer: "My daughter is going to absolutely *die*. She had the Christmas movie memorized. Hell, *I* had the Christmas movie memorized." Her voice has the nasal quality of Chandler's girlfriend on *Friends*. For all Fiona knows, this *is* the woman who played Chandler's girlfriend on *Friends*, and she's just had so much plastic surgery that she's now virtually unrecognizable. It occurs to Fiona that perhaps that's a strategy she should try.

"I have to call her," the woman continues, pulling her phone out of a massive Louis Vuitton tote bag and dialing. "Maddie, honey," she says, looking at the screen—of course it would be a FaceTime, not a regular call—"you are never going to guess who is standing in front of me right now." The woman spins the phone around so the camera is facing Fiona. "Say hi to Riley Bird!"

Maddie blinks at Fiona for a moment, her face slightly distorted on the smudgy screen. *I didn't agree to this*, Fiona thinks of saying. She imagines grabbing the phone from the woman's hand and hurling it across the shop.

Instead she smiles and waves. "Hi, Maddie!" she says.

"I almost didn't recognize you," the woman says, looking at Fiona curiously. "Did you put a little weight on? Maddie, don't you think she put a little weight on? I don't mean that in a bad way," she adds quickly, though it doesn't sound like she means it in a good way, either. Fiona keeps smiling.

Once she's finally alone she sits down behind the counter: not in a chair or on the stool, but actually behind the counter on the floor, which is where Richie finds her twenty minutes later when he comes back from his lunch break. She feels like all the energy has been leached right out of her, like that little space rover who eventually ran out of juice and had to stay alone on Mars forever.

"You okay?" Richie asks. By the smell of him he did not actually eat lunch, he sat in the parking lot behind where the old Blockbuster Video used to be and hotboxed his car.

"Fine," she assures him, leaning her head back. "I'm good."

Richie nods. He pulls one of the messed-up flyers from the recycling bin and sits down next to her, leaving six inches between them. She watches as he turns and folds the paper this way and that, his hands moving with the kind of quick, efficient confidence Fiona doesn't think she's ever brought to anything in her entire life. She thinks again of asking him how he does it, but then it would be just another thing for her to fuck up or fail at. On top of which it looks pretty hard.

When he's finally finished he's got a perfectly rendered dog, which he hands over to her with zero fanfare. "Break over," he says, and boosts himself up off the floor.

Fiona looks from the dog to Richie, then down at the dog again. Then she gets up and gets back to work.

"Shouldn't you be getting ready?" Claudia asks late that afternoon, sitting at the kitchen table eating ranch-flavored popcorn and working on some precalc homework that Fiona doesn't understand. "Don't you have rehearsal tonight?"

Fiona shrugs. She does, technically, though all day long she's been thinking about skipping it. Permanently. Like she told Sam the other day: it's community theater, that's all. It's not like it actually matters. She could just stop showing up, disappear into the ether never to be heard from again. It's not like it would be the worst thing she'd ever done.

Claudia would know, though, and in the end that's what has Fiona stuffing a granola bar into her bag and shuffling crabbily out to her car.

She spends the whole ride downtown bracing herself, trying to figure out how she's possibly going to explain to them all about the pictures—about lying to them for the better part of two years like something out of some cheesy Lifetime movie. She should have known there was only so long she could pretend. She *did* know, if she's being honest with herself. But she also just . . . really liked being an Angel City Player.

It was a role, that's all, she reminds herself firmly, squaring her shoulders and marching inside the theater. *And now the show is over.*

But to Fiona's surprise, when she gets downstairs the only thing anybody wants to talk about is the set their tech guy has started building and whether or not it's ugly, which it emphatically is. "Frances!" Larry shouts irritably, as Georgie wrings her hands by the listing plywood backdrop. "Are we serious thespians, or are we a bunch of fucking dilettantes? What kind of hack do you have putting this thing together?"

Fiona grins. "The kind who works for free," she reminds him, the relief flooding through her stronger than any narcotic she's ever tried. "We'll fix it."

That night is their first full run-through. It's a little bit of a misery—all dropped lines and clumsy transitions, a rickety Goodwill chair collapsing into kindling when Hector sits down in it halfway through the second act. Still, it's the most fun Fiona has had at rehearsal in a long time. She feels like she's gotten away with something. She feels almost . . . *light.* By the time Nora slams the door at the finale, Fiona is having a hard time remembering what she was so worked up about to begin with—after all, it was just a couple of trashy gossip sites. She's not actually even that famous anymore. Maybe it's true, what Claudia and Estelle are always saying—the only person still holding her past against her is herself.

And whatever, Fiona thinks as she tucks her script back into her bag. If she feels a tiny pang of longing every time she remembers the way Sam looked at her in his bed the other night—well, it's not like anything real was ever going to happen between them anyway. He's probably at Kimmeree's house at this very moment, scrolling through his own tag on Instagram and drinking low-cal malt beverages. Frankly, the very idea of it makes Fiona want to eat a bacon cheeseburger.

"Are you guys hungry?" she asks as they're all heading out of the theater. "Do you want to go get food?"

Hector glances at her sidelong. "Really?" he asks.

"Really," Fiona echoes, frowning. "Why do you sound surprised?"

"I don't know," Hector says. He's in his thirties, with a day job at a marketing firm and two little girls who live with their mom in the Valley. "You just normally kind of keep to yourself, I guess."

"Oh." Fiona guesses he has a point. "Well," she says after a moment, "this is me . . . keeping to other people."

"I'll go," Pamela says, winding a gauzy black scarf around her neck, and Georgie and DeShaun nod amicably.

"I could eat," Larry agrees.

Fiona smiles, trying to come up with a restaurant nearby that isn't guaranteed to give them all hepatitis. There's a dive bar with mostly passable burgers, or a Mediterranean place she picks up from sometimes on the way home. But DeShaun has a gluten thing, Fiona remembers vaguely, and Larry is a vegetarian . . .

She's so busy thinking about it that she doesn't notice the photographer leaning up against the hood of her car until it's too late.

"Fiona," he calls, and she's never been mugged but she imagines this is what it feels like, her whole body going ice-cold stupid. For a moment she only just stares.

"How are you, honey?" he asks, waving at her like they're old friends. He's one of Darcy's guys, Fiona recognizes him, the shutter on his giant camera clicking away like a mutant robot insect from *The Hunger Games*. Were there mutant robot insects in *The*

Hunger Games? Fiona doesn't know. He's got another guy with him for backup, a younger one holding a phone. "Congratulations on the reboot!"

"There is no reboot," she blurts, which is amateur hour on her part, because the absolute worst thing you can do is engage with these guys, and Fiona knows that. "I mean——"

"Frances?" That's DeShaun, his voice soft and full of uncertainty; the rest of the cast is watching in silence. "Is everything okay?"

Fiona waves a hand. "It's fine," she says automatically, making a move to sidestep the photographer, but he shifts his broad shoulders so she can't get by him on the sidewalk, the camera still stuttering away.

"You don't need to play it so close to the vest, honey," he tells her, continuing on as if it's just the two of them having a conversation. "From what I hear, it's already in production. You looked great in those pictures from Sam's apartment the other night, PS. It's nice to see you happy after all this time."

Fiona shakes her head. She'd forgotten this, or tried to——the way these guys monologue, the way they act like they're your friend. "Enough," she says, her face flaming as she glances over at her castmates' curious faces. "You got your pictures, can you just——"

"I think she asked you to stop." That's Georgie drawing herself up tall and regal; Pamela stands at her shoulder like a pale, goth bodyguard.

But the photographer shakes his head, teeth flashing in a lascivious grin. "Trust me," he assures them. "She wants it."

That's when Fiona loses her temper.

Later she won't remember consciously deciding to lunge for the guy's camera, but she must, because the next thing she knows Hector and Larry are holding her back while she thrashes, her limbs flailing in every possible direction. She thinks she catches Hector in the nose. "*Fuck* you," she's yelling, and for a second she's not even sure who she's talking to.

"Frances," Larry is saying, "take it easy, will—"

"That's not my name," Fiona interrupts—still fighting, shrugging them off once and for all. She doesn't want any of them touching her for one more second. She doesn't want anyone touching her ever again.

"Enough," she says again, once they finally release her, reaching out and slapping at the camera one more time. "Enough! Is this what you wanted? Congratulations, I'm a fucking psycho! You win!"

It's a hurricane, noisy and furious: DeShaun and Georgie are trying to soothe her. The photographer is yelling about a lawsuit. The kid with the cell phone got the whole thing on film. And here's Fiona at the eye of it just like always, leaving a trail of chaos and destruction in her wake.

Finally she takes a deep breath, raking her hands through her hair and setting her shoulders. She is not not *not* going to cry. "I'm going to take a rain check on dinner," she manages quietly. Then she gets into her car and drives away.

CHAPTER TWELVE

Sam

"I mean," Erin says the following morning, both of them staring wide-eyed at the grainy video on her laptop, "the girl's got a flair for the dramatic, that's for sure. It's almost a shame she doesn't act anymore."

"Yeah," Sam says distractedly, scrubbing a hand through his hair as Erin hits play one more time, Fiona's wild-eyed face filling the computer screen. She looks feral—her hands flying around like demented birds, her hair enormous—but more than that, Sam keeps thinking, she looks *scared*. "I mean, she actually does still act, sort of, but—whatever." He shakes his head. "Can we go out?" he asks abruptly, shutting the laptop harder than is probably necessary and standing up. "Let's go out."

Erin takes him for a breakfast beer at the dive around the corner from her apartment: cool and dark and a little bit grimy, the floor slightly sticky underfoot. It's early enough that they're the only people sitting at the bar, a friendly drunk scratching lotto tickets at a table in the corner and some daytime talk show carping away on the TV—a talk show, Sam realizes belatedly, on which they're playing the footage of Fiona outside her theater over and over. *Fiona St. James at It Again in New Viral Video*, the chyron reads.

"For fuck's sake." Sam drains most of his beer in two long gulps. "Hey," he calls, signaling the bartender before he quite knows he's going to do it, "sorry. Would you mind turning this off?"

The bartender looks dubious. "You object to *The View*?" he asks.

"No, I don't object to *The View*, I just—sports?" he begs. "There must be a sport on somewhere, right? There's always sports on."

The bartender rolls his eyes, but dutifully flips over to competitive bowling on ESPN2. When Sam turns back to Erin, he finds her staring at him, her eyes wide and triumphant. "Holy shit," she says quietly, "did you catch feelings for Riley Bird?" She says *feelings* but it sounds like what she means is *chlamydia*.

Sam finishes his beer instead of answering. "Better not let her hear you call her that," he says finally. "She'll eat your heart in the fuckin' marketplace."

Erin shakes her head. "Don't try to put me off."

"I'm not trying to do anything," Sam replies, knowing he sounds peevish. "We hung out a couple of times, that's all. I barely know her."

"Can you not be full of shit for one second?" Erin asks, setting her glass down. "Like, now that I'm actually looking at your face I'm realizing I've been kind of an asshole about the whole thing, so

I probably owe you an apology, but putting that aside for a minute, it doesn't have to be some bullshit game of who can be the coolest guy in Hollywood. If you like her, which you clearly do, and she's going through a thing, which"—she gestures at the TV—"shit, she clearly is, then what are you doing sitting here with me? Go be a decent human person and make sure she's okay."

"It's not—" Sam breaks off. "I mean, we aren't—" He sighs. "She's not taking my calls, okay? I tried her last night, and again this morning, but she doesn't want to talk to me. Is that what you wanted to hear?"

"Yes, actually." Erin smiles, reaching for her glass again before kicking him gently underneath the bar. "I am sorry, for the record. I wouldn't have been so cavalier if I knew it was, like, a real thing."

"It's not," Sam says reflexively. "But maybe it could be?" He drops his head back. "I don't fucking know."

"Liar," Erin says cheerfully. Sam orders another beer.

When he gets home there's a residuals check waiting for him from a Hallmark movie he did a couple of Christmases ago, which cheers him up for a minute, though after he pays down his credit card enough to be able to use it he's basically right back where he started. Sam frowns. He hasn't been this broke since he was living with Erin, doing push-ups on the nasty carpet in their tiny apartment and splurging on ten-dollar haircuts. He can't believe he let himself wind up here again.

He walks around the apartment for a while. He eats half a bag of baby carrots standing up at the sink. He thinks about taking a nap, but he can't settle, even after he jerks off and watches two episodes of an afternoon court show and checks to see if maybe Russ emailed him with news about the firefighter thing, which he has not. He pulls up Fiona's video one more time. He remembers a night back in the third or fourth season of *Birds*, a big party at a fancy hotel out in Malibu—the network threw one every year the week of the Television Critics Association press tour, when everyone came out to LA to watch next season's pilots and take corny pictures of themselves in front of the Hollywood sign. The party was always black tie, candles floating in the pool and tuxedoed waiters scurrying by balancing trays of champagne and canapés. Thandie and Fiona used to call it the Sexless Prom.

Attendance, while not strictly mandatory, was strongly encouraged, and though Sam had dutifully shown up every year he'd been on the show, the whole thing never got less weird to him, all the big Family Network names mingling together: the second lead from a vaguely racist period piece about a feisty pioneer nurse chatting up the host of a morning talk show that was best known for showcasing new and novel recipes for ground beef every single day. He was angling for a little bit of face time with the star of a marquee drama about a small-town sheriff—the guy had just booked a role in a Coen Brothers movie, and Sam wanted to know how—when he spotted Fiona standing near the edge of the pool talking to a couple of older women from one of the executive teams, clutching a rocks glass in one hand and tiny appetizer plate piled with a mountain of fruit from the cheese board in the other. Judging by the expression on her face, she was seriously considering drowning herself in the shallow end.

"There you are," Sam said, striding over and swinging an arm around her shoulders before he quite knew he was going to do it. "I've been looking for you. We're all getting in the photo booth." He grinned his most winsome grin at the executives. "Sorry, ladies. Need to find this gal a feather boa and some novelty sunglasses, stat."

"What the hell?" Fiona asked once they were alone, sitting down hard on the edge of a massive stone planter overflowing with tropical flowers and taking a sip of her drink. "How do you know I wasn't dying to talk to those women?"

Sam raised his eyebrows. "Were you?"

"No," she admitted. She was wearing a short, fringe-y dress and sky-high heels, a bunch of chunky rings on her fingers. Also, though she was holding it together decently well—not to mention the fact that she was only eighteen—he was pretty sure she was shit-faced. She'd started showing up on the gossip sites by then, a few dicey scenes at clubs in West Hollywood and a well-publicized fling with a two-bit pop star whose biggest hit featured a chorus that consisted entirely of the words *my junk, my junk* repeated over and over. Sam had asked Thandie about it when they'd broken up, just casually, in response to which Thandie had fixed him with an extremely dubious look and told him that if he was interested in Fiona's personal life for any particular reason, he could damn well ask Fiona about it. "But I could have been."

"You could have been," he agreed, "and I apologize."

"I forgive you," she said politely.

"Magnanimous," Sam teased, plucking a grape from her plate. He *wasn't* interested in Fiona's personal life for any particular reason, for the record. He'd just been curious, that was all. "Worried about getting scurvy?" he asked, nodding down at the pile of fruit.

"Cute." Fiona rolled her eyes, fingers brushing his as she picked up a strawberry and popped it into her mouth. "I'm on a diet, technically."

"Really?" That surprised him. "Why?"

"Jamie says I'm getting fat."

"Seriously?" Sam blinked. It didn't sound like something Jamie would say. It was certainly not something Jamie had ever said to *him*, and Sam found himself almost unable to picture it. He wondered if maybe Fiona had misunderstood, somehow, but knew better than to ask. "What the hell?"

Fiona shrugged. "Lucky for me," she said, raising her glass in a little toast, "vodka is a low-calorie food."

Sam grinned, charmed in spite of himself. "How drunk are you right now?"

"Fuck off," she said immediately, but she was smiling. "How drunk are *you* right now?"

"Moderately," he admitted, and Fiona laughed. In the glow of the patio lights she looked—he tried to think of another word, and couldn't—*luminous,* full mouth and long eyelashes and something faintly glittery slicked across her collarbones. Then, all at once, her face fell. "This," she said quietly, setting her glass down on the planter between them, "is not a good idea."

Right away Sam felt himself blush, like he'd gotten caught doing something he shouldn't have; and yeah, okay, there *was* a tiny part of him that had been thinking about asking her if she wanted to get out of here, that was in fact more than passingly interested in her personal life and wondered if there might be a place for him in it. Still, he didn't think he'd been so obvious that she needed to shut him down preemptively.

But Fiona didn't seem to be talking about whatever intentions might or might not have been forming in the back of his mind for the rest of the evening. In fact, she didn't seem to be talking about him at all. She ran a hand through her hair, her rings catching at the tangles. "I'm fucking up," she said, so quietly she might have been saying it to herself.

"What?" Sam shook his head, not understanding. This conversation had taken a hard swerve when he wasn't paying attention, and he wasn't sure how to get it back on track. "Why, because you're drunk at Sexless Prom? Nobody can even tell."

Fiona shook her head. "No," she said, "I don't mean that. I mean—"

"You're okay," he said reflexively, and the words were out of his mouth before he realized how stupid they were. It reminded him of his mom running across the playground after he'd fallen off the jungle gym when he was seven: *You're okay*, she'd promised, presumably so he wouldn't be scared, only then he'd looked down and realized his arm was twisted at an unnatural angle, his hand splayed limp as a dead bird. He wasn't okay, and—he saw it now, in her panicky expression—neither was Fiona. He felt young and clueless and out of his depth all of a sudden; he was relieved when he looked up and saw Jamie crossing the patio in their direction.

"Children," he greeted them, lips quirking. "You guys plotting your escape?" He was wearing dark jeans and a tuxedo jacket, this afternoon's sunglasses poking out of the breast pocket. He nodded at Fiona's drink. "I'm assuming that's water."

Just like that, Fiona was herself again, saucy and wry; she took a long sip, gestured with the glass in Jamie's direction. "My warden," she said, smiling sweetly.

"That's me," Jamie said. He squinted. "Can you pull it together?" he asked, plucking the glass from her hand and placing it on the nearby tray of a cater waiter as they passed by in a blur of black and white. "Or do we need to leave?"

Fiona shrugged. "Only one way to find out," she said cheerfully. She wobbled a bit as she got to her feet, and for one horrifying second Sam was sure she was going to take a header directly into the deep end of the pool, but in the end she corrected with impressive grace, finishing with a spunky little dance right there on the patio. "Look at that," she said, and her smile was dazzling. "Right as rain."

"Very nice," Jamie said, sounding distinctly unimpressed. "Still, I think that's your cue."

Fiona frowned. "I'm having fun," she protested. "I'm hanging out with my friend Sam."

Jamie's gaze flicked to Sam for an instant, then back to Fiona again. "I see that," he said. "I also see that you're about half a vodka tonic from making a fool of yourself in front of every entertainment reporter in America and possibly a Canadian or two, so I'm suggesting again that you call it a night."

"Oh, is that what you're suggesting?" Fiona looked at him balefully. "You realize, James, that you're not actually my father."

Jamie didn't react to that, though Sam thought he could see a muscle ticking in his jaw. "No," Jamie agreed evenly, "I'm certainly not." Then he sighed, his voice softening. "Come on, sweetheart," he said, wrapping his hand around her elbow. "It's time."

"Jamie, dude," Sam said, the words out before he could stop to consider whether or not this was a situation he wanted any part of; a minute ago he'd been relieved to see Jamie—their boss, a grown-up, a rational person in charge—but now he just kind of felt like a snitch. "She just said she was good."

Both Jamie and Fiona looked vaguely shocked at that, and Sam thought he probably couldn't blame them. After all, he was pretty sure it was the first time he'd ever contradicted Jamie about anything. Still, something about the vibe Fiona had been giving off a minute ago made him want to protect her—which was why he was doubly surprised when she shook her head. "No," she said, and her voice was all surrender, "he's right. I need to go."

Jamie nodded. "Atta girl," he said, the relief audible in his voice. "Let's get you the fuck out of here. Sammy, my man, you're in charge. Get 'em to write something nice about us, will you?"

Sam nodded vaguely, certain he'd missed something important and entirely unsure what it might be. Still, in the end he guessed it didn't actually matter. Jamie was right—the last thing any of them needed at this point was *Fiona St. James Gets Sloppy Drunk at Sexless Prom* to be the lead story on every gossip website on the internet come morning. He was doing all of them a favor.

"I'll do my best," Sam finally said, though he didn't think either one of them actually heard him. They'd already disappeared into the crowd.

Now, seven years later, Sam gets up off the couch and changes his T-shirt, checks his teeth in the bathroom mirror. "This is fucking ridiculous," he tells his reflection, then grabs his keys off the table by the door.

He's half expecting Fiona's house to be dark and deserted, like possibly her whole family will have packed up and skipped town in the middle of the night like a traveling circus in an old-fashioned storybook, but Claudia answers the door ten seconds after he rings.

"I don't know if this is really a good time," she says, glancing out the door at the street behind him before crossing her arms like a bouncer at Soho House. She's wearing a flowy skirt and cowboy boots, her hair in a complicated braid over one shoulder.

Sam nods, trying to swallow down the disappointment in his throat. "I get it," he says. He likes her, her big glasses and serious expression. She looks like Fiona ten years ago, if Fiona had been cosplaying as Stevie Nicks. "I don't want to make things worse for her. But if you could just tell her that I came by—"

That's when Fiona comes around the corner into the hallway.

"Claud?" she calls. "Who the fuck is at the—hi," she says,

eyes widening. She's wearing a sports bra and a pair of men's basketball shorts about ten sizes too big for her, her long hair wet from the shower. She puts a hand on her sister's back, looking out at the street the same way Claudia did a second ago—for photographers, Sam realizes belatedly, feeling like a total fucking fool. It didn't even occur to him to check. Fiona squeezes Claudia's shoulder. "It's okay," she promises. "I got it."

Claudia looks unconvinced. "Are you sure?"

Fiona nods, stepping outside and shutting the door behind her. She's barefoot and she looks younger suddenly, her face scrubbed clean. She smells like drugstore shampoo.

"Hey," he says.

"Hey," she says.

"Thinking about trying out for the NBA?"

"Considering it," she tells him, glancing down at her clothes. "My jump shot could use work."

Sam nods. "Maybe Michael Jordan can give you some pointers when he comes by to get his pants back."

Fiona huffs a laugh but then it turns into something else halfway out, her face falling. In the second before she rearranges her expression, she looks like she might be about to burst into tears. "Sam—"

Sam takes a deep breath. "Do you want to go for a drive?"

Now she really does laugh, shaking her head at the Tesla in the driveway. "Not in your car, I don't."

That makes him smile. "Fair enough."

They look at each other for a long moment. He can see her

weighing something in her mind. "Wait here," she says finally, then turns and goes back inside the house.

Sam shoves his hands in his pockets and looks out at the neighborhood, at a couple of kids playing freeze tag and the bald guy dragging his trash cans up the driveway across the street. Two ladies in workout clothes power walk by him, then execute a sudden about-face three houses down and power walk by him again. Just when he's starting to wonder if maybe Fiona isn't coming back, if she's planning to leave him out here indefinitely to get eaten by coyotes as a final fuck you from the other day, the front door opens again.

"Come on," she says, holding up her car keys. She's changed into a pair of denim shorts and a white T-shirt, the deep V revealing the tan jut of her collarbones and the skinny gold chain she wears around her neck. Her sunglasses are red plastic hearts. "I'm driving."

As soon as they're out of the driveway, Fiona rolls the windows down and turns the radio up, presumably so he doesn't do anything crazy like try to start a conversation with her. Sam likes watching her drive. He's not stupid enough to ask where she's going but pretty soon he realizes she's headed to Zuma Beach, past the tourists and the souvenir carts to where the sky is huge and the sand is cold and empty. The waves are enormous today. Sam had never been to the ocean before he moved to California, and even all these years later the sight of it still makes him a little uneasy—the bigness of it, he guesses, even though he knows it's corny to think about. The smallness of everything else.

"I guess I should warn you," Fiona says, once they're sitting side by side on the hood of the car. "If you're looking for an apology, you're not going to get it."

Sam glances at her sidelong. "Why would I be looking for an apology?"

Fiona shrugs. "For what I did outside the theater. For dragging you into it. For being myself, I don't know." She sighs. "It felt good, to lose it on that guy like that. The adrenaline rush, all of it. It's been a long time since I let myself do something like that." She looks out at the water for a moment, watching the breakers. "Sometimes I wonder if that's what it's like to be an addict. If I was in recovery this whole time from, like . . . my own personality."

"Taking it one day at a time?" he asks with a smile, but Fiona doesn't laugh.

"I'm serious."

Sam shakes his head. "There's nothing wrong with your personality," he tells her. "That guy was a dick."

"Oh, I know he was," she says immediately. "And I can grandstand all day long about, like, consent, or what you sign up for or don't sign up for when you're a kid in this business, or whatever. But the end result is the same."

"The end result being?"

"That everybody who ever called me a crazy fucking train wreck can go to sleep feeling secure in their assessment this fine evening."

"Okay." Sam boosts himself off the hood of the car, turning to face her in the late afternoon sunlight. "I'm going to say something to you, and I don't want it to go to your head, all right?"

Fiona lifts an eyebrow. "All right . . . ?"

"I think you're kind of incredible."

She laughs out loud, throwing her head back in apparent hilarity. "Okay," she says, holding a hand up. "Look, Sam, just because we fooled around half a time doesn't mean you have to, like—"

"Can you stop it?" Sam shakes his head, irritated. The truth is that the public side of his job has never bothered him—the opposite, actually. Sometimes he thinks he likes the attention more than he likes the acting itself. But he's also never gotten anything even close to the kind of scrutiny Fiona did, and it's starting to occur to him now that he never really stopped to think about what it must have been like for her—the grinding relentlessness of a million casual cruelties, everyone in America saying the same poisonous shit about her until finally there was nothing to do but believe it herself. The whole thing makes Sam feel like a complete and utter dickhead. "I do. I think you're moody as all hell, and I have no idea what's going on in your head most of the time, but you're incredible. Smart and talented and beautiful and—" He breaks off, embarrassed. "Whatever. That's what I think." He raises his eyebrows. "And for what it's worth, I don't know what rubric you're using, but we definitely fooled around a whole time."

Fiona smiles at that, just faintly. "Okay," she agrees. "A whole time."

Sam climbs back onto the car beside her, leaning against the windshield so he's staring up at the sky, the heat from the Plexiglas bleeding through the thin cotton of his T-shirt. It's uncomfortable, but not uncomfortable enough for him to do anything about it. It doesn't seem to bother Fiona at all.

"My mom is sick," he hears himself tell her. He doesn't even know he's going to say it until the words are already out, loud and stark in the salty air. He hasn't told anyone in LA, not even Erin. He thinks he had it in his head that if he could keep it contained safely in Wisconsin, thousands of miles away, that meant it wasn't actually happening. "She has breast cancer."

"Shit, Sam." Fiona turns to face him, pulling one leg underneath her and pushing her sunglasses up into her hair. Her eyes are wide and serious. "Is it . . . I mean, is she going to be okay?"

"Probably not," he admits. Saying the words out loud feels like getting a piece of popcorn stuck in his throat in a darkened movie theater, like he's choking and also trying not to make any noise.

Fiona doesn't reply for a moment, absorbing that information. "She gave me a maxi pad once," she tells him finally. "At the callback for *Birds*. Do you remember that?"

"My mom giving you a maxi pad?"

Fiona makes a face. "The callback, dumbass."

Sam does. He was sixteen at the time; he and his mom flew out from Milwaukee in the middle of January, slinging their heavy winter coats over their arms when they landed at LAX. The callback itself was like a middle school square dance or summer camp, a dozen kids in a rehearsal room playing theater games, all of them switching scene partners until finally it was just a few of them left. Fiona had dyed a hot pink streak in her hair, which he guesses is where Jamie got the idea for Riley. "Sure," he says.

"I got my period right in the middle of it—like, for the first time, I mean. And Caroline was the one who'd driven me over and I was too embarrassed to tell her, so I'm just standing there in the ladies' room trying to figure out what the fuck I'm going to do, and your mom came in and took one look at me and that was it. She fixed my pants with a Tide pen and sent me back out there, like the fairy godmother of feminine hygiene products." Fiona smiles. "She always seemed like a good mom."

"Yeah," Sam agrees, scrubbing a hand through his hair. "She is. And I should be there with her, and instead I'm out here trying to be a movie star like some kind of joke."

Fiona shakes her head. "That's not what you are," she says.

"No?" He laughs a little. "Then what am I?"

He's fully expecting her to say *a hot corpse* but instead she seems to think about it, her bare knee just brushing his thigh through his jeans. "You're a magician," she says.

Sam looks at her in the golden pink twilight: her mouth and her eyelashes, her hair going a little frizzy now that it's all-the-way dry. He wants to tell her he's afraid of how much he likes her. He wants to tell her he's afraid of being alone. He wants to tell her that he's sorry, that he didn't mean it last time when he said he wouldn't bring the show up again but he means it this time, it's finished.

That it isn't worth more to him than whatever this potentially is here with her.

"Come over," is what comes out.

Fiona raises one eyebrow, the possibility of it unspooling between them like the first day of summer. "Are you going to promise not to put a move on me again?"

"No," Sam says quietly.

Fiona gazes at him for a long minute. Then she nods. "Okay," she says. She scoops her keys up off the hood of the car, metal glinting in the setting sun. "Let's go."

CHAPTER THIRTEEN

Fiona

Sam takes her hand as they climb the steps to his apartment, the skin all over her arms and back prickling at the contact, his thumb just grazing the underside of her wrist. She smells eucalyptus and jasmine and something else, a nighttime-in-Los-Angeles kind of smell that blows hot out of the desert. One of his neighbors is having a party and she can hear the sound of people laughing as Nancy Wilson caterwauls away.

"Do you want a drink?" he asks, once they're inside.

Fiona shakes her head. As soon as they came in here she gravitated toward the bookcase, her back bumping gently against the shelves. "Not particularly," she says.

Both of them are quiet for a minute. Fiona can hear the faucet dripping in the kitchen sink. She wants to say, *I haven't had sex with nearly as many people as everyone thinks I have.* She wants to suggest they put on *Wives with Knives.*

Sam looks at her across the living room. "Shit," he says, rubbing a hand over the back of his head and smiling a little sheepishly. "I don't know why I'm nervous right now."

Fiona shrugs. "It's normal to be nervous your first time," she manages.

Sam snorts. "Fuck you," he says, "get over here," only then he's the one to close the distance between them and kiss her, and all at once Fiona forgets to be tense.

She wraps her arms around him, her fingertips working through the soft, dark hair at the nape of his neck. He's starting to smell familiar, his soap and his shampoo and his skin. "Hi," he mumbles against her mouth, his hands creeping up underneath her shirt as he turns them around and walks her backward down the narrow hallway.

"Hi yourself." The bedroom is at the back of the apartment, a triptych of arty minimalist movie posters framed on the far wall and the dense branches of a fig tree visible through the window above the dresser. The wall behind the bed is painted a close, moody gray. "I've been thinking about your sheets for two days," Fiona confesses, the backs of her knees bumping the edge of his bed.

"My sheets?" he asks, lifting his head to look at her. "That's it?"

"Yes," she says immediately, pushing aside the collar of his T-shirt so she can bite at the hard ridge of bone there. "You were never actually in them."

Sam nods like he expected about as much. "Makes sense," he says, nudging at her with his hips and chest until she sits down hard on the mattress. "I can't land a fucking part to save my life right now."

Fiona smiles, sliding her hands under his shirt and across his stomach, feeling the muscles flex under her hands. He's built like a Ken doll, all slopes and sharp curves, and when she runs her nail across the jut of his hip bone she feels his whole body shudder. "Poor you," she says.

"Poor me," Sam agrees. He gets one knee up on the bed beside her, kissing her back into the pillows and tugging her T-shirt up over her head. He goes to work on her bra next, flicking the clasp open with two fingers and pulling the straps down her arms, then sits up to gaze at her in the half dark.

"You," he says slowly, reaching out to touch her with one careful finger. "Are. Really pretty."

Fiona makes a face, feeling her cheeks get warm. "You don't have to flatter me," she tells him, fighting the ridiculous urge to cross her arms across her chest. It's not that she doesn't want him to look at her, exactly. It's more like she's scared of how much she likes it when he does. "I'm going to sleep with you either way."

But Sam isn't laughing. "I mean it," he says, boosting himself up into a kneel and slinging one leg over her hips, looming a little. He's still wearing all of his clothes. "You can insult me all you want, that's fine, I like that. But you are."

Fiona swallows hard. "Not as pretty as you," she says. "*Heart Surgeon*, et cetera."

Sam makes a face like he's getting exasperated and for a moment she's worried she pushed him too far, that he's going to stop what he's doing on account of her shitty attitude, so she arches her back underneath him, hooking one leg around his and pulling at his shoulders until he drops all the way down on top of her, close enough to grind against. Sam groans, and she smiles a secret smile over his shoulder.

After that it feels like it's happening in flashes: She wrestles his shirt off, tossing it onto the rug. Sam peels her shorts down her legs. It's like he knows instinctively how to touch her, thumbing along the undersides of her breasts and stroking the creases of her elbows, nipping his way down her ribs until her skin feels tight and hot and her whole body is humming. When he hooks his finger in the elastic of her underwear, letting it snap gently back against her hip bone, it's all she can do not to gasp.

Still: "Sam." She's about to tell him he doesn't have to do *that*, either, but Sam must know it's coming because he drops his forehead against the lowermost part of her stomach, the day's worth of beard on his face scratching against the sensitive skin of her inner thigh.

"Fee," he says, his breath hot through the fabric of her underwear, "let me, okay?"

So. She lets him.

He takes his time about it, his hands and his mouth and his body pinning her down against the bed, her heel sliding against his back. He's thorough. Fiona clutches at her hair, at his shoulders, at the mattress, trying not to make an embarrassing amount of noise.

She overcorrects, probably: after a couple of minutes he glances up at her, his brow creased like he's worried she's running lines for *A Doll's House* in her head. He's got two fingers curled inside her as he draws slow, purposeful circles with the flat of his tongue. "That okay?" he asks against her skin.

Fiona nods up at the ceiling. "It's not terrible," she allows, breathless, then squeezes her eyes shut and immediately comes apart in his hands.

When she opens her eyes again, Sam is grinning at her. His hair is sticking up every which way. "Was that—?" he asks, looking openly delighted with himself. "I mean, did you just—?"

"Maybe," Fiona says, already yanking at his shoulders. The pleasure is still fizzing wildly through her, like her whole body is full of seawater. She wants to grab him like a life raft and hold. "Come up here."

"In a minute," Sam says, still smiling his curly smile against the inside of her thigh—and fuck, the way he's *looking* at her. "I want to enjoy this."

"I'm pretty sure you're going to enjoy it," she promises, hoping she sounds more confident than she feels. As much as she's spent the last few days trying to convince both of them otherwise, the truth is she's a little overwhelmed by him, Sam Fox with his Big Three TV show and his smile and his six-pack, all the pretty girls he's probably seeing. She's afraid of accidentally getting her heart broken. She's afraid of letting him know he could.

He's still got his jeans on, the hot length of him pressed against her as he works his way back up the mattress. Fiona reaches for his zipper with clumsy hands, pulling at them and at his boxers.

At least, she's expecting to pull at his boxers, before she realizes all at once that he isn't wearing any.

"Oh my god," she says, and just like that she isn't overwhelmed anymore. God, he is a ridiculous person. "Are you seriously one of those guys who thinks he's too cool for underwear?"

Sam sighs theatrically. "I'm not too *cool* for anything, thank you," he says. "I just—"

"I'm confused, though, because you were wearing them the other night. So this is a mystery."

"Yeah, better call up Robert Stack." Sam fixes her with a withering look. "I'm sorry, sweet pea, would you have stayed the night if I had strolled in here bare-assed for a long winter's nap?"

Fiona nods. "Point taken." She's got her hand around him now, stroking experimentally. His skin is very, very warm. "So is this like a laundry thing, or—"

"Oh my god, fuck you," he says, but also he's thrusting into her palm so she doesn't actually think he's too mad about it. "Brad Pitt doesn't wear underwear, for the record."

Fiona bursts out laughing. "How do you know that?" she asks. "I mean, who told you that? Sam, I don't think that's true."

"It's true," he says firmly. He leans over and roots around in the nightstand until he comes up with a condom, ripping the foil open with his teeth and working it on. Fiona sinks her teeth into her bottom lip as she watches—his hand on his cock and the muscle bunching in his stomach, the way he lines himself up close enough so she can just barely feel him. He stays there a long time, teasing, only just grazing the place where she needs him to be. Fiona tries to move, but he's stronger than he looks.

"Do you want to make fun of me some more?" he asks quietly, the ghost of a smile pulling at the corners of his mouth. "Because if you want we could just call this whole thing off, maybe go get some frozen yogurt, and you could try out some more of your hilarious materi—"

"Shut up," Fiona mutters fiercely. "*Sam.*"

Sam grins and lets go.

This time she does gasp: the size and the stretch of him, the rangy weight of his body on top of her. "That okay?" he murmurs into her hair.

"Yeah." It's better than okay, if she's being honest—the slow, purposeful way he's moving inside her, like there's nowhere on earth he'd rather be. Fiona shifts her hips. "I—*yes.*"

He smiles then, or at least it sounds that way. "Okay."

It goes on like that for a while, his mouth on her jaw and his hands everywhere he can reach her, her waist and her thighs and her hair. "Wanna see you," he tells her finally, rolling them so she's on top, and before Fiona can think of anything to say to that his fingers are between her legs and she's coming again, no warning, shocked by the speed and the intensity of it. "Oh my god," she says. "Oh my god, Sam." She catches her breath, lifts her head to look at him. "Don't be smug."

Sam laughs up at her, the corners of his eyes crinkling. "I'm a little smug," he says.

"Yeah." Fiona swallows. "Keep going," she murmurs, rocking her hips to encourage him. Up close he's not entirely perfect, with a tiny acne scar near his hairline she's never noticed before and the beginnings of crow's-feet at the corners of his eyes. She reaches down and collects his wandering hands, curling her fingers around his wrists and pushing them up against the pillows. Sam's eyes get very dark.

"Fiona," he says, so quiet, and there's a ragged edge in his voice that sounds unfamiliar and strange. "Fiona, *please*."

Fiona nods. "I lied," she confesses, dropping her head down so her mouth is pressed right up against his ear. "When I told you I was only imagining the sheets."

"*Fuck*," Sam says, and then it's happening for him—his whole body going taut, his face as vulnerable and undone as she's ever seen it. Fiona feels like the most powerful person in the world.

Once it's over Sam yanks her down on top of him, their chests pressed together, Fiona's face tucked against his salty neck while their breathing slows down to something like normal. After a while she starts to wonder if he's sleeping, and she bites gently at his collarbone to check. "Eventually I'm going to want dinner," she tells him softly, rubbing her thumb across his flat brown nipple. "Just as, like, a heads-up."

Sam laughs at that, the low, satisfied rumble of it echoing all down Fiona's limbs. "I'll get you dinner," he promises, his fingers trailing sleepily up her backbone. "Fuck, Fee. I'll get you whatever you want."

Fiona closes her eyes even though he can't see her. Just for a second, she lets herself believe he's telling the truth.

CHAPTER FOURTEEN

Sam

Sam blinks awake early, the light just barely turning blue outside the window, and finds Fiona lying on her back beside him, staring at the ceiling with one hand tangled in her hair.

"This time I did hide your shoes," he announces, rolling over and sliding his palm across her naked stomach, thumb dipping into her navel. Last night they ordered dinner and ate it on the couch in front of a two-part Ted Bundy documentary, then had sex again in Sam's kitchen before crawling back into bed and messing around a little more for good measure. Sam likes hearing her sounds. "Just in case you were thinking about trying to clumsily sneak out again."

Fiona's eyes narrow. "It wasn't *clumsy*," she protests, turning to face him and propping herself up on one elbow.

Sam shoots her a dubious look. "You were like a herd of water buffalo unwrapping cough drops at the opera," he says.

"Evocative."

"Louder than Paula Deen calling her weird adult sons in for a fried chicken dinner down on the farm."

"Okay."

"You made a monster truck rally sound like the quiet car on the Amtrak Acela."

That makes her smile. Her face is sweet and sleepy, her mouth smudged from kissing and her hair operating at nearly twice its normal volume. She looks like a Renaissance painting, actually, though Sam 100 percent knows better than to say anything like that out loud, so instead he just keeps on touching her—tracing her lips and the bridge of her nose and the seashell curve of her ear, connecting the dots of three or four closed-up piercings until he gets to the tiny pearl still fastened securely in her earlobe.

"They're my mom's," Fiona admits after a moment, her fingertips brushing his as she reaches up to fiddle with it. Her voice is very quiet.

"Ah," Sam says. "I was wondering."

"She works at a pottery studio in Seattle," Fiona explains, rolling her eyes like the tweeness of it offends her to her very core. "She moved there to, like, find herself after she left my dad."

"When was that?"

"Long time ago. Second season of the show, I guess?" Fiona flops onto her back, shrugging into the pillows. "I was sixteen."

Sam nods, trying not to look eager. She hardly ever talks about her family. "Was it a surprise?"

"I mean, yes and no," she admits, still talking up at the ceiling. "Don't get me wrong, my parents always had their problems. I think they had Claudia more or less explicitly to try and fix their marriage and then were shocked and dismayed when it didn't work. But I will admit to being *slightly* taken aback that she felt the need to cross state lines to get far enough away from us for her comfort." Then she grins. "And that was when I was still basically normal! Imagine if she'd waited around a year or two? She'd have had to go to New Zealand and farm alpacas."

Sam doesn't know whether to laugh at that or not. She's got the same tone she had when she was talking about *Weetzie Bat* the other night, like she's kidding around but also not really. "Do you guys talk?" he asks now, and Fiona shakes her head.

"Not really. I'm sure this will come as a shock to you, the beneficiary of my sparkling conversational repartee, but we don't usually have a ton to say to each other."

"Not even when everything was, like . . ." He trails off.

"No," Fiona says quietly. "Definitely not then."

Sam doesn't reply for a moment. Not for the first time, he thinks about asking her what the hell was actually going on with her around the time *Birds* got canceled, why she was so bent on blowing up her entire life, but he's pretty sure that as far as she's concerned he'd be buying himself a one-way ticket to Fuck Yourself Junction, and he doesn't want to do that. He might not know what's happening between them, exactly, but he knows he doesn't want to ruin it just yet. "That must be hard," is all he says.

"Not as hard as you'd think." Fiona shrugs. "I feel like she can go screw, mostly. But I'm also stupidly attached to these earrings, so you do the math."

"And your dad?"

Fiona smiles. "My dad's a really decent guy," she says, "but he has a lot of problems that he either cannot or will not get help for."

She lifts her eyebrows. "I keep telling him, a few weeks in a psych hospital? Fix you right up."

Sam reaches out to tuck her hair behind her ear. "Your sister is lucky to have you," he says, but right away Fiona shakes her head.

"Other way around, dude," she says. "Other way around."

It's fully light now, the sky turning pink and yellow and warm out in the courtyard. The sun streams in through the windows, bounces off the gold in Fiona's hair. She's a marvel, this girl. This *woman.* He wants to tell her that, too, but a) he thinks she'd probably never let him live it down and b) he's afraid of the feeling, a little, the force of it in his own stupid chest. It's way too much, way too soon.

Thankfully, she seems to have had enough of talking about herself for one morning. "What about you?" she asks, slouching down into the bed again. Sam can see the dark outline of her nipples through the white cotton of the sheet. "Good dad? Bad dad?"

"I don't know, really," he admits, lying back down beside her and tucking one arm behind his head. "They split up when I was a real little kid. I've only ever met him a handful of times. So: bad dad by default, I guess?"

Fiona frowns. "Is that the truth?" she asks, reaching out and running a speculative finger along the cut of his bicep. "Or is it like, a sad-sack story you tell girls to make them want to sleep with you?"

Sam's mouth drops open. "Fuck you!" he says with a laugh. "I was just so nice to you about your fucked-up parents!"

That makes her smile. "You were," she admits—scooting a

little bit closer, pressing herself against his side. "You were very nice."

"Also, for the record, some might point out that it probably says more about you than about me if my bad dad story turns you on."

Fiona tilts her head. "Some might," she agrees, swinging one leg over his hips and bending down to kiss him. "Some might also point out that *you're* sounding pretty offended for a guy with a *hey ladies aren't I deep* Van Morrison guitar nailed to his living room wall. For all I know your dad is back in Wisconsin right now making chocolate-chip pancakes and wearing unflattering jeans, with no idea you're besmirching his good name."

"Uh-huh." Sam bucks against her, involuntary. He's been half-hard since he woke up. "For all *you* know I'm a guitar virtuoso."

Fiona drags herself along the length of him, teasing. "Are you?"

Sam bites back a groan. "No," he admits, swallowing hard as she ducks her head to nip along his jawline, "but I could be."

"You could be," she agrees, then reaches toward the night-stand for a condom.

When they're finished they doze for a little while longer, a warm breeze ruffling the curtains and the birds calling to each other outside the window. Sam keeps waiting for that familiar surge of regret or impatience, that feeling of wanting her to leave—it happens more often than it doesn't when he brings someone home, though it's not a trait he particularly likes in himself, because it makes him feel like a meme or a cad character in a low-end romantic comedy—but instead he's just kind of glad she's here.

Eventually his stomach starts to growl, though, and he nudges her with his knee under the covers. "You know," he points out quietly, "we never got eggs."

As soon as the words are out Sam *does* regret them, a little bit—like maybe he's trying to drag this thing out past its sell-by date, to make it something other than what it is. On the other hand, *Let's get eggs* isn't exactly a marriage proposal. Not to mention the fact that, historically speaking, it's not like Fiona is the type to turn down an offer of breakfast food.

Also: he doesn't want to say goodbye to her just yet.

If Fiona thinks he sounds thirsty or desperate, it doesn't seem to bother her. "I could eat eggs," is all she says. She flips back the covers and pads down the hall toward the bathroom, not bothering to pull her clothes on. Sam takes a moment to enjoy the view—the graceful slope of her backbone, the high round curve of her ass. She doesn't look back at him until she reaches the bathroom, curling one hand around the doorjamb and calling down the hallway.

"Hey, Sam?" she says—sounding distracted, almost, scratching the back of her knee with her opposite foot. "Your dad's a giant loser, and him not being there for you every day of your life is one hundred percent his loss." Then she steps into the bathroom and shuts the door, the lock clicking neatly behind her. Sam stares down the empty hall.

For breakfast they go to a place he knows with a tiny patio out back, bougainvillea winding through an arbor over the rickety round tables, and plinky pop-folk music piping through a tinny outdoor speaker. Sam orders an acai bowl with blueberries and flaxseed. Fiona orders bacon and three eggs. "It's you!" the waitress says, looking at her wide-eyed. "I read on the internet you were dead."

Fiona nods, smiling sweetly. "I was," she admits.

The waitress doesn't react. "My brother had a poster of you in his room," she muses instead. "The trashy one, with the nudity and the lizard?"

Fiona keeps smiling, shaking her head. "I don't know it," she says.

The waitress frowns, confused, then evidently decides she's not interested in pursuing this conversation. "Acai bowl, bacon, and eggs," she repeats, glancing down at her notepad, then shuffles grumpily away.

Once she's gone Sam raises his eyebrows across the table. "That happen to you a lot?"

Fiona shakes her head. "Oh, that was nothing," she says, scooping her hair into a knot and securing it without the benefit of an elastic. "Sometimes they're rude."

Sam takes a sip of his coconut latte. "I have to ask," he says. "The thing with the lizard."

Fiona brightens. "Oh, I love that poster!" she says immediately, clapping her hands like a delighted child on Christmas morning. "It came out exactly how I wanted it. It was my artistic vision from the very beginning. Actually, if you ever visit my family home you'll see a life-size version of it framed above the fireplace with one of those special museum spotlights on it, so we can all behold it with appropriate reverence every time we walk in the—"

"Okay," Sam says, holding his palms out in surrender. He knew it was a mistake to ask. "Okay. Point taken."

Fiona is quiet for a moment, like she's debating how much she wants to tell him. Finally she sighs, sitting back in her chair and wrapping her hands around her coffee mug. She has delicate-looking hands, Fiona does, like maybe they're the one part of her body she hasn't been able to properly disguise.

"They told me Annie Leibovitz was going to shoot it," she says, her voice so quiet Sam has to lean across the table to hear her. "And it was going to be this hugely artistic thing with birds— like a play on ballerinas, *Swan Lake*, whatever." She makes a face. "There was a point when I was trying to start over, you know. There was a point when I was trying to get people to take me seriously again."

"Okay," Sam replies, feeling a little bit sick. "So what happened?"

"Well, in case you've never seen it yourself, Samuel, I can tell you it was not an artistic fucking ballerina picture with swans shot by Annie Leibovitz." Fiona shrugs violently, her whole body suddenly made of angles. "I showed up on the day and they said she had a conflict. And then something happened with the swans— like, they didn't *die* or anything, they were just unavailable that day, probably they were booked for the wedding of, like, an actual famous person, but then it turned out that one of the lighting assistants was also, like, a reptile guy." She sighs. "You see where this is going."

Sam does. Listening to her tell it reminds him of sitting through a horror movie, watching some skinny blond ingenue creep down a darkened hallway to meet her inevitable demise. Shouting *Don't do it* and knowing full well she can't hear him. "Yeah."

"I could have said no," she points out, running her thumb around the lip of her mug. She isn't quite meeting his eye. "I *should* have said no, which you'll notice was sort of a recurring theme in my life back then, but I just thought—hell, all these people are already here, I'm the one who got myself into this, so. I did it. I grit my teeth and I went somewhere else in my head and I did it. And now for the rest of my life, when people hear my name, that's what they're going to think of."

Sam opens his mouth to tell her that's not true, then shuts it again. She's probably right—it *is* true, at least a little. A past like Fiona's isn't the kind of thing people tend to forget. He glances over her shoulder instead of meeting her eyes, trying to ignore the sneaking suspicion that being out here with her is the worst thing he could possibly be doing for his career and his reputation and wishing, not for the first time, that he wasn't the kind of person who cares about things like that. He *is* that kind of person, though; he always has been, and the truth is he's not sure how much longer he's going to be able to pretend otherwise.

Thankfully the waitress returns with their plates just then, setting them down without fanfare and stalking off again. "You forgot to tell her she's the woman of your dreams," Fiona observes mildly.

"I didn't forget anything," Sam tells her. "Eat your eggs."

Fiona needs to get a birthday present for her sister, so after breakfast they duck into a little shop a few doors down, the kind of place that's full of crystals and leather bracelets and those little felt pennants girls like with slogans about coffee and feminism. It smells like patchouli and citrus, a little like Fiona herself. "Which?" she asks, holding up two gold necklaces, each of them strung with a bead no bigger than his thumbnail. "Jade or tigereye?"

Sam sifts his hand through a basket of tiny enamel pins shaped like avocados. "Tigereye," he decides, though he doesn't actually know which one is which. He just likes the way it sounds when she says it.

Fiona pays for the necklace, plus one of the avocado pins and a card with a cartoon of an ostrich wearing a party hat. They're walking back to the car when Sam's phone dings with a text from Erin. Just filed that giant-ass *Vanity Fair* piece, she reports. Taking myself to drunk lunch if you want to meet up?

Sam hesitates. Drunk Lunch is a celebratory tradition that dates back to their days of living together, when both of them were still scraping for whatever work they could get. Back then it usually meant splitting a burger and as many cheap shots as they could possibly afford, then passing out in front of *Bones* reruns in the middle of the afternoon. Nice work, killer, he texts back. Can't meet up now but I owe you a plastic bottle of gin.

BORING, Erin chides. Too busy with Riley Bird?

Sam blinks, his gaze flicking instinctively in Fiona's direction. The safest strategy here would be bald denial, but part of what makes Erin so good at her job is her ability to detect the faintest whiff of bullshit even over text, so instead he just shoots her the eyes emoji and hopes that's enough of an admission to satisfy her.

No such luck. Holy shit, she volleys back immediately, are you with her right now??? Bring her to me at once.

Then, a moment later: Unless you're, like . . . She sends him three eggplant emoji.

Sam snorts. "For fuck's sake," he mutters, shoving his phone back into his pocket as they reach the car.

Fiona glances over at him, curious. "What?" she asks.

Sam opens his mouth, fully intending to make up something innocuous. "You don't want to meet my friend Erin, do you?" he blurts instead.

This time, the regret is searing. Right away he wishes he could reach out, grab the words from the air, and shove them back into his mouth. It's way too fast, the stakes are way too high, and by the way Fiona blanches he can tell she feels the same way.

To her credit, it only takes her a moment to recover. "Don't lie," she says airily. "You don't have any friends."

"Oh, you're a gut-buster." Sam smirks, relieved. "Really, if this whole community theater thing doesn't work out, you should give stand-up a try. I bet Jerry Seinfeld would love to take some pointers from you."

Fiona raises her eyebrows. "I'm sorry, is Jerry Seinfeld your gold standard of a hilarious comedian?"

Sam frowns. "What's wrong with Jerry Seinfeld?"

Fiona shakes her head faintly, gazing at him over the roof of the car. It's like Sam can see her brain working—how she's weighing all the possible outcomes, cataloguing the ways it might go wrong. Then she takes a deep breath. "Sure," she says, and oh, she is so, so casual. "Let's go."

Shit. "Okay," he fires back immediately. If they're playing chicken here—and he's pretty sure they are—he's definitely not going to be the one who blinks first, even if he'd rather shave off his eyebrows or compete on *Dancing with the Stars*. Fuck, there's no way this isn't going to be such a massive crash and burn. "Yeah. Let's."

Erin is sitting at a corner table at their usual place reading *The Paris Review* and nursing a bourbon, a half-eaten Cubano on the table beside her. "Oh my god, you actually came," she says, standing up and wiping her hands on a paper napkin. She's wearing jeans and a T-shirt that says THE FUTURE IS NONBINARY, her dark hair in a long braid over one shoulder. "I thought for sure you were going to bail."

"We almost did," Sam and Fiona say in unison, then whirl to look at each other with naked horror.

Erin's eyes widen. "Oh, you guys are already gross."

Sam ignores her. "Fiona St. James," he says, gesturing between them, "Erin Cruz."

"Why do I know that name?" Fiona asks as they shake.

"Erin's a writer," Sam explains. Even as the words are coming out of his mouth he's filled with an irrational fear that Erin wrote something horrible about her somewhere—fuck, how did he not think to google that?—but then all at once Fiona's whole face lights up.

"You wrote that piece in the *Times* a few months ago," she

says, sitting down across from Erin, "about the gross coach at St. Anne's."

Sam looks at her, surprised. He always reads the stuff Erin writes, because she's his best friend and she sends it to him, but he wouldn't exactly have pegged Fiona for a connoisseur of long-form investigative journalism. "Guilty," Erin says, ducking her head, but he can tell she's dorkily pleased to have been recognized. She's more like him in that way than she'd probably want to admit.

"That was, like, *incredible* reporting," Fiona says, her face open and earnest. It's . . . actually the most sincere he's ever heard her sound. "Can I ask you something? When you're writing something like that, do the sources come to you, or . . . ?"

"It can work a few different ways," Erin says. "That time I got a tip from a friend of a friend who worked at the school and knew that the administration was trying to clean up the mess without anybody finding out."

"Of course they were," Fiona says. "Did you read that thing on the *Cut* about the equestrian camp—"

"—in Greenwich," Erin finishes, nodding excitedly. "A friend of mine wrote that."

In the end it turns out Sam was worrying for nothing. By the time they drain their first round of drinks, Erin and Fiona are deeply engrossed in a conversation about the *New York Times*, TikTok, and the flattening of the media landscape, and Sam finds himself totally extraneous to the entire proceedings. "Honestly, it's probably only a matter of time until I have to start pitching stories via viral video," Erin says wryly.

"Let me know if you need any pointers," Fiona replies, grinning. "I'm something of an expert myself." Then, glancing across the table at Sam and seeming to realize suddenly that he is, in fact, still here: "Another round, please, bartender." She slides her empty glass in his direction.

Well. Sam can take a hint. He gets up and heads over to the bar, watching the two of them with their heads tipped close together and trying not to feel like this is somehow weirder and more stressful than the alternative. He's waiting for the bartender to look up from what appears to be Grindr when his own phone vibrates in his pocket.

"Hey!" he says, picking up quickly when he sees Russ's name on the screen. "How's Tulum?"

"Miserable," Russ says. "Hot as shit, my daughters both hate me, and the Wi-Fi at the resort is garbage."

"Any word on the firefighter thing?"

"What?"

Sam frowns. "The thing from the other day," he clarifies. "My audition?"

"Ah," Russ says, like possibly he'd forgotten all about it. "No, not yet. I'm calling about *Birds of California*."

"Oh. Um. Hang on a second?" Sam glances over his shoulder at Fiona and Erin, neither of whom are paying him any attention, before heading for the door of the bar. "It's dead in the water, right?" he asks once he's out in the parking lot, blinking in the raw brightness of the midday sun. "I mean, after what happened with Fiona and that photographer . . . ?"

"You'd think that, wouldn't you?" Russ sounds triumphant. "But I just got off the phone with Arkin, and if anything, they want it more."

"Wait." Sam feels the blood drain right out of his face. "Seriously?"

"All publicity is good publicity, et cetera," Russ says. "And according to Bob, they're going for an older audience with the streaming platform—edgier, more sophisticated. 'Family After Dark,' or some fucking thing."

"That . . . is a terrible way to brand it," Sam says. "It makes it sound like all the shows are going to be about vampire incest."

"For fuck's sake, Sammy." Russ makes an impatient sound. "Can you focus, please? I'm on vacation here. The point is he and Hartley want to know if you've made any progress with the girl."

"Progress?" Sam echoes.

"Hartley said he ran into the two of you together on the UBC lot," Russ reports. "And don't think I didn't see those pictures of you all canoodling outside your apartment." He chuckles. "I gotta say, when I told you to sweeten the pot, I didn't mean literally."

Sam winces. "It wasn't like that," he protests. He glances over his shoulder again, feeling slightly panicky. It's cheesy, but the truth is he completely forgot about the reboot the moment Fiona came to the door yesterday afternoon. The last thing he wants is for her to come outside and hear him talking about it now.

"Sure looked like something, pally." Russ sounds positively cheerful, though Sam guesses that could be the unlimited daiquiris at whatever fancy all-inclusive resort he's working from this week.

"Don't get me wrong, I'm not complaining. The whole thing is great PR. Frankly, I wish I'd thought of it myself."

Sam's stomach roils. "We're friends," he insists, "that's all. And I gotta be honest, I don't know if I love the idea of trying to convince her to do something she's been pretty clear she doesn't want to do."

Russ laughs. "That girl doesn't know what the fuck she wants," he declares, with a casual certainty that takes Sam's breath away. "Now, if *you* don't want to do it, on the other hand—"

"No no," Sam says quickly. "I do, I just—"

"Are you sure?" Russ interrupts. "Because if you're not interested in the work, I've got plenty of other clients I could be busting my ass to try and—"

"No, it's not that." Sam hesitates, scrubbing a hand through his hair. Shit. It's not like he doesn't need a job—at this point he'd be crazy not to do whatever it takes to book anything Russ can scrounge up for him, up to and including that imaginary *Dancing with the Stars* gig. But there's another part of him that was hugely relieved by the idea of the reboot drifting forgotten to the bottom of the pile so that he and Fiona could . . . do whatever it is they're doing without the specter of it sitting there breathing heavily on the table between them. Sam doesn't like the idea of lying to her. But it's already too late to tell her the truth. "I'm working on it, okay? It's a delicate situation."

"Yeah, I'll bet." Sam can hear the smirk in his voice. "Listen, Sammy, I gotta go. Cara signed us up for scuba lessons. I'll talk to you soon, unless I somehow mysteriously drown, in which case you'll know she finally made good on her threats and murdered me."

Russ hangs up without saying goodbye. Sam stuffs his phone into his pocket, then goes back inside, squinting in the sudden dimness. When his vision clears he sees that Fiona and Erin have bellied up to the bar on their own, still chatting busily away.

"We helped ourselves," Fiona reports, raising her glass when she sees him, "being two independent women."

"We got you one, too, even though you don't deserve it," Erin chimes in.

"Like I always say, you're a couple of classy broads." Sam picks up the pint glass and drains the beer in two long gulps, feeling edgy and out of sorts. He's worried his conversation with Russ is sticking to him in a way Fiona is going to notice, that she'll be able to smell it on him like cheap drugstore cologne. "What did you guys talk about?" he asks.

"Same stuff girls always talk about," Fiona says immediately.

"Gel douches," Erin deadpans, and Fiona grins.

"You know what?" Sam says. "I deserved that." He looks down with some surprise at his empty glass. "Another round?"

By the time they say goodbye to Erin an hour later, Sam has that slightly woozy feeling of being buzzed in the afternoon—confused by the sun, by the fact that it's still daylight. "I was nervous," he explains when Fiona looks at him with raised eyebrows, "so I drank a lot."

Fiona nods like, *No shit.* "What were you nervous about?"

Sam opens his mouth, shuts it again. He could just say it, he thinks, a little sluggishly. He could just tell her the truth. "A lot of things," he says.

Fiona thinks about that for a moment. "Yeah," she says finally. "Me too."

Sam pushes her up against the driver's side door instead of answering, cupping his hand around the back of her neck and putting his mouth on hers. Fiona makes a quiet sound of surprise. He's expecting her to tell him to keep it in his pants—she doesn't strike him as a person who encourages PDA, particularly in broad fucking daylight—but instead she lets him do it for a minute or two, fitting her hips against his and widening her stance so he can slip his thigh between hers. Sam groans against her mouth.

"Okay," she gasps finally, pushing him gently away. "Enough."

Sam nods, backing off and tucking his hands into his pockets. It isn't enough, though. It isn't enough by a long shot.

"Come on," she says, "I'll drive you back to my house so you can pick your car up. Maybe I'll even let you feel me up for a couple of minutes when we get there."

But Sam shakes his head. "Wait," he says, lacing his fingers through hers and squeezing. "There's actually one more place I think we should go."

"I will tell you, Samuel," Fiona says twenty minutes later, slowing her car in front of a wall of dense green shrubs high in the lush quiet of the Hollywood Hills, "I'm confused about what I could possibly have said or done in the time we've known each other that would have made you think I'm the kind of person who likes surprises."

"Yeah, yeah." Sam points. "It's this one right up here." He unbuckles his seat belt and leans over her, breathing in the smell of her hair as he reaches an arm out the driver's side window and enters the code into the keypad. A moment later the sleek, minimalist metal gate swings open.

Fiona peers out the windshield as they creep up the driveway, eyes narrowed like she's trying to squint through a blizzard. She hangs back as he gets out of the car and unlocks the front door, like possibly she's getting ready to do a runner. "Whose house is this?"

"My agent's," he admits.

"Who else does he represent besides you?"

"Rude," Sam says, but he's smiling as he shoos her inside.

Fiona looks around in wonder. Russ's place is like something out of an HBO show: all wood and stone and metal, soaring ceilings and sharp modern lines. The floor is polished concrete, the furniture severe and architectural and frankly uncomfortable-looking. The back wall of the house is made entirely of glass. "He just . . . lets you hang out here?"

"I know this is probably hard for you to understand," Sam tells her, "but most people like me."

Fiona shrugs, not quite looking at him. "It's not that hard for me to understand."

Sam laughs, nudging her forward through the cavernous house. "Was that a compliment?"

"Enjoy it," she shoots back. "It's the only one you're going to get from me today."

"I'll be sure to write about it in my diary."

He leads her through the sliding door out to the pool deck, where the air is fragrant with hibiscus and citrus and enormous succulents spill from terra-cotta pots. The water is still in the rosy afternoon sunlight, a view of the hills down below. It looks like the kind of place no one should actually live in. It looks like a place where you could hide for a long time.

Fiona slips her shoes off and dips a toe in the pool, then looks at him with naked suspicion. "You're sure the cops aren't about to come?" she presses.

Sam smiles. "I am sure the cops are not about to come."

"Because that's all I fucking need, you realize. Fiona St. James arrested for trespassing at luxurious mansion in the Hollywood Hills."

"Darcy Sinclair would love that."

"I already sent Darcy's kids to private school six times over," she reminds him. "I'm not inclined to do her any more favors."

"Uh-huh."

"I'm just saying, it seems like at the very least I should be getting residuals checks."

"Get in the water, duchess."

Fiona scowls at him for another moment, the skepticism written all over her face like possibly she thinks Ashton Kutcher is about to pop his head out of an upstairs window and announce a punking. Finally she pulls off her tank top, then shimmies out of her denim shorts and slips into the water, barely making a splash. She surfaces a moment later, her hair wet, water sticking to her eyelashes and beading on the smooth skin of her breasts above her bra.

Sam stares at her openmouthed for a second, then almost trips over his own feet in his hurry to get his pants off.

Fiona lifts an eyebrow. "Oh," she teases, "*now* you're wearing underwear, I see."

"Is this just going to be hilarious to you forever, no matter what I do?"

"I'm sorry!" Fiona laughs. "I'm not trying to shame you out of walking around in your natural state like God made you—"

"Uh-huh," Sam says, and cannonballs into the deep end.

They float on their backs for a while, a warm wind rustling the palm trees and a dragonfly buzzing idly on the patio. "I love being in the water," Fiona admits quietly. "I used to be on the swim team at my middle school, before I quit."

Sam glances over at her. "The swim team?"

"Middle school."

"You ever think about going back?"

"To middle school? I'm probably a little bit too tall."

"Wokka wokka wokka." He rights himself. "You got your GED, didn't you? You could go to college."

Fiona snorts. "Do I look like Elle Woods to you?"

"You're smart," he says with a shrug.

He's expecting some snotty reply in response but instead Fiona tilts her head to the side. "Thank you," she says.

"You're welcome. It's true."

"I'd want to do it right," she confesses, "if I did it. Like, a real campus, going to the library, taking boring required classes. The whole thing."

From the way she says it he can tell that she's pictured it before. "Drama major?"

"English," she says immediately, then smiles. "Minor in drama."

"You could," he says again.

"Maybe."

"No maybe." He wants to tell her that he thinks she could do anything she wanted to, star in an Emmy-winning TV show or found a company or run for president. He wants to tell her she makes him feel like he could do anything, too. Instead he closes the distance between them and curls his hand around her waist under the water, pulling her close. "I just want to kiss you," he promises softly, which is a lie; every time he looks at her he wants too many things to name. "I'm not going to do anything else."

Fiona smiles. "Well, that's too bad," she says, then pushes him up against the side of the pool and shoves his boxer briefs down over his hips.

Sam breathes in, all the blood in his body immediately rushing to his dick. "What are you doing?" he asks.

"Not putting a move on you," she deadpans, wrapping her fingers around him and stroking. Sam bucks up into her hand. He lets out a quiet groan as she touches him, his eyes slipping closed at the rush of pleasure.

"Nice try," Fiona says immediately, letting go and stepping back. "Look at me."

Sam's eyes fly open again, his gaze locking on hers.

"Good," she says softly, and goes back to what she was doing.

She takes her time about it, experimenting—learning what he likes, Sam realizes belatedly, like maybe this is a thing she intends to do again in the future. The thought of it has him fisting his hands in her hair. "Please," he mutters. "Fiona. Please."

Fiona smiles, teasing. "Please what?"

"Please don't stop."

Fiona doesn't stop. It's technically not even sex and still it's one of the most intimate moments of Sam's entire life: her touch warm and steady, her eyes flecked with hazel and gold. He feels like she can see the tissue underneath his skin. "Fee," he murmurs finally, wanting to warn her. "I'm gonna—"

Fiona smirks. "That's the plan," she says, and keeps going.

Sam keeps his eyes on hers for as long as he can manage before his forehead falls forward onto her shoulders, his breathing dense and ragged against her ear. Fiona rubs the back of his neck until he's finished, the hot wind rustling the leaves of the palm trees high above them.

CHAPTER FIFTEEN

Fiona

They get back to Fiona's just at the shadows are starting to get longer—the sunlight taking on that golden, late-afternoon toastiness and the outlines of the palm trees going a deep, moody blue. "So, um," he says as the car idles in the driveway, looking suddenly bashful. "I guess I'll text you? I mean, if you want—?"

Fiona presses her lips together to keep from laughing. Her hair is wet from the pool, the weight of it damp against her shoulder. Her mouth is still swollen and stinging, a low sweet ache throbbing between her legs. "Sure," she says, casual as she can manage. "That'd be fine." Then she fists her hand in his T-shirt and yanks him close for a kiss.

Inside the house she finds Claudia eating an after-school snack of potato chips dunked in peanut butter and watching *Nosferatu* on her phone. "Hi," Fiona says, opening the fridge to see if there's anything in there that could conceivably become dinner. "How was your day?"

Claudia raises her eyebrows, popping a chip into her mouth. "Long drive," is all she says.

Fiona shrugs. "Hit some traffic," she shoots back, then completely fails to keep her cool about it, smiling goofily across the kitchen.

Claudia grins back.

By the time she throws together some pasta and heads into her room to change for rehearsal, though, Fiona's mood has plummeted to somewhere below sea level. Spending the day blowing off her responsibilities and running all over town with Sam may have been distracting, but the idea of marching back into the Angel City Playhouse after the little one-woman show she put on makes her want to stroll directly off the end of the Santa Monica Pier. She hasn't talked to anyone from the cast since she sped off in her car the other night. It felt easier to try and forget it had happened altogether, to leave them to their shock and gossip. She thinks again about disappearing, letting herself become a ghost story for them to tell at cast parties: *Remember when Riley Bird joined the company for a while and then it turned out she was just as batshit as everyone said?*

It would be easier that way, Fiona thinks. Cleaner. Less humiliating.

But as she stares at herself in the mirror above the dresser, she's surprised to realize she doesn't actually want to do it.

Sure, there's a part of her that feels obligated to finish what she started. And yeah, she doesn't want her sister to think she's a coward. But the plainer truth is she loves that stupid theater—the sweat-and-greasepaint smell of it, the lights going down on opening night—more than she ever loved working on *Birds of*

California. More than she's loved working on almost anything. She doesn't want to let anyone to take that from her, especially Darcy Sinclair.

So. She goes to rehearsal.

When she opens the door to the theater, the whole cast is already assembled onstage, gathered close together like a cluster of flamingos riding out a hurricane. They fall silent as she walks down the center aisle, their expressions wary. She feels like she's going to puke. "Hi," she says finally, holding up one sheepish hand. The set looks better, she notes distractedly, though it still needs a little bit of work. "I owe you guys an apology."

None of them says anything for a minute, a silent game of hot potato playing out on the stage. "For what?" DeShaun finally asks.

"I mean." Fiona runs a hand through her hair. "I think that's pretty obvious, don't you?"

Another too-long moment of silence; shit, this might be the longest any of them have been able to keep their mouths shut since Fiona joined the company. Then Hector clears his throat. "First of all, that douchebag deserved it," he says, surprisingly emphatic. "Second of all . . . it's not like this was some giant shock."

Fiona feels her eyes narrow. "Meaning what, exactly?"

"Frances," Georgie says gently. She's wearing flowy pants and a culturally appropriative kimono, her hair up in a little blond-gray knot on top of her head. "Fiona. We knew."

Fiona blinks. "What do you mean, you *knew*?" She shakes her head, looking around the circle with a mix of horror and dark hilarity. "Like, this whole time?"

"Of course we knew," Pamela tells her. "We're theater actors, not mole people."

"No, I know that," Fiona says, though *mole people* is basically exactly how she described them to Sam just the other day. "I just—"

"Give us a little credit," Larry says from his cool-dad perch on the arm of the Helmers' couch. They're going to need throw pillows, Fiona notes distractedly. "You were on the cover of every gossip magazine in America every week for like three years."

"My son has the picture of you with the alligator on his wall," Georgie tells her.

"I saw a rumor on Twitter that you were dead," DeShaun chimes in.

"Okay," Fiona says, holding a hand up. "Maybe I don't need all the details." She shakes her head. "You guys all just . . . collectively decided to let me get away with it this whole time?"

"It seemed like you needed some privacy," Hector says with a shrug. "I think everybody here can relate to what it's like to want to be someone else for a little while."

Fiona nods, looking around at this group of spectacular weirdos—Pamela boredly gnawing the chipped black polish off her fingernails, Larry scowling under his thick, bushy brows. She's filled with an emotion that feels physical, like something inflating inside her chest. After a moment it occurs to her that it's love. She wants to tell them that, but she doesn't know how and also it's corny as shit, so instead she swallows hard and claps her hands once.

"Well, in that case," she says brightly, "let's put on a fucking play."

The next couple of weeks pass by in a blur. She works at the copy shop. She goes to rehearsal. When she finishes at night, instead of going home and watching *Homicide Hunter* in bed, she goes to Sam's house and they listen to music on his ridiculous sound system and drink beer on his terrace and fool around.

They grab a six-pack and catch a movie at the Hollywood Forever Cemetery. They eat breakfast burritos on the beach. They go to Richie's ska show at a club downtown that's almost definitely about to be shuttered by the health department; neither of them has any idea how to dance to the music so instead they jump up and down for a while, holding hands so they don't get separated in the crowd and emerging sweaty and damp-haired and laughing an hour later, a strange exhilaration fizzing through Fiona's veins.

"You came!" Richie says when his set is over, beaming at them. He wraps Fiona in a slightly smelly hug, then shrugs like *What the hell* and wraps Sam in one, too. For once, he looks one hundred percent sober.

"Sweet guy," Sam says once Richie has been absorbed back into the crowd, another band clanging their introduction onstage. Sam likes people, is a thing Fiona has noticed about him; he's pals with everyone, from his publicist to his trainer to the barista at the coffee shop around the corner from his apartment.

"Richie? He is, actually," she agrees. "I mean, he's basically my best friend, so." Then, feeling weirdly embarrassed: "Well, Thandie, obviously. But other than her."

Sam nods. "How is Thandie?" he asks.

"Good!" she says immediately, then feels herself sag a little bit under the weight of the lie. She shakes her head, leaning back against a metal support post. "Honestly, I have no idea. I haven't had a real conversation with Thandie in years."

That surprises him, she can tell. "Really?" he asks. "You guys were, like, inseparable."

"Yeah," she says slowly, remembering it: Thandie's bawdy laugh and steady hand with liquid eyeliner, how much she loved art museums and string cheese. For Fiona's eighteenth birthday Thandie rented a vintage convertible and they drove up the coast to San Luis Obispo, where they ate rib eyes and shrimp cocktail in the gilded pink dining room of the Madonna Inn. "We were."

"What happened?"

Fiona hesitates, gazing out at the teeming, writhing crowd. It occurs to her that if she keeps on casually telling him about all the people who have literally fled the Los Angeles area rather than spend one more second in her proximity, eventually he's going to figure out it's the only logical course of action and abscond back to the Midwest under the cover of darkness just to get away from her. A Milwaukee goodbye. "I think we both just got busy," she says lightly. "You know, she's got SAG awards to accept, and I've got informational posters about gonorrhea to proofread for the DTLA free clinic."

Sam shoots her a look like he suspects she's full of shit, but he doesn't press her, which she appreciates. Instead he heads over to the bar to get them another round, but he must find somebody he knows over there, because he's gone for what seems like forever, and the close heat of the club is starting to feel oppressive, the incessant noise grating on her nerves. She can only handle being out like this for so long. She's just about to go find him and tell him she wants to get out of here when a hand lands on her shoulder. "Fiona St. James!" says a deep voice behind her. "I thought that was you."

Fiona flinches at the unexpected contact, spinning around and coming face-to-face with a vaguely familiar guy in glasses and a Henley unbuttoned halfway down his skinny chest. "It's me," she agrees, trying to place him. A minor UBC actor, she thinks, or maybe some tangential member of the crew she used to party with? It's also possible she's never actually met him before and he's trying to fake her out; that's happened before, too. She wishes she remembered more about the couple of years after the show got canceled, except for the part where she doesn't actually wish that at all.

"I always meant to text you," the guy says, ducking his head close so she can hear him over the clamor. "After . . ."

"Ah." All at once it comes to her: a wet, sloppy makeout in a booth at a club in West Hollywood, his hand creeping up the inside of her thigh. Josh, she thinks. Or Joss? "And here I've been waiting by my phone all this time."

Joss/Josh's lips twist. "Okay," he says, taking a step closer, "I deserved that."

You don't deserve anything, Fiona thinks, her temper prickling.

He may not have texted her, but he definitely called up Darcy Sinclair to tell her all about his wild night out with the Family Network's most notorious young ingenue. The headline, if she recalls, was *Bird in Heat*.

"It's good to see you out," Josh/Joss is saying now, though it's hard to hear him over the relentless clatter of the music and the dull buzzing sound filling her own head. "Who are you here with?"

Fiona shakes her head. "What?" she asks, his words only half registering. Pam once tried to get her to describe what the inside of her brain looks like when this happens, rage firing fast and powerful through every single one of her synapses. "It doesn't look like anything," Fiona told her finally. "It's all noise."

"I *said*," the guy repeats—curling his fingers around her waist now, squeezing a little—"who are you here with?"

Well, that does it. "What the *fuck*, dude?" Fiona bursts out, batting him away just as Sam finally turns up, clutching a bottle of Pacífico in either hand. "Don't touch me."

Sam's eyes widen. "Um," he says, gaze darting back and forth between them, "everything okay?"

Fiona whirls on him. "Why does everyone think they can touch me?" she demands, loud enough to carry over the cacophony in the club. "Like, would you walk up to Sir Ian McKellen and pinch him on the ass? You fucking would not, so I don't understand why—"

"Whoa whoa whoa," Josh/Joss interrupts, holding his palms up, looking beseechingly at Sam. "Bro, I definitely did not pinch her ass."

"Don't talk to him!" Fiona snaps. Dimly she's aware of people starting to look over at them, though she can't bring herself to care. "You were delighted to talk to me two seconds ago, so it seems to me that the very least you can do is—"

"Okay," Sam interrupts, glancing nervously at the bouncer, who's eyeing them from his post by the door. "I think it's probably time to blow this particular banana stand, don't you?"

"Really?" Fiona asks dryly. "But I was having so much fun."

"Uh-huh." He hands the two bottles of beer over to Josh/Joss. "Peace offering," he announces, with an infuriating little salute. "Have a good night, dude."

"Don't give him the beers!" Fiona protests, suddenly and deeply annoyed by Sam's pathological need to be everybody's best friend all the time. By his refusal to defend her, even if she knows she would have immediately made him regret it if he'd tried. "What the fuck are you giving him our beers for?"

"I mean, I don't think they're going to let us take them to go," Sam points out. He takes her hand and tugs her toward the doorway; Fiona yanks her arm away, but she follows him, seething with the kind of weird exhilaration that always floods through her after she loses her temper. All at once she feels very, very calm.

"That fucking guy," she says, shaking her head as they burst through the front door and out into the cool, breezy night. "I am so sick of guys like that fucking guy that I could vomit."

"Did he actually pinch your ass?"

"Did he—" Just for a second she thinks about explaining to

him, about Josh/Joss and Darcy. Then she shakes her head. "How is that in any way the point, Sam?"

"It's not," Sam clarifies immediately. "It's not, of course it's not, I just mean—okay, can you lower your voice, please?"

"Lower my—" Fiona frowns, stopping short in the middle of the sidewalk. "Oh my god. Are you *embarrassed?*" she realizes suddenly, whirling on him. "Seriously? Because you think I made a scene in front of some random aspiring screenwriter, or whoever the fuck that guy just was?"

"What? No," Sam counters immediately, but he blanches as he says it. All of a sudden he isn't looking her in the eye.

Oh, Fiona cannot believe him. "You are," she accuses as she stalks across the parking lot. Anger and shame bloom inside her again like two desert flowers, vining up around her spine. "You absolute piece of shit."

"First of all, take it easy on the name-calling, will you?" Sam says irritably. "Second of all, I just said I'm not, though one *could* argue that you made a scene in front of a lot more people than just one aspiring screenwriter. On top of which, how do you even know he was an aspiring screenwriter? He could have been Martin Scorsese's assistant, for all you know, and—"

"You're worried about *Martin Scorsese's* opinion of you?"

"Martin Scorsese is arguably the greatest director of all time!"

"And now he's never going to put you in a picture, by proxy?"

Sam—for god's sake—Sam actually *blushes*. "I'm just saying, I don't understand why you need to take a flamethrower to every single bridge you encounter."

"And I don't understand why you need to be such a striving little pissant, but here we are."

"Wow." Sam's eyes widen, his expression stung. "Fuck you, Fiona."

"Fuck you, Sam!" It feels good, to be mad. It feels familiar and energizing and significantly less terrifying than whatever else she feels for him, like her guts are about to fall out all over Sunset Boulevard for anyone to see. "You think you're the first person—the first *guy*—to be embarrassed of me? Take a fucking number. Call Darcy Sinclair yourself, why don't you, tell her what a psycho I am. Talk to her about it. Because honestly, I've heard it more than enough for one lifetime. I don't need to hear it from you, too."

Her voice wavers dangerously on that last part; Fiona sets her jaw. She's not about to let him hurt her. At the very least, she's not about to let him know he has.

She turns to walk away and call an Uber—ugh, she really needs to start driving herself places if she's going to make a habit of leaving in a huff—but Sam grabs her arm. "I'm sorry," he says, pulling her flush against him, burying his face in her hair. "I'm not embarrassed of you. I'm a jerk; I like you and I'm scared about it, I don't know."

Fiona breathes in, squeezes her eyes shut. There's a part of her that wants to keep fighting—to end this now, to get it over with once and for all—but she's surprised to find that another, bigger part of her just wants to hold on.

"I wouldn't blame you," she admits quietly, her voice muffled against his button-down. "I mean, that's not true, I'd blame you until the day I died, I'd find someone to put a hex on you and I'd start a rumor that you're terrible in bed, but it's not like I wouldn't understand." She shrugs inside his grip. "I know I'm too much."

Sam shakes his head. "You're . . . the perfect amount, actually."

That makes her laugh for how ridiculous it is. "I'm sorry I called you a striving little pissant," she says.

"I am a striving little pissant," Sam says easily, "for all the good it's doing me right now." He ducks his head to kiss her—just once, so quick and light she almost doesn't feel it. She can't tell if she's imagining that he looks around to make sure no one saw. "Want to go make up?"

Fiona raises her eyebrows. "Didn't we just do that?"

Sam laces his fingers through hers, tugging her in the direction of the Tesla. "Not yet."

He takes her home to his apartment and kisses her backward into his bed, then flips her onto her stomach and goes down on her until she's keening quiet sounds into his pillows, her fingers tensing and relaxing in the sheets. Afterward they eat leftover takeout from cereal bowls, sitting cross-legged on the rumpled covers while the neighbors play a rowdy game of Celebrity across the courtyard. "How did you get started acting?" Sam wants to know.

"Oh my god, don't ask." Fiona smiles, clapping an embarrassed hand over her face. "I got discovered," she admits, peeking out from between two fingers.

"Shut up." Sam laughs. "You did not."

Fiona nods. "I did. I was like, what, thirteen? I was hanging around at the print shop being a fucking ham when Caroline came

in to pick up some bridal shower invitations—she was still an assistant at LGP back then, she was probably younger than I am
now. She asked my parents if she could take a video of me on her
phone, and here I am."

"Here you are," Sam says, trailing a finger over the thin, sensitive skin on the inside of her arm. "Did you want to do it?"

"What, acting? I mean, sure," Fiona says with a shrug. "Or . . .
I guess I kind of didn't think about it as a choice at the time, more
like. And then by the time I got it together enough to have an
opinion . . ." She trails off. "Anyway. What about you?" she asks,
spearing the last of the broccoli from her picked-over noodles and
setting the bowl aside. "Did you come out of the womb, immediately hand over your headshot, and deliver a monologue from an
Aaron Sorkin movie?"

"Pretty much," Sam says, flopping down beside her. "I'm sure
this will come as a shock to you, but I liked the attention."

"You?" she asks, feeling her lips quirk. There's a little bit of
stubble on his chest and she strokes it absently with one finger—
liking the soft porcupine-y bristle of it, how weirdly intimate it is.
She tries not to think about the look on his face at the club earlier
tonight, that cold flash of panic in his eyes like he'd suddenly realized he was in over his head and needed to get away from her
as soon as humanly possible. She can feel his heart tapping away
underneath his skin. "I'd never have guessed."

Sam looks down, watching her. "I go to a Hungarian woman
named Renate," he confesses, covering her hand with his. "The

first couple of times I screamed like that scene in *The 40-Year-Old Virgin*, but now I'm very stoic about the whole thing."

Fiona props herself on one elbow. "Does Renate give you a lollipop at the end and tell you what a brave young man you've been?"

"That is the kind of positive reinforcement I require, yes."

"I thought so," Fiona says with a smile, and climbs on top of him one more time.

"Did you know that Eartha Kitt had a threesome with Marlon Brando and James Dean?" Claudia asks on Saturday morning. They're sitting on Estelle's screened-in patio doing foot masks, which Estelle bought on Amazon and which promise to slough layers of dead skin off and leave their heels as soft as a baby's.

Fiona raises her eyebrows. "Where did you hear that?" she asks, at the same time as Estelle says, "She wasn't the only one."

Fiona and Claudia look at her, then at each other. "Say more about *that*," Claudia instructs Estelle, as Fiona ducks her head back over the thank-you card she's writing. Across the yard and inside her house a beautiful orchid is sitting on the windowsill above the kitchen sink, alongside a note from Thandie that says she hopes Fiona is taking good care of herself. She didn't mention the video—Thandie wouldn't—but still Fiona has been working on her reply for the better part of an hour, trying to strike the right balance of gratitude and *actually this was completely unnecessary, as I'm extremely fine and sane*. The whole thing is mortifying, even though she knows Thandie meant it sincerely. It's mortifying, even though she knows Thandie's just being a good friend.

"Okay," Fiona says finally, bending down and sliding the disposable cotton booties off her feet, which are slimy with some kind of gel. She actually has no idea what's in this mask, though the package had a bold-print warning against using it if she was pregnant or nursing. "On that note, I've gotta get ready for rehearsal."

"Are you coming home tonight?" Claudia asks. "Or are you sleeping at Sam's?"

That gets Estelle's attention. "How often is she sleeping at Sam's?" she asks, crossing her elegant ankles and eyeing Fiona with interest.

"Three nights this week," Claudia reports.

Fiona's mouth drops open. "Claudia!"

"Well, you are." Claudia shrugs.

"Good for Fiona," Estelle says, toasting her with a coupe glass full of V8. "And as for you, *principessa*"—she turns to Claudia—"you know Brando and I are always happy for company if you find yourself getting lonely over there."

Fiona frowns. "Are you?" she asks. She's been worrying about this, her sister alone in the house with only their dad for company, even though Claudia has been very clear that she's graduating in a couple of months and certainly doesn't need babysitting. "Getting lonely?"

"Desperately," Claudia says, her fox-like face going serious. "In fact, I've been meaning to talk to you about it. I think I'm going down a bad path. Some other latchkey kids at school got me hooked on huffing whipped cream and I feel like it's probably only a matter of time until I'm creeping into your room at night and stealing your Nickelodeon Kids' Choice Award to hock for Reddi-wip money."

Fiona snorts. "All right," she says, wiping her sticky feet with a towel and standing up. "You've made your point."

"I like Sam," Estelle announces, taking a sip of her V8—which, upon closer examination, seems to be mostly vodka. "He seems *extremely* virile."

Fiona manages to keep a straight face, but barely. "I'll be sure to let him know you think so."

"Has he said anything else about the show?" Claudia asks.

Fiona shakes her head. "He hasn't," she admits, a little grudgingly. "He said he wouldn't, and he hasn't."

"Almost like he just wants to spend time with you because he likes spending time with you," Estelle says pointedly.

Fiona feels herself prickle, though she isn't entirely sure why. "Almost like," she agrees.

"I'm happy for you, *ma chérie*," Estelle continues. "You deserve it."

"Don't go picking out our wedding china just yet," she says. "We barely know each other."

"Seriously?" Claudia sounds surprised now, the joke drained right out of her voice. "Fiona," she says quietly. "You've been half in love with him since you were like fifteen."

"I—what?" Fiona sputters, her cheeks flaming. "I have not!"

"Easy," Claudia says, holding both hands up. "I'm not saying it to be an asshole."

Fiona eyes her. "Aren't you?"

"No," Claudia says evenly, sitting perfectly still in her lounge chair. "I'm saying it because I think it's, like, kind of true."

Fiona gazes at her sister for a long moment, still holding her ridiculous cotton booties. "I'm going to be late," is all she says.

CHAPTER SIXTEEN

Sam

Sam figures Russ will call him when he gets back from Tulum, but after a week goes by and he doesn't hear anything he calls and leaves a message with Sherri, who promises to pass it along. "Nothing urgent," he tells her, trying not to sound desperate or sweaty. He would have thought he'd heard back about the firefighter show by now. "Just, you know. Checking in."

He drops in on his old acting class in the Valley. He spends a lot of time at the gym. He goes on YouTube and watches old *Birds of California* clips for a while, which is weirdly enjoyable—turns out it was a pretty good show, with sharp dialogue and the occasional bit of slapstick and a knack for tearjerker montages set to acoustic covers of classic rock songs. He'd forgotten what a gifted comedian Fiona could be when she wanted to, all perfect timing and elastic expression, her delivery always dead-on.

Sam blows out a breath, leaning his head back against the couch and sifting his hands through his hair. He knows he needs to be honest with her, to talk to her about *Birds*, but he doesn't trust her not to bite his head off the second he brings it up. The last thing he wants to do is lose her. But it feels like he's running out of time.

Still, Sam reminds himself, they might have gotten famous for playing precocious teenagers on television, but they aren't actually kids anymore. They can have actual conversations. He'll take her out, he decides—somewhere nice with white tablecloths and flattering lighting, the kind of place where they call french fries *frites*.

And okay, he doesn't really know how he's going to afford to do that at this particular moment, but whatever. He'll figure it out.

He shuts his laptop with a confident click, then digs his phone out from between the couch cushions. Want to hang out tonight? he texts.

Can't, she replies. It's Claudia's birthday.

Sam thinks about that for a moment. Asks himself, not for the first time, exactly how deep he's prepared to get in here. I like birthdays, he types, then hits send before he can talk himself out of it.

Seriously? Her reply is immediate. You want to come to my sister's birthday?

Well, now he feels like an asshole. But: in for a penny, et cetera. I mean, only if you want me to. I'm not going to bust in through the wall like the Kool-Aid Man.

The dots appear, then disappear, then appear again. It's close to a full minute before her reply comes through. Yeah, okay, she says. I want you to.

He's expecting a dozen teenyboppers but instead it's just Fiona and her dad and Estelle when he shows up, with Sam Cooke on the stereo and the sliding door wide open to the warm evening breeze.

Claudia is wearing a long pink skirt made of tulle that looks like cotton candy, a crop top, and a pair of Nikes. "Samuel," she says, sounding exactly like Fiona. "Nice to see you again."

"Um, you too." He had no idea what to get her but he didn't want to show up empty-handed so finally he went to a costume shop in West Hollywood and got her a five-dollar plastic tiara. "Happy birthday," he says, handing it over. Claudia grins and pops it on top of her head.

"She had a party with her friends, too," Fiona assures him, passing him a pitcher of lemonade spiked with basil and ginger and nodding in the direction of the backyard. "My family is tragic, but it's not *that* tragic."

Sam shakes his head. "This doesn't feel tragic," he says, and it actually doesn't. They've draped a cloth over the patio table and lit candles, strung little white lights all through the trees. There are glass jars full of herbs and flowers lined up at the center of the table alongside an enormous spread of food: chicken, hummus, pita, all kinds of pickled veg. "This is amazing," Sam says, taking a second helping even though technically he's only supposed to be eating 1,500 calories a day right now. "Did you guys cook all this?"

"Oh god no," Fiona says, reaching for the tabbouleh. "It's murder chicken."

"Murder chicken?" Sam repeats, and Claudia nods.

"The guy who owned the restaurant put on a white silk suit and went out one day and murdered his mom and sister," she explains pleasantly, scooping some hummus onto her pita. "Then he shot himself in the head."

Sam stops chewing. "I'm sorry," he says, "*what* now?"

"Hey," Fiona's dad says with a tired-looking smile, pointing a drumstick in his direction, "you asked."

"I did," Sam admits faintly. He wasn't sure what he was expecting, but the guy seems nice enough, if a little schleppy and quiet. "And the whole operation didn't shut down after that?"

Claudia shrugs. "I mean," she points out, "it's very delicious chicken."

Sam shakes his head, looking across the table at Fiona. "That *would* be your restaurant of choice."

"It's her birthday," Fiona says, nodding across the table at her sister. Sam likes watching them together: how easy they are with each other, how comfortable and funny they are. He and Adam get along fine, but it isn't like this. "I just made a helpful suggestion."

Sam helps her clean up after dinner, wrapping the murder chicken in plastic and loading the plates into the dishwasher. As Fiona is boxing up the leftover birthday cake she swipes one sneaky finger through the frosting, but before she can lick it off Sam catches her hand and slips it into his own mouth instead, tasting the cloying sweetness of the sugar mixed with the salt of her skin. Fiona swallows hard, the muscles in her throat moving. "That was mine," she protests softly.

"Oops," Sam says, and goes back outside to get more plates.

Fiona's dad has disappeared into the house, but Claudia and Estelle are taking glamour shots in the fading light, cooing about the magic hour; Sam is gathering up the glasses when Estelle puts a hand on his arm. "Sam, honey," she says quietly. She's wearing a long sparkly gown and a pair of heels so high he's immediately concerned about her old-lady ankles. "Listen."

Sam turns to look at her. Something about the tone in her voice has him expecting the kind of speech Jamie's character might have given to one of Riley's potential boyfriends on *Birds of California*: *If you hurt her I'll cut your balls off and put them in the Vitamix* or something. Well, Jamie's character wouldn't have said that, exactly—the Family Network had very strict rules about vulgarity of any kind—but that would have been the gist. Maybe the dialogue will be a little spicier on Family After Dark.

Now he looks at Estelle and holds both hands up, conciliatory. "Whatever you're about to say," he blurts, "I know you all are protective of Fiona. And rightfully so. She's been through a lot. But I care about her, and I wouldn't do anything to hurt her on purpose. So you don't have to worry about that."

Estelle looks at him for a moment, a wry, knowing smile playing over her brightly painted lips. "Those champagne flutes can't go in the dishwasher, cupcake," she tells him. "They're crystal."

Sam feels himself blush from the bottoms of his feet clear up to his hairline. "Oh," he says, nodding vigorously. "Um, good to know."

"They're the real thing, and they're delicate." She raises her eyebrows. "That's all I was going to say."

Eventually Sam wanders down the hall to pee, then stops in the door of Fiona's room on the way back. He's not sure what he's expecting—chaos, maybe, shit everywhere—but instead it's calm and tidy, a pale quilt smoothed over the queen-size mattress and little jars of essential oils lined up on the dresser. There are framed photos of her and her sister, plus one of her and Thandie with their arms around each other, so young they look like they're going to a middle school dance. The smell of vanilla and sandalwood hangs in the air. He's just wandering over toward her bookshelf when he hears Fiona's voice behind him: "Looking for drugs?"

Sam turns to look at her leaning in the doorway, arms crossed and a half smile on her face like she's onto him. "Guns, actually."

Fiona nods seriously. "Guns are in Claudia's room."

"I was going to check there next." Sam turns back to the bookcase, his gaze skipping across the titles: plays, mostly, but a decent amount of fiction, an essay collection or two. The shelves are stuffed to the gills, bowing a little bit. It's no wonder she and Erin got along. "Oh-ho!" he crows, prying a paperback copy of *The Alchemist* out from between a gruesome-looking true crime book and a battered hardcover of *The Velveteen Rabbit*. "What do we have here?" he asks, holding it aloft in victory.

Fiona rolls her eyes. "I never said I hadn't *read* it," she says, crossing the room and taking it out of his hand before tossing it onto the bed. "I've read a lot of things."

"I know you have," Sam says quietly. He turns back to the bookcase and runs his finger along the spines until he gets to *Weetzie Bat*, pulling it off the shelf and holding it up. "Can I borrow this?" he asks.

Fiona's eyes narrow. "Why?"

"Why do you think?" He shrugs. "You've read mine. I want to read yours."

Fiona looks at him for a long moment like she's waiting for the gotcha. "Fine," she says, when she's satisfied there isn't one coming. "If you promise to bring it back."

That makes him smile. "Do you want to write your name in it first?"

"Maybe," she says, but before Sam can reply she's already kissing him, hooking her fingers in his belt loops and yanking him close. Sam groans quietly against her mouth—dropping the book and curling his hands around her waist, running his thumbs along the soft skin just above the waistband of her jeans. He tries to remember the last time he wanted someone like this, and he can't. He wants to hand her a Sharpie and hold his arm out, to look down and see *Property of Fiona St. James* scrawled in her handwriting across his skin.

He starts to walk her backward toward the bed, his hands creeping higher, but Fiona stops him when the backs of her legs bump against the mattress. "Not here," she mumbles.

Sam groans low and quiet, presses his hips against hers. "Why not?"

Fiona arches, then pushes him gently away. "Because my entire family is watching *The Bachelor* in the next room, perv."

"Oh." Sam swallows. "Right." He stands there for a moment completely unable to problem solve, dizzy with desire. Finally Fiona laughs, reaching down and lacing her fingers through his.

"You want to get out of here?" she murmurs.

Sam does.

They don't talk as he winds down Laurel Canyon toward his apartment, the windows down and the warm night air blowing Fiona's hair around her face. There's a part of Sam that wants to speed east until they get to Palm Desert, to lay her out on a blanket and gaze up at the massive bowl of stars; there's a part of him that wants to drive north to see the redwoods, to walk across the Golden Gate Bridge. Sam's lived in California for fifteen years and he's never done any of those things, but with Fiona in the passenger seat beside him he thinks maybe he'd like to.

Then she slides her hand up his thigh and squeezes his cock through his jeans, so casual, and Sam completely forgets about doing anything but getting her naked in his bed.

It takes him forever to find a parking spot. They drive around for what seems like hours, Sam feeling increasingly desperate as he circles the block again and again. "I can't believe you park your fucking Tesla on the street," Fiona says finally, sounding agitated. "Like, in all seriousness, how has nobody slashed your tires?"

"I got so excited about the apartment that I forgot to ask if there was parking," he says, gritting his teeth. "And then it was too late."

"So you didn't think to, like, rent a spot somewhere, or—"

"There's usually plenty of parking in this neighborhood!"

Finally he finds a spot that's really too small, jerking the wheel back and forth as he tries to wriggle in. "Do you want me to do it?" Fiona asks, her voice a full click higher than normal.

Sam makes a face. "What are you, some kind of parallel parking expert?"

"Yes, actually," she says. "My dad grew up in Queens, it's a point of pride for him." She glances out the window. "You're definitely not going to make it."

"I'm going to make it!" Sam insists. He does, too, though not before gently kissing the car behind them with the bumper of the Tesla. "It's fine," he decides, glancing perfunctorily at the damage before grabbing Fiona's hand and yanking her toward his apartment, both of them nearly tripping as they race up the stairs to his place. The door has barely shut when they're on each other, Sam grabbing her ass and boosting her up, her back thumping against the wall as she wraps her legs around his waist.

The bedroom is too far away so he sets her down on the couch and drops down on top of her, rucking up her T-shirt and yanking down the cups of her bra instead of bothering with the clasp. Fiona gasps. It feels like her hands are on him everywhere: her fingers raking over his chest and back and stomach, reaching down to work the button on his jeans.

As soon as they're both finally naked Sam pushes himself as deep as he can and then just stays there—bracing his elbows on either side of her shoulders, brushing the hair off her forehead. They stare at each other for a moment, both of them silent. Sam bites his tongue before he says something he can't take back.

"Sam," she whispers finally, her eyes dark with pleasure; she's rocking underneath him now, restless, hands clutching at his biceps and hair. *"Sam."*

Sam blinks at her dazedly. "Hm?"

Fiona grins. "Nobody's ever keyed your car out there before?" she asks, lifting one hand and miming a little scraping motion. "Really? Not even a little bit?"

Sam growls and flips her onto her stomach, wrapping an arm around her waist and finding her clit with two fingers; she's still laughing right up until the moment she finally comes apart against his hand.

They do it again in the shower a while later, then one more time in his bed, her wet hair soaking into the pillow and their skin warm and damp from the spray. "You ever been to Palm Springs?" he asks when they're finished, propping himself up on one elbow.

"No, actually." Fiona raises her eyebrows. "Isn't it all influencers and, like, the occasional cactus?"

"Maybe," Sam says with a shrug. "You wanna find out?"

He's expecting her to say no like a reflex but instead she thinks about it for a moment before nodding, her eyes like a cat's in the dark. "Sure," she says. "Let's go."

"Okay," he says, and lets himself believe that she means it. "Let's."

He falls into a sweaty, sated sleep almost as soon as his eyes close, only to jerk awake in the dark what feels like a few seconds later, disoriented. Sam blinks for a moment, then looks over at

Fiona, who's tossing violently in bed beside him, muttering something he doesn't understand. The clock on the nightstand says it's just after two.

Sam sits up. "Fiona," he says quietly, not sure what to do. His instinct is to touch her, but for some reason he doesn't think it's a good idea. "Fiona."

"Wha—?" She startles awake all at once then, dazed, shaking her head and looking around like she doesn't know where she is. Her eyes narrow, like she's never seen him before. "What the fuck?" she demands, drawing sharply back.

"It's me," he says, holding his hands up. Then, just in case: "It's Sam. I think you were having a nightmare."

Fiona blinks at him for a moment in the darkness, then sags. "Oh," she says, scrubbing a hand over her face. Her hair is one big tangle. "Sorry."

"No, it's okay." He almost asks her what she was dreaming about, but that seems like a bad idea, too, on top of which there's a tiny part of him that doesn't actually want to know. Instead he smiles, smoothing a hand down her arm. Fiona smiles back—at least, he thinks she does; it's hard to tell in the dark—and lies down beside him.

He doesn't mean to, but he must fall asleep again, because the next time he wakes up she's gone, the mattress cool beside him. He gets out of bed and shuffles into the living room, where he finds her curled up in a ball on the couch watching something called *Evil Lives Here* on cable. "Hey," he says sleepily, scrubbing a hand through his hair. "What are you doing?"

Fiona doesn't look at him. "I mean." She shrugs, gesturing at the TV. "That's pretty obvious, no?"

Sam frowns. "Are you okay?"

"Yep."

"Okay." He's used to her giving him a hard time about things, but she sounds really and truly annoyed, and he's not sure why. "Do you want to talk to me?"

"What?" Fiona stares at him blankly. "There's nothing to talk about. I'm fine."

"You . . . don't look fine," Sam says carefully. She doesn't, either: there are dark rings under her eyes; her hair is a little bit matted. He wonders how long she was tossing and turning before she gave up and came out here.

Fiona laughs hollowly. "Thanks a lot."

"No, I didn't mean—" Sam breaks off. Her jaw is set, her shoulders somewhere up in the neighborhood of her ears. He can see her closing up shop, sure as the lights blinking out in the strip malls back home. "Do you want to come back to bed?"

She shakes her head. "You go," she says, nodding in the direction of the bedroom. "I'm going to watch this."

Instead he crosses the living room and lies down at the other end of the couch. Their feet brush, but she pulls hers away, curling her knees up and keeping her eyes on the television. "Fee," Sam says, gazing at her in the half dark. Then, even though he has a pretty good idea of how it's going to go: "Do you get nightmares a lot?"

Sure enough: "Sam," she snaps, reliable as winter in Wisconsin. "Leave it, okay? I can go home, if I'm keeping you up."

"What?" Sam startles. "No, hey, that's not what I want."

"Okay." Fiona shrugs. "Well then. Let me watch this, okay?"

"Okay."

He doesn't sleep for a long time, and he can tell she doesn't, either. Instead they lie there in uneasy silence, the light from the TV flickering across the rug.

He wakes up the next morning, and she's making pancakes.

"Something approximating pancakes, anyway," she says when he pads into the kitchen, popping up onto her toes to plant a cheery kiss on his mouth. She's wearing underwear and one of his T-shirts, her hair piled high on top of her head. "There's coffee."

"I—thanks." Sam scratches at the back of his neck, cautious. Fiona has never, in all the time they've been hanging out, made coffee in the morning. Honestly, Sam didn't even know he *had* coffee in this house. "Wow."

"I don't have rehearsal until tonight," she continues, moving busily around the kitchen. "Want to do something? A hike?"

Sam raises an eyebrow. "Since when do you like to hike?"

"I like to hike!" she defends herself. "I could like it, conceivably. I've never actually done it." She shrugs. "But that's a thing normal people do, right? With the person with whom they're engaging in various and sundry sexual acts?"

Sam smiles. "I think it's a thing people do, yeah." His brain catches on that word, though, *normal*, like a snag in the knit of a cashmere sweater. He can't get over the feeling that she's playacting, like she accidentally dropped some important façade and now she feels like she has to compensate. "Fiona," he says. "About last night."

"Yeah," she says with a self-deprecating smile. "Sorry. I don't sleep so well sometimes and it makes me an asshole."

"You weren't an asshole," he says.

"You know what I mean." She waves her hand, like him finding her half-catatonic in his living room is cigarette smoke she can swat away. "I'm going to shower."

"Wait," he says, "what about the pancakes?"

Fiona shrugs, like she hasn't considered it. "I'm not actually hungry. I mostly just wanted to make them. You should eat, though."

"Okay . . . ?" Sam frowns. "We showered last night, you realize."

"I mean." Fiona presses another kiss against his mouth, though he can't figure out if he's imagining that it feels a little bit forced. "I don't think it counts when there's no soap involved."

"We used soap."

"Not for washing."

That makes him smile. "Fair," he admits.

Fiona heads down the hallway, pulling off her T-shirt as she goes. Sam watches the long line of her bare back, muscles flexing underneath the smooth expanse of her skin. He stands there for a moment once she's gone, stuffing a couple of pancakes absently into his mouth. He definitely didn't have the right ingredients, and they taste distinctly sandy; still, nobody has made Sam breakfast in years.

Fuck it, he thinks, setting a half-eaten pancake down on the counter. He's being a dick. Everybody's entitled to a bad night every once in a while—not to mention the fact that when one considers the complete, collected history of Fiona St. James meltdowns, last night barely registered. He's overthinking it because he feels guilty about lying to her, that's all. Enough is enough. It's time to come clean.

He's just about to head down the hallway when his phone rings on the counter. Sam frowns. It's a number he doesn't recognize— the firefighter thing, he realizes suddenly, his heart lifting in his chest. And yeah, usually something like that would come through Russ, but it's conceivable they wanted to talk to him direc—

"Sam Fox," he says.

"Sam!" comes the familiar voice on the other end. "Jamie Hartley."

Sam startles. Jamie hasn't called him in—well, Jamie hasn't called him ever, actually. "Um, hey," he says, glancing over his shoulder at the bathroom door. "Can I call you back?"

"No," Jamie says cheerfully. "This is important. Do-or-die time here, buddy. Look, I talked to your agent, and he says you're just as excited to get this thing off the ground as I am. And I know you've been making time with our girl."

Sam can just imagine Fiona's face if she heard Jamie refer to her as *their* anything. "I don't know if that's what I'd call it," he manages, trying to keep his voice as quiet as he can without actually whispering. "And dude, I gotta tell you, it really seems like any negotiations you're trying to have with her should probably be between the two of y—"

"Listen to this guy!" Jamie laughs. "Okay, man, you don't want to talk about it, I can respect that. I think that's very classy. But listen. Why don't the three of us have lunch, at least? We'll go somewhere nice, have a few drinks, you and I can make our pitch in person. And if I can't close, then that's on me. At the very least, you can tell her she'll get a free meal. Really, no strings attached."

"I—" Sam has to admit, it sounds reasonable. Fun, even, if not for the fact that Fiona is probably going to rip his balls off for even suggesting it. "Yeah, maybe." He remembers Jamie taking him for burgers at the end of every season of *Birds of California*. He remembers that his rent is due in eleven days. "Okay," he says finally, scrubbing a hand through his hair. He was going to tell her the truth anyway, wasn't he? This will just be . . . part of it. "Look, Jamie. You know as well as I do that nothing I say is going to make her do anything she doesn't want to. But I'll talk to her about it, okay? And I'll keep trying to convince her."

"Good man," Jamie says. "Let's say one o'clock tomorrow? I'll have my assistant make a reservation and send you guys the details."

Sam feels himself blanch. "Wait," he tries. "I didn't say—"

But Jamie is already gone.

Sam swears quietly under his breath, staring at the darkened screen for a moment. It's only after he sets the phone down on the counter that he realizes at some point when he wasn't paying attention, the water shut off down the hall.

"Convince her to do what?" Fiona asks.

Sam closes his eyes for a moment. Opens them again. When he turns around, there she is, standing at the mouth of the hallway in a towel, gazing at him evenly. Her hair is wet, her face scrubbed. She looks very, very young.

"Fee," he starts, then snaps his jaws shut. His first instinct is to lie. Did he use her name just now, on the phone with Jamie? He doesn't think so. He could tell her they were talking about something else. Hell, he could tell her it was another Jamie entirely, someone she doesn't know and who's never even heard of her, calling about something entirely unrelated to—

"He wants to have lunch," Sam says quietly. "The three of us. To talk about the show."

Fiona nods slowly, absorbing that information. Then she smiles. "This whole time, huh?"

"Wait, what?" Sam shakes his head, not understanding. "No, I—"

"What did you think, exactly?" She sounds sincerely curious. "That if you plowed me enough eventually I'd just roll over and do whatever you wanted? Or was the sex just, like, a fun bonus for you?"

Sam flinches. "I—no," he insists, "of course not. That's not what this is at all."

"Was," Fiona corrects.

"What?"

"Whatever this *was*," she repeats. She's still smiling. She looks . . . almost pleased, actually, like she's been waiting for this moment and is relieved it's finally arrived. "It's definitely over."

Sam feels that like a fist through his ribs. "Fee," he says again, voice cracking a little. "Come on. Can we just——"

"Can we just *what*, exactly?" Fiona's eyes flash dangerously; for the first time, her smile falls. "Talk some more about the supposed merits of a project I've been very clear I have no interest in doing? Have a friendly little lunch with a person you're fully aware I *truly* fucking hate? Forget about the fact that you've been lying your flat ass off the entire time we've been sleeping together?" She tilts her head. "What is it specifically that you want me to do here, Sam?"

Sam blinks at that, caught off guard. "Wait a minute," he blurts stupidly, before he can stop himself. "You think my ass is flat?"

"Oh my god." Fiona laughs out loud, a sharp, mean-sounding cackle. "Okay. This is ridiculous. And you know what the worst part is? I *knew* it was ridiculous, every single day I was saying to myself, *Fiona, this is fucking ridiculous*, and still I let myself——" Fiona breaks off, shaking her head in disbelief. "Forget it. I'm gonna get dressed." She turns toward the bedroom.

"I'm sorry, what about it was so ridiculous?" Sam takes a step toward her, reaches for her arm. "Because I have to say, you didn't seem to think it was so ridiculous when you were——"

Fiona yanks her arm away. "Do not touch me."

"Okay." Sam holds his hands up, backs off right away. "Okay." He knows he's in the wrong here, obviously; he knew this was inevitable, on some level, the same way he knew it was inevitable that his show was going to get canceled even if he never really let himself think about it. He's fully aware that the only possible course of action is to own this as the massive fuckup it is, to prostrate himself and beg her forgiveness and hope eventually she forgets the whole thing.

He picks a fight instead.

"You know what I want from you, actually?" he asks, hands still in the air. "I want to have an actual adult conversation about this for once in our entire relationship. The reboot. Because I think you owe me that much."

"First of all, our *entire relationship* is, like, three weeks," Fiona scoffs. "And second of all, I don't owe a damn thing to you or anybody else."

That stings—the idea that he's been in this more than she has, that he's trying to make it something other than what it is. "Oh, right," Sam says, clapping himself theatrically on the head, "sorry. For a second I forgot what a tortured lone wolf you are. Won't make that mistake again. Although I guess tortured lone wolves don't usually have cushy little family businesses to fall back on when they irreversibly fuck up their career."

Fiona's eyes fly wide. "Oh, *that's* what you think I'm doing?"

"I think you're in the position of not having to hustle, that's for sure."

"Having to *hustle*?" Fiona bursts out laughing. "Look at your apartment, Sam! Look at your fucking car! Are you really going to stand here and try to convince me you're hurting for cash?"

"I'm completely broke, Fiona!"

"What?" That surprises her, he can tell. "You are not."

"Yeah, I am." It feels gross and good to say it, like ripping off a scab. "Quite seriously, how have you spent basically every waking minute with me for the last three weeks and not noticed that? Congratulations, you were right, I'm exactly as much of a fuckup as you've always known I was. I have tens of thousands of dollars in credit card debt. I have no idea how I'm going to pay my rent next month. My mom is dying"—he almost gags on the word—"and I'm desperately trying to get my shit in order while she's still around to see it."

Fiona smirks. "And doing the *Birds of California* streaming revival is the thing that's going to convince her that you've really made it?"

Sam feels his whole body flush with shame and anger. "Fuck you."

"Fuck *you*," she counters immediately. "I'm the one person in your life who refused to be manipulated by you, and you couldn't deal with it, so you spent a month lying to my fucking face instead."

"Can you blame me?" he bursts out. "You wouldn't even consider it. Not only would you not consider it, you wouldn't even do me the courtesy of telling me why."

"I've given you plenty of reasons!"

"Not a single one that isn't bullshit, you haven't. What the hell was I supposed to do?"

"Gee, I don't know." Fiona looks at him like he's a clown. "I mean, you could have been the one person in America who respected my fucking boundaries. Just, like, to start."

"Your *boundaries*?" Just like that, Sam has had enough. "Come off it, Fiona. You love to act like Darcy Sinclair and whoever else just randomly started picking on you for no reason, but, like: you *did* all that shit. You did it! I'm sorry, but if you wanted people to stop looking at you all the time then maybe you shouldn't have walked around for five years of your life acting like a total fucking sideshow!"

Fiona doesn't say anything for a moment. Right away, Sam knows he's gone too far. "Fiona—"

"Well!" She cuts him off. "You feel better, now that you finally got that off your chest?"

Sam's stomach plummets. "I'm sorry," he tells her, scrubbing both hands through his hair. "I didn't mean—" He can tell by the expression on her face that he's just confirmed something for her, some secret fear she's had that she's tried to talk herself out of or ignore. He *is* embarrassed of her, a little bit—more than a little bit, on occasion—and judging by the way she's looking at him right now there's a part of her that knew it this whole time. Sam has never felt like more of a coward in his entire life. "I shouldn't have—look. We're both worked up, obviously. Why don't we just—"

"Here's what's going to happen right now," Fiona tells him crisply. She definitely isn't smiling anymore, but nothing about her is out of control, either. Mostly she just looks . . . blank. "I'm going to go into the bedroom and put my clothes on. You're going to go out onto the balcony and wait until I'm gone."

"Fiona—"

"I never want to see you again," she says calmly. "And I'd like for *again* to start as soon as possible. So please go."

Sam stares at her for a long beat, his mouth opening and closing uselessly. Fiona doesn't wait for his answer before she turns and walks away.

CHAPTER SEVENTEEN

Fiona

Fiona gets all the way downstairs before she remembers he drove her here last night, the two of them groping each other like teenagers in his stupid fancy car. It feels like a lifetime ago, like it happened to someone else entirely—his hands on someone else's body, the engine rumbling behind someone else's knees. She digs her phone out of her bag and calls for an Uber, then stands outside Sam's apartment for three endless minutes while she waits for it, mostly hoping he won't come down here after her. Hoping a little bit that he will.

He doesn't.

She thinks about going to a bar and getting so drunk she can't see straight. She thinks about calling Richie and seeing if he can hook her up. She thinks about doing something so weird and public and fucked that she winds up back at Cedars, but in the end it all feels like a lot of work for nothing, so instead she rides home in the back of the Uber with her head against the window, looking numbly at Instagram photos of Martha's Vineyard cottages on her phone.

"Hey," says the driver, glancing at her in the rearview. "Aren't you—"

"No," Fiona says flatly. "I'm not."

Back at home she gets into bed, puts *Wives With Knives* on her laptop, and passes out like someone has decked her. When she wakes up, the screen saver is on, and she can tell by the light spilling in through the blinds that it's already the middle of the afternoon. Her head is throbbing, a dull persistent ache at the back of her skull; the foot masks she did with Claudia and Estelle have finally started to do their thing, and her feet are weird and wrinkly, little shreds of skin flaking off her toes. When she looks at her phone, there's nothing from Sam—not that she was expecting there to be. There are, however, eleven missed calls from Georgie.

"I have bad news," Georgie announces when Fiona calls her back, sounding darkly excited to be the bearer of it. "Larry broke both his ankles."

"What?" Fiona sits upright in bed. "How?"

"He stepped off a curb wrong."

Fiona shakes her head even though Georgie can't see her. "That's . . . not real."

"It's real."

"I—okay," Fiona says, scrubbing a hand over her face. Larry is their Torvald, Fiona's onstage husband. Without Torvald, there's no show. "Well, DeShaun can do it, can't he? That's what we have understudies for."

"That's the other thing," Georgie says. Fiona can't decide if she's imagining the glee in her voice or not. "Apparently DeShaun booked a three-episode guest spot on *Malibu Nights*."

Just for a minute, Fiona can't breathe. "That's not real, either," she manages.

She sends out a group text canceling tonight's rehearsal, pending a plan she has no idea how she's going to come up with. Then she pulls the blankets over her head and goes back to sleep.

She stays in bed for a long time. It's embarrassing; she hasn't cried in years and she doesn't intend to start now but she can feel that familiar heaviness in her chest and throat and sinuses, like clouds gathering before a storm. She knew better. She *knew* better, and still she let him—

Still she let *herself*—

Ugh, she is the stupidest fucking person in the world.

"You're here?" Claudia asks at some point later that night, stopping in the doorway. "This whole time I thought you were out."

Fiona shakes her head. "I'm sorry," she says. "I'm going to get up in one second and make dinner."

"It's like ten thirty," Claudia tells her gently. She's wearing a pair of white coveralls that make her look like a trendy Ghostbuster, Fiona's heart-shaped sunglasses perched in her hair like a headband. "Are you okay?"

Fiona sighs. "No," she admits.

"Do you want to talk about it?"

"No."

"Is it about your play?"

"Sort of."

"Is that all it's about?"

"No."

"Okay." Claudia looks at her for another minute, then crosses the room and gets into bed beside her, pulling the sheet up over them both and scooching so close Fiona can smell the peanut butter toast she must have been eating before she came in here.

"My feet are peeling off," Fiona warns her.

"Mine too," Claudia assures her, brushing her gross, flaky toes against Fiona's legs.

"That's disgusting," Fiona says—laughing in spite of herself, trying to wriggle away.

"You're disgusting," Claudia says, and snuggles her harder.

It's the middle of the night when she finally gets hungry. Fiona climbs out of bed as quietly as possible—Claudia is sleeping beside her, one arm thrown over her face—and pads into the kitchen, where Brando is snoozing on the tile beside the door. He cracks one eye open when he hears her, like possibly he knew they needed reinforcements and wants to reassure her that he's available in case of emergency. She opens the fridge, which is basically empty except for the last of the murder hummus and some birthday cake, because Fiona is the person who shops for groceries in this house and she didn't go to the store today. She shuts the door again, tears of frustration rising in her throat.

"Couldn't sleep?"

Fiona gasps and whirls around. Her dad is standing in the doorway in a battered pair of moccasin loafers and the Caltech sweatshirt he's had since college, a couple days' worth of beard on his face. "I'm sorry about Sam," he says.

Fiona blinks. She had no expectation that he was familiar enough with the comings and goings in this house to even know something was wrong, let alone to intuit what that something might be. It must show on her face, because her dad fixes her with a look in return. "I'm depressed," he reminds her, nudging her gently out of the way with his shoulder and opening the fridge one more time. "I'm not in a coma." He nods for Fiona to sit at the table, then pulls a dozen eggs out of the fridge.

"What are you doing?" she asks him, even as she's sinking down into the wobbly wooden chair.

"What does it look like I'm doing?" He pulls a frying pan out of the cabinet, turns the knob on the stove. "I'm making Special Scramble."

He says it like it should be obvious—and it is, she guesses—but also she doesn't think her dad has even been in the kitchen in three months, let alone cooked anything. Fiona sits and watches him work. They used to have Special Scramble every Saturday morning when Fiona was little, her mom whisking eggs at the counter and her dad slicing up a loaf of bread; it wasn't until she was older that she realized the whole production was really just a way to get whatever was wilting in the crisper onto their plates and into her stomach without too much complaining.

Tonight it's the very end of a brick of cheddar cheese, plus some purple spinach Claudia picked out when they went to the farmer's market and then promptly forgot about. There's ham from the deli drawer and some tomato. Salt and pepper. Her dad tops the whole thing with some yogurt sauce leftover from the murder chicken, then sets the plate in front of her, along with a paper towel and a fork. "Eat that," he instructs.

It's the first time he's told her to do anything in five years, so Fiona does it, cleaning her plate while he gazes out the back door at the yard. "I ruined my life," she tells him when she's done.

Her dad shakes his head. Her mom always used to say her dad looked like Mandy Patinkin in *The Princess Bride*, and he did, but now he looks like Mandy Patinkin in the later seasons of *Homeland*. "You're twenty-eight years old," he tells her. "You haven't ruined anything."

That annoys her; Fiona feels her temper flare. "I'm sorry," she says, immediately furious at him for trying to comfort her and at herself for saying anything at all. "How would you know that, exactly?"

Her dad looks bewildered, and she guesses she doesn't really blame him. She can't remember the last time she talked back. "Fiona—"

"I mean it," she interrupts, unable to stop herself. It feels good and terrible to say it after all this time. "At what point in the last ten years have you cared enough to have the vaguest idea whether my life is ruined or not? Or like—forget my life, even. What about Claudia's?"

Her dad looks at her for a long moment in the darkness. "Okay," he says softly. "I deserve that."

"You do deserve it!" Fiona agrees, then immediately feels like an enormous gaping asshole. "I just—I know you're sick, Dad. I get it. But like, if you had diabetes or whatever and you were always saying you couldn't do stuff because of your diabetes but also you never took your insulin . . ." She shrugs. "Eventually your diabetes would stop sounding like such a great excuse."

Her dad nods, holding his hands up. "You're right," he says. "I know you're right."

"I don't want to be right!" she counters. "I want you to see a doctor!"

"Fiona—" He sits down in the chair across from her, heavy. "Okay."

That stops her. Fiona's eyes narrow, looking for the trick. "Wait," she says, "really?"

He nods again, running a hand over his thinning hair. "Really. I know I haven't been around for you girls—for both of you—in a long time. And I know how much you've done around here to pick up the slack." He sighs. "You should be able to have your own life, sweetheart. You should be able to move on."

Fiona opens her mouth, shuts it again. "Okay," she finally says, her voice barely more than a whisper. It occurs to her to wonder what might have happened if she'd lost her temper with him a long time ago. It occurs to her that maybe, just possibly, losing it isn't always the absolute worst thing she could do.

Her dad gets up again, taking her plate and setting it carefully in the dishwasher. "I'll call my GP in the morning," he promises. "In the meantime, you should try to rest."

I'm fine, Fiona starts to tell him. Then, on second thought, she only nods.

She tries, heading back to bed and staring at the ceiling for the better part of an hour before finally giving up and taking her phone out onto the patio—flicking through her contacts in the cool of the predawn morning, thumb hovering over Sam's name. She hesitates for a moment, then closes out the window and types *Erin Cruz* into the search bar of her browser instead.

The article about the private school coach is the fourth result down; Fiona clicks the link and reads the whole thing start to finish one more time, her heart thumping wildly at the back of her mouth. She commits the smallest details of the story to memory: the coach sneaking these girls drinks and making them playlists, driving them home at the end of the night. "None of us thought anyone would believe us," Erin quoted one of them as saying—a senior in high school now, just the right age to have watched *Birds of California* when she was younger. "It wasn't until we finally started talking to each other that we realized that was exactly what he wanted us to think."

By the time she's finished reading Fiona is crying, tears slipping quietly down her nose and cheeks and gathering in the jagged cracks that crisscross the screen of her phone. She thinks of the Ryan Adams album Jamie always used to play in his trailer. She thinks of the acrid, smoky scent of his cologne. She thinks of him calling her parents to tell them how worried he was, how erratic she was acting. How untrustworthy she'd suddenly become.

Now she wipes the screen on her sweatpants, then takes a deep breath and opens her contacts one more time, hitting the screen to dial before she can talk herself out of it. She has no idea what time it is in Paris, and she's fully expecting to get voice mail or be shunted to an assistant who will promise to send along a message with no intention of actually doing it, but a moment later a familiar voice says hello. "Fiona?" Thandie asks, her voice soft and wary and achingly familiar. "Are you okay?"

"Not really," Fiona says, clutching the phone so tight her hand aches. "Do you have a minute to talk?"

CHAPTER EIGHTEEN

Sam

He doesn't get the firefighter gig.

"It's fine," Russ reassures him across the table at Soho House, his perpetual tan an even deeper shade of toasty after his trip to Tulum. "It's going to get canceled after two episodes anyway. Derivative."

"Did they say anything?" Sam asks, picking at his salad. The early afternoon sun shines cheerily over the crowded patio, but instead of filling him with a buzzing kind of energy like usual, today it just makes him feel like an imposter, like someone who has no business being here in the first place. He might as well be wearing a sandwich sign that says *Out of Work*. Shit, he might as well be wearing a sandwich sign with an actual advertisement on it. At least then maybe he'd be getting paid.

"Just that they're going in a different direction," Russ says, shaking his head in a way that makes Sam suspect that is not, in fact, all they said. "Look, don't pack your bags just yet, all right? Something always comes along."

"No, I'm not," Sam says, frowning a little uncertainly. "Wait, who said I was packing my bags?"

"It's an expression, Sammy." Russ looks at him a little strangely. "Take it easy, will you?"

"I'm easy," Sam mutters, which is of course a lie. What he *is* is an out of work never-was with $27,000 in credit card debt and a ridiculous electric car he's pretty sure is about to be repossessed. What he *is* is a guy who doesn't know how he's going to pay next month's rent. Just for a second, he thinks about asking Russ to float him until he books something, but that would make him desperate—that would make him poison—so instead he pastes a smile on his face and signals the waitress across the patio for another vodka tonic.

"I'm easy," he says again.

He goes off his diet. He smokes a lot of weed. He reads *Weetzie Bat*, which is a weird fucking book—an eighties fairy tale about a version of LA he's pretty sure never actually existed, with a lot of white girls wearing headdresses in a way that feels distinctly not okay. Still, he thinks he gets why Fiona would have liked it when she was a kid. It's about finding people who love you no matter what inadvisable shit you go out and do, drinking too much or running away from home or accidentally impregnating a witch who casts spells using Barbie dolls. It's about making a family where there wasn't one before.

Sam lets out a quiet groan, tossing the book onto the coffee table and telling himself he doesn't miss her. It keeps hitting him at weird moments: finding one of her hair elastics in his bathroom, scrolling past some creepy fucking murder documentary Netflix now thinks he might enjoy. He clicks her name in his contacts list a thousand times—thumbs the screen to dial, even—then immediately hits the button to end the call before it can connect. For fuck's sake, what does he think he's possibly going to say to her? He's never felt like such a piece of shit in his entire life.

He fucked it up, that's all. Of course he did; he always does. It was only a matter of time. He remembers the last time he saw her before that day at the print shop, the cast party his last season of *Birds*. It was at some trendy restaurant in West Hollywood—long since closed now—with exposed brick and industrial lighting, the tall warehouse windows flung open to the cool night air. He'd bummed a cigarette from one of the sound guys, and when he headed out into the alley to smoke it he found Fiona sitting on an overturned bucket beside the dumpster, wearing a dress stitched with a million purple sparkles and reading a skinny paperback book. Her eyes widened at the sight of him. "What are you doing out here?"

Sam blinked, then recovered. "Looking for you, obviously." He held up the cigarette, leaning back against the wall of the restaurant beside her. His thigh brushed the side of her arm.

"Obviously." Fiona used her index finger to mark her page: *King Lear*, he saw when he glanced at the cover, which he'd never read but which looked like a total downer. "Since when do you smoke?" she asked, eyes narrowing as she watched him light up.

"Since when have you been paying attention?" He shrugged. "Awhile."

Awhile like since right now, truth be told—in fact he'd only wanted one for the sake of something to do with his hands. He'd been weirdly edgy all night, awkward in conversations, fighting a strange feeling of embarrassment at being at this party in the first place now that everyone knew he wasn't coming back next season. It felt risky to be leaving a job without having anything else lined up, even though Russ, his new agent, kept saying he was going to start booking films no problem.

Now Fiona was quiet as Sam took a drag, then held her hand up wordlessly for the cigarette. Sam looked down at her, surprised, but handed it over, the tips of his fingers grazing hers. She inhaled, then passed it back, the silver smoke heavy around her face in the half dark.

"So," he said—doing what he always did when he felt like he was out of his depth, which was turn on the charm—"you gonna miss me?"

Fiona laughed out loud. "No," she said decisively. "In fact, I'm looking forward to being the prettiest person on set for a change." She leaned her head back against the brick and looked up at him, all eyelashes and collarbone. "You glad to be leaving?"

Sam shook his head. "*Glad* is the wrong word," he said, although until two minutes ago he would have said exactly that. Still, standing next to her in this alley, all at once he was starting to have second thoughts. "Excited to do some other stuff, is all."

Fiona nodded, her expression filled with—there was no other word to describe this—*longing*. "I would love to do other stuff," she confessed.

That surprised him; even on her weirdest, drunkest tabloid days he'd never seen her anything but prepared and professional when the cameras were rolling. He'd always thought that must mean she liked it, disappearing into Riley Bird every day of her life, but suddenly he wasn't so sure. "Why don't you?" he asked.

"Can't," she said with a shrug, a dead kind of acceptance in her voice. "Contract."

"So?" Sam asked. "Contracts expire."

Fiona smiled at that, just faintly. "Not soon enough." She held her hand up again, expectant; he helped her climb to her feet, then just . . . didn't let go, their fingers knitting quietly together at their sides like possibly it was something they'd done a million times before, which it emphatically wasn't. Neither one of them looked down. "I should get back inside," Fiona said.

Sam nodded. "Okay," he agreed, even as he was angling his body in her direction. He'd already decided he was going to kiss her. He thought it was possible he'd decided a long time before now, somewhere in the very back of his secret brain.

Fiona knew it, too: "I'm going," she told him, her full mouth quirking.

Sam nodded. "You should."

"I intend to," she promised, and that was when Sam ducked his head.

It wasn't particularly raunchy, as far as kisses went, lips and tongue and the barest graze of her teeth at his bottom lip; still, the force of it surprised him a little, his entire body humming wildly to shocking neon life. *There you are*, he thought, the notion popping into his head fully formed like possibly it had always been there, waiting. He had no idea why he'd never done this before.

Fiona pulled back, her expression all amusement. "What the fuck took you so long?" she asked him, but before he could answer, the back door of the restaurant swung open with a clatter and Jamie poked his dark head outside.

"What are you two knuckleheads doing out here?" he asked, his canny gaze flicking back and forth between them. "Get your asses back inside and eat some cake."

Just for a moment Fiona's eyes flashed with pure, animal hatred; then Jamie raised an eyebrow, and she sighed and shuffled inside. Sam was about to follow when Jamie grabbed his arm. "You," he said. "Wait a minute."

"Me?" Sam asked with a laugh. "What did I do?" Fiona glanced over her shoulder as the heavy metal door shut behind her.

"Yeah," Jamie said once they were alone, "you. What were you guys doing out here?"

Sam hesitated, a little taken aback by the intensity in Jamie's expression. "Easy, Dad," he joked. "We were just hanging out, that's all. Taking a break from this excellent party so we didn't get overstimulated."

Jamie didn't smile. "I'm not screwing around, Sam. You think I haven't seen you making eyes at her?"

"I'm not 'making eyes' at anybody," he said, equally offended by both the accusation and the corniness of the phrasing. "Also, isn't my personal life kind of . . ." He trailed off, hoping the *none of your business* was implicit even if he wasn't entirely sure that was true. Sometimes it seemed like everything was Jamie's business, at least as far as the show was concerned.

"I'm not talking about your personal life, idiot." Jamie rolled his eyes. "I'm talking about your future. Fiona is a great kid and a brilliant actress, but you know as well as I do that she's got a lot of fucking problems."

Sam didn't know what to say to that. "I mean," he hedged finally, "everybody has problems, right?"

"Not like Fiona, they don't," Jamie countered. "Look, I know you're on your way out the door here to do bigger and better things, and that's great. Fuck, I *want* that for you, which is why the last thing I want to see happen is you fucking it up because you can't keep your dick in your pants around a pretty girl, do you know what I'm saying?" He shook his head. "We've got one, maybe two colossal Fiona screwups to go before the network shitcans us altogether. You're smart to be getting out now. Don't let yourself get sucked back into her drama-queen bullshit."

Sam thought of the way Fiona had looked at him in the second before he kissed her. He thought of the way her hair had felt in his hands. He thought of what it had been like to be around her for the last few months, like watching a not-very-experienced swimmer paddle out past the breakers; and yeah, for a second tonight it had felt like she was about to tell him what her deal was, that maybe she was about to let him see some secret part of herself she kept hidden from the rest of the world, but who even knew if any of that was legit or not? After all: she was a brilliant actress.

On top of which, he trusted Jamie. The guy might not have

been his real dad, but the embarrassing truth was that for the last four years he'd been the closest thing Sam had to one. And if Jamie was telling him to get as far away from Fiona as humanly possible, then in all likelihood there was a damn good reason for that.

"Yeah, no, totally," Sam said now, waving him off. "I hear you; you're right. I don't exactly think we're going to be hanging out a whole lot once I'm done here."

Jamie relaxed. "Smart guy," he said with a grin, slapping Sam on the shoulder. "Let's go get a beer."

Fiona was standing by the bar when he got back inside, something clear and icy sweating in the glass in her hand; Jamie had stopped to talk to some studio guys near the doorway, his expression bright and animated. "What did he want?" Fiona asked, jerking her chin in Jamie's direction.

Sam shook his head. "Nothing," he said—his voice noticeably colder than it had been outside, even to his own ears. "Just career stuff." He ignored the pang of regret in his gut as he watched Fiona's expression flicker warily, reminding himself of all the opportunities waiting for him outside this studio: all the big-budget films he was going to star in, all the famous women he was going to meet. Jamie was right. He didn't need anybody's immature Family Network baggage dragging him down.

"I should go talk to some people," he told Fiona, squeezing her arm before turning away toward the party. "I'll see you around."

Erin stages an intervention the following night at a hipster Mexican place she hates but knows he likes, with spicy cilantro cocktails

and carnitas made of tofu. Sam orders a tequila gimlet, trying not
to think about that first night with Fiona at his apartment. The
bartender smiles as she sets the glass in front of him; Sam can tell
objectively that she's beautiful, with her dark red hair and a body
for days, but just . . . nothing. She might as well be a dude.

"What's the latest with Hipster Glasses?" he tries, wanting to
talk about anything else besides his own ridiculous bullshit. "You
guys still hanging out?"

"Every night this week," Erin admits a little shyly. "Turns out
I knew the right amount of feminist theory after all."

Sam grins. "That's awesome," he says, and means it. Erin deserves somebody great. He listens as she tells him about some arty
movie they saw and the day trip they took to the botanical garden,
asking questions and holding his drink up so they can toast, but
the truth is that as glad as Sam is for her, his heart just isn't in it
tonight. Finally he swallows the rest of his drink in two big gulps,
then reaches for his jacket. "I'm going to go," he says.

"Wait, already?" Erin's eyes widen. "Come on," she says,
catching his arm. "It can't be that bad."

Sam opens his mouth, then closes it again, realizing with no
small amount of horror that there's an actual lump rising in his
throat. "Dude," he says finally, swallowing it down with some
effort, "I'm broke as shit. Like, seriously, cannot-pay-for-these-
drinks broke. My career is completely stalled. Russ didn't even say
anything about another audition. I'm doing a fat lot of nothing for
my family, and I just took a gigantic steaming dump all over the
closest thing I've ever had to a real relationship with a girl I might

actually be in—" He breaks off abruptly, snapping his jaws shut one more time.

Erin's eyebrows creep, just slightly. "A girl you might actually what, exactly?" she prompts.

"Actually nothing," Sam says, glancing around the noisy restaurant to avoid meeting her eyes.

"Liar," Erin says primly, and nods at the bartender for the check.

Back at his apartment he puts *Supermarket Sweep* on streaming and makes a list of things he could do for a living besides acting. Barista, he thinks. Gym teacher at a private school where you don't have to have a teaching certificate and they don't care if you've never taught gym, or anything, ever before. He's just typing *how to become a referee in the NBA* into Google when his phone rings on the coffee table. "Is this Sam Fox?" a woman's voice asks when he answers.

Sam hesitates, a quick orange lick of anxiety flaring inside his rib cage. He just talked to his mom a couple of days ago, he reminds himself; if anything was really wrong, Adam would have called. Still, for a second he almost says no. "Yes . . . ?"

"This is Estelle Halliday," the voice reports. "What are you doing tomorrow morning?"

Sam blinks in surprise, then looks around his filthy apartment. "I—probably nothing," he says honestly.

"Good," Estelle says, her diction crisp and regal. "I was wondering if you might like to try out for a play."

CHAPTER NINETEEN

Fiona

Fiona spends the better part of Saturday morning flat on her back on the stage at the theater, staring up at their fire hazard of a lighting rig and trying to figure out how to tell everybody that they're going to have to cancel the show. She thought it was the noble, grown-up thing, to deliver the news in person, but now that she's actually waiting for them to show up she feels like an asshole of the first magnitude for dragging the entire cast all the way downtown to attend the epitome of a meeting that could have been an email. She wonders if it's too late to call them all again and tell them not to come. She's just digging her phone out of her pocket when she hears the door open at the back of the theater and the sound of someone clearing his throat.

Fiona sits up so fast she gets dizzy, blinking out at the dark, empty house. She can't see his face in the glare of the stage lights but right away she recognizes the broad, solid outline of his body, the TV-star line of his jaw.

"Hi," he calls, lifting a cautious hand in greeting. "I'm Sam Fox. I'm here for an audition?"

Fiona snorts to cover the sharp, hopeful sound of her inhale, using her hand to shade her eyes. "Excuse me?"

"A gulf has opened up between us," he tells her, voice booming as he strides up the center aisle, "I see that now. But Nora, couldn't we bridge that gulf?" He plants his feet just before he reaches the stage—shoulders back and chest puffed, completely in character as a wounded, arrogant husband. "Can I never be more than a stranger to you?"

Fiona laughs, but the laugh turns into something else halfway out, her breath catching like broken glass inside her chest. "Why are you reciting my play to me?" she asks.

Sam drops his arms and just like that he's himself again, his smile a little bit sheepish. "I learned it," he confesses quietly. "I stayed up all night. I learned the whole thing. I'm ready."

Fiona gazes at him for a moment, not understanding. *"Why?"*

Sam shrugs. "Because I think maybe I'm falling in love with you," he explains, "and because I heard you needed a Torvald." He shakes his head. "Estelle told me your guy fell off a curb or something? I don't understand how you break your ankle falling off a curb."

"It's not a real thing," Fiona agrees faintly. Then, in spite of herself, never quite as tough or cool or unbreakable as she wants to be: "Go back to the other part."

"Sorry." Sam smiles at that, slow and teasing. "Which part, exactly?"

"Don't be an asshole," she tells him. She's still sitting on the stage, her legs out in front of her. She hasn't washed her hair in three days. "The part about maybe . . ." She trails off, waving her hand. "You know."

"There's no maybe," Sam corrects. "I shouldn't have qualified it just now. I'm scared you're going to tell me to go fuck myself, but still I shouldn't have qualified it." He wrinkles his nose. "Is that weird?"

"That you qualified it?"

"That I'm sure."

"I mean, yes." Fiona squeezes her eyes shut, opens them again. No guy has ever said it to her before. Nobody has ever even gotten close. "But keep going."

"Well," Sam says—taking one step toward her, then another. "I am. I'm sure. And I get why you wouldn't trust me, and I'm not asking you to say it back." He sits down on the edge of the stage, turning his body to face her. "I just think we should, you know. Plug into the love current, like *Weetzie Bat* says."

"Shut up." That makes her laugh, loud and disbelieving. "You read *Weetzie Bat*?"

Sam nods, shifting around and digging the battered paperback out of his pocket. "I brought it back in case you told me you never wanted to see me again," he admits, his fingertips brushing hers as he hands it over. "You seemed serious about me returning it in a timely fashion."

"I was," Fiona says. She flips instinctively through the soft, worn pages, then glances at him sidelong. "And I still might."

"Yeah." Sam smiles a little sadly, there and gone again. "You do need a Torvald, though."

Fiona raises her eyebrows. "You seem very confident that I'm going to give you this part."

Sam shrugs. "I mean, I can do my monologue if you want," he offers, then jerks a thumb toward the door. "I've got my headshots in the car, we can do the whole—"

"That won't be necessary."

"I owe you an apology."

"That won't be necessary, either."

Sam's face falls then, his broad shoulders sagging. He lifts his hand like he's going to touch her, then seems to think better of it. "Fee," he says, his voice cracking a little. "Yeah it is."

Fiona leans back on her palms and tilts her chin up, staring into the lights and concentrating on keeping her bottom lip steady. She didn't want to let him hurt her. She didn't want to be the kind of person who could get hurt. She didn't want to be the kind of person who felt much of anything, period, but then he strolled into the print shop like he couldn't possibly imagine she'd be anything but delighted to see him, and now it's all these moments later and here they are. "Yeah," she admits finally. "It is."

"I'm sorry," he says immediately. "It doesn't matter why you didn't want to do the fucking show, obviously. You said you didn't want to, and that should have been enough. But I felt desperate— not that that's an excuse—but I felt desperate, so I acted sneaky, and I acted like a piece of shit. And I'm sorry. Again."

Fiona tilts her head to the side, considering. "That's . . . a pretty good apology," she admits.

Sam smiles goofily. "Thanks," he says, the relief audible in his voice. "I practiced in the car."

She considers him then for a long, loaded moment—his open face and the uncomplicated way he's looking at her, his green merman eyes—and feels something unlock deep inside her. She closes her eyes, breathing in the dust and sweat smell of the theater. The soap and cologne smell of Sam. "Do you want to know the real reason?" she asks, and opens her eyes again.

All at once Sam gets very, very still. "Yeah," he blurts. Then, like he's worried she's going to change her mind if he isn't polite enough: "I mean. Yes please."

Fiona huffs a laugh, though nothing about this is actually funny. Already she's regretting saying anything at all. "You're not going to think you love me anymore once I tell you," she warns him. "Or like me, even."

"Doubtful," Sam says, and now he does reach for her, his fingertips just grazing the edge of her sleeve. "Try me."

Fiona pulls her arm away, instinctive—drawing one knee up and tucking her foot underneath her, making herself small. She never imagined telling him, and now that she's come this far she finds she isn't entirely sure how. It's very possible he won't even believe her. It's very possible nobody will.

She's quiet for a moment longer, rubbing her thumb back and forth over a fray at the hem of her jeans. "I *was* a late bloomer," she finally tells him. "But you weren't my first kiss."

Sam looks at her curiously. "Okay . . ." he says, shaking his head like he thinks she's setting him up for some kind of riddle. "Who was your first kiss?"

"Jamie Hartley."

For a too-long beat Sam just stares at her like she's fried his motherboard, like his brain is glitching and he needs to unplug himself and wait thirty seconds to reconnect. "I—what?" he finally says.

Fiona hesitates, not particularly wanting to repeat it. Makes herself say it again. "Jamie Hartley was my first kiss."

"Jamie Hartley is, like, pushing fifty years old."

"Is he?" Fiona barks another laugh, dry and brittle. "No shit, Sam."

And—yeah. He gets it this time. Fiona watches as everything reshuffles in his head like those Magic Eye books Claudia used to like when she was a kid—how suddenly he can see the secret picture hidden inside what happened that day at the UBC lot. Inside what happened when she heard him on the phone the other morning.

Inside what happened at the end of her career.

"Fuck," he says slowly, reaching back and running a rough hand over the back of his head, yanking a little at his hair. "I—*fuck*, Fiona."

"Yeah," Fiona agrees, lips twisting; she's trying to sound tough and nonchalant about it all but her voice wobbles, dangerous. "That too."

Sam doesn't say anything for a moment. Fiona keeps her eyes

on her sneakers, wanting to postpone the inevitability of whatever blame or incredulity or disgust she's going to see in his expression, but when she finally pulls herself together and glances over in his direction the only thing she finds on his face is—

"So first of all, you were wrong," Sam says quietly. He catches her gaze and holds it, steady on. "I still love you. I still don't need to qualify it. And I am really, really fucking sorry that happened."

Fiona blinks. She thought she was prepared for every possible reaction on his part—that by now she'd lost the ability to be surprised—but somehow she didn't account for this one. "I could have said no," she points out, worried that maybe he isn't understanding. "I knew it was wrong, I knew it was messed up. I wasn't so divorced from reality that when he said *Don't tell anyone* I thought he was, like, protecting our true and abiding love. I could have said no. And I didn't. Not at first."

"Are you kidding me?" Right away, Sam shakes his head. "You were, what, seventeen? Eighteen? If it happened to your sister, would you say, *Well, you didn't say no?*"

"Of course not," Fiona says immediately, the thought of Claudia like a bucket of ice water dumped directly over her head. "That's different."

"How is it different?"

"It's just different, Sam!" She scrubs a hand over her face. Of course she knows it isn't different, not really. But there's an entire world of shame and weirdness between knowing something intellectually and feeling it in her cells. "Anyway. It went on for . . . a while. And I didn't know how to tell him I wanted him to stop. So instead I told him I wanted to quit the show."

Sam raises his eyebrows. "And I bet he was just falling all over himself to let you out of your contract."

"He fully laughed at me," Fiona remembers, her cheeks warming with old embarrassment. She hasn't let herself think about it in a long time. "So then I told my parents I wanted to quit, but I had already kind of started acting like a freak by then—"

"Understandable," Sam points out.

"I mean, sure," Fiona allows, "but they were already getting tired of my bullshit. My mom especially, even though she was up in Seattle by then. She told me I'd signed a contract, I'd made a choice. I didn't have to re-sign if I didn't want to. But I had to see it through until then."

Sam winces. "So that was—"

"Right around the end of your last season, yeah," Fiona says. She remembers the night of the cast party: Sam finding her hand and pulling her closer, his warm smile pressed against hers. How just for a moment he'd made her feel like a normal person. How for one moment she'd been able to forget.

"I just kind of lost it after that," she says now, making a conscious effort to drop her aching shoulders; she's been hunching without meaning to do it, her whole body up around her ears. "I'd started doing all this batshit stuff—stealing, constantly yelling at everybody, crashing my car—and then it was like I couldn't stop."

"You were trying to get fired," Sam says reasonably, but Fiona shakes her head.

"It wasn't like that," she confesses. "That makes it sound like I had a plan, like it was calculated, and it wasn't. *I* wasn't. I was just . . . flailing."

"Nobody helped you?"

"Nobody knew," Fiona points out. "I mean, Thandie suspected. She flat-out asked me once. But I told her she was crazy, and projecting, and that she was the one who had a crush on Jamie to begin with. I pushed her away and I pushed her away until finally— you know. She went away." She clears her throat. "Anyway. Eventually I *did* get fired, obviously, but by then it was like I'd created this whole other person and I didn't know how to quit being her. Or even if I wanted to quit." She shrugs, looking out at the empty theater. Remembering how safe it can feel to play a part. "Sometimes I still want to be her, to be completely honest with you. She's tough."

"*You're* tough," Sam counters. "You're ferocious. And that fucking guy deserves—"

"Don't," Fiona interrupts, holding her hand up.

Sam frowns. "Don't what?"

"Whatever you're going to say, just—" She shakes her head. "I didn't tell you any of this so that you could rescue me or, like, go out and defend my honor."

"I've never met anyone who needed rescuing less than you do," Sam says immediately. "And your honor is fine. Jamie fucking Hartley's, on the other hand—" He breaks off. "I cannot believe that asshole has just been glad-handing his way around town this entire time."

Guilt flares fresh in Fiona's chest at that—for years, she's had the sneaking suspicion that in all likelihood glad-handing isn't the only thing Jamie's been doing all over town. She thinks again of the high school girls at St. Anne's, how many of them there were. "I can," she says quietly.

Sam nods. "Yeah," is all he says, and after that he's quiet for a long time. "Well. I'm really glad you told me. And whatever you want to do or not do is the right thing, obviously, which doesn't mean I don't want show up at his house and beat the living shit out of him."

Fiona smiles, she can't help it. "What's that called, a Sheboygan How Are Ya?"

"A Green Bay Bear Hug," Sam says absently.

Fiona nods seriously. "In any case," she says, "I think have a better idea. But I'm going to need Erin's number."

"Oh yeah?" Sam asks, tilting his head to the side. "What for?"

Fiona is just opening her mouth to tell him when the door at the back of the theater opens and Georgie and Pamela hurry in. "We're canceled, right?" Pamela calls, her face hidden under an enormous black hat. "There's nothing to do but cancel."

But Fiona shakes her head, climbing to her feet and standing tall and proud in the middle of the stage. "This is Sam Fox," she says, reaching for Sam's hand and pulling him upright. "He's going to be our new leading man."

CHAPTER TWENTY

Sam

A week later, Sam stands in the humid dark of the tiny backstage at the Angel City Playhouse, sweating his ass off in a mothball-smelling Goodwill suit. "Can't I just wear my own clothes?" he begged Fiona again this morning, but she shook her head and told him it was a nonstarter.

"People are going to have a hard enough time forgetting you're you to begin with," she pointed out, gesturing across the room at his closet. "If you wear some skinny little Hugo Boss or whatever the fuck expensive getup you've got hanging in there, there's no way they're ever going to look at anybody else."

Sam raised his eyebrows. "It's Tom Ford, actually," he told her, trying without a lot of luck to bite back his smile. "And I'm sorry, was that you telling me I'm distractingly handsome?"

"No," Fiona countered immediately, and since she happened to be naked on top of him as she was saying it, Sam didn't argue. "It was me telling you that I'm the director, and you have to do what I say."

Sam nodded, swallowing hard as she raked her short nails

through the hair at the nape of his neck. "Yes, ma'am," he promised solemnly, and flipped her onto her back.

Now he takes a deep breath as the stage manager calls two minutes, running his tongue over the back of his teeth. He hasn't been in a play since he made his stage debut as the Tin Man in his eighth-grade production of *The Wizard of Oz*. He doesn't think he's been this nervous since that night, either.

"Are you going to barf?" Fiona asks him quietly. She's dressed in full Lululemon as Millennial Nora, helicopter mom of the twenty-first century. "Because I have to say, you kind of look like you're going to barf."

"I might," Sam replies, "but only because apparently this suit was soaked in formaldehyde at some point before it came into my possession."

Fiona smiles, sliding one hand into his back pocket and squeezing. "Pretty sure that's your cologne, cowboy."

"Cute." Sam nudges her back into the corner. "Didn't they just call two minutes?" he murmurs, even as his fingertips are creeping up inside her hoodie. "Shouldn't you be, like, centering yourself or whatever serious theater actors do?"

Fiona nods. "In a second," she promises, tipping her face up. "Don't smudge my lipstick."

Sam smiles against her mouth. He likes seeing her like this—lighter, maybe. Energized about something. Earlier this week she sat down with Erin for the first in a series of interviews for a long piece set to run in *New York* magazine about dropping out of Hollywood—and about what happened with Jamie. "Realistically

I'm not the only one he did it to," Fiona pointed out when she asked Sam to help her set up a call with Erin. "Or even if I am, there's still no guarantee he won't do it again. If I can make it even a tiny bit harder for him to get away with it, then it'll be worth it."

"It's going to be a nightmare," Erin warned her immediately. "He's going to try and make your life a living hell. And not to put too fine a point on it, but . . ."

"I'm not exactly a perfect vessel?" Fiona didn't flinch. "Whatever he throws at me, I've had worse," she said, and Sam believed her. "And I'm not afraid."

Erin nodded. "Okay then," she said, digging her notebook out of her massive tote bag. "In that case, let's get the bastard."

Now Angel City's ancient backstage speakers crackle, a burst of static making Sam wince. "One minute," comes the half-garbled announcement from the stage manager. "Have a good show, everyone. Full house out there."

Fiona grins. It's the first sold-out run in the history of the Angel City Players. Claudia and Estelle are out there. Erin is in the front row. Thandie flew in from Paris last night just in time to catch the end of their final dress rehearsal, sneaking into the back at the last moment; Sam watched as Fiona hopped off the stage and ran up the aisle to meet her, the two of them wrapping their arms around each other and clinging. Neither one of them said anything for a long time.

Now Fiona digs into the pocket of her hoodie, coming up with what looks at first like a crumpled piece of paper and tucking it into his hand. "I made this for you," she tells him quietly. "I thought I was making it for you, anyway. I think actually I made it for me."

Sam squints at the gift in the darkness, realizing after a moment that it's an intricately folded bird—its tail tall and proud and delicate, its narrow beak sharp as a blade. He shakes his head, not understanding, but before he can ask what it means: "Say it again," Fiona tells him, her voice muffled against his shoulder. Sam's heart stops deep inside his chest.

"Fiona——" he starts, but she's pulling back now to look at him, her expression calm and steady and sure.

"Sam," she says. "If you meant it, say it again."

Sam doesn't have to ask what she's talking about. He's said it to her half a dozen times in the last week, in the car and in the morning and in bed buried deep inside her; he'll keep saying it as long as she'll let him. He'll keep saying it until she believes.

"I love you," he tells her as the lights go down out in the theater, his voice barely carrying over the applause of the crowd. "Fiona. I love you so much."

Fiona smiles like the dawn coming up over the hills at sunrise. Then she ducks her head and whispers in his ear. She squeezes his hand and they step out onto the stage together, taking their places side by side.

ACKNOWLEDGMENTS

I've been lucky enough to publish a good number of books in my career, but in a lot of ways *Birds of California* has felt like the very first all over again. I'm so grateful to all the people who have helped make it happen:

My brilliant editor, Mary Gaule, whose keen eye (and encyclopedic knowledge of all things Los Angeles) made this book one thousand times better, and whose boundless enthusiasm had me excited to open the document every day. The entire team at Harper Perennial but especially Amy Baker, Megan Looney, and Heather Drucker for welcoming me aboard so warmly. Joanne O'Neill and Andrew Davis, I legit gasp every time I look at this cover. Thank you so much.

My inimitable agent, Elizabeth Bewley—I truly just adore you. Finally getting to work together was so, so, so worth the wait. Let's keep doing it forever, okay great. And to everyone at Sterling Lord Literistic—you are incredible, and I feel so lucky to be a part of this amazing team.

Robin Benway, Bri Cavallaro, Brandy Colbert, Lauren Gibaldi, Corey Ann Haydu, Emery Lord, Jennifer Matthieu, Julie Murphy, Iva-Marie Palmer, Eric Smith, Elissa Sussman, and Sara Zarr for their friendship and good humor and insight. I can't wait to eat large quantities of snacks at conferences with you all again one day soon.

Lisa Burton, Jennie Palluzzi, Sierra Rooney, Marissa Sertich. Always, always, always.

My family, for their love and encouragement and extreme generosity with childcare. My sister, for being the person I write every single book trying to impress.

Tom, Annie, Charlie + Avon: you are all my very favorite love story.

ABOUT THE AUTHOR

Katie Cotugno is the *New York Times* bestselling author of seven romantic young adult novels, including *99 Days* and *You Say It First*, and is the coauthor, with Candace Bushnell, of *Rules for Being a Girl*. Her books have been honored by the Junior Library Guild, the Bank Street Children's Book Committee, and the Kentucky Association of School Librarians, among others, and translated into more than fifteen languages. Katie is a Pushcart Prize nominee whose work has appeared in the *Iowa Review*, the *Mississippi Review*, and *Argestes*, as well as many other literary magazines. She studied Writing, Literature and Publishing at Emerson College and received her MFA in fiction at Lesley University. She lives in Boston with her family.